Princess Songbird was not the diva he'd first thought.

Whether she was dressed up in her fancy stuff or mud-splattered from working with him, she radiated kindness and beauty. He'd never known a woman quite like her and enjoyed watching her having fun.

"You really do know how to fix everything," Liz said. They were facing one another, and she moved close enough to brush a leaf from his shoulder.

Her nearness made him very aware of his heartbeat. Travis glanced across to the other side of the fountain and his unusually good mood took a nosedive. Her ex-boyfriend, Jeff, was standing there staring at them with that annoyingly smug look on his face.

His protective instincts flared to a new level. This guy was begging for something he was not going to like, and if he made one wrong move, he'd find out. He needed to keep her from seeing the jerk.

Travis made a quick decision. He lightly grasped her shoulders. "Liz, don't freak out. Just trust me and go with it."

"Okay." Her eyes widened, and she swayed toward him.

He surprised himself even further when he slid his arms around her shoulders, pulled her close...

And kissed her.

Dear Reader,

Welcome to Channing, Texas! *The Rancher's Love Song* is the first book in my new series, The Women of Dalton Ranch, set in a fictional small town near Dallas. I love starting a new series because there are so many possibilities.

City girl Lizzy Dalton is spending the summer on her twin aunts' Texas horse ranch to prepare for an opera audition. Travis Taylor, ranch foreman and rodeo cowboy, took the job on Dalton Ranch for peace and quiet after too much drama in his life. Lizzy is anything but quiet, and little miss sunshine is his opposite. Her fostering an orphaned baby boy with Down syndrome adds to the chaos and taps into Travis's wounds. How will an opera singer and a tiny baby rope this cowboy's heart?

I hope you enjoy *The Rancher's Love Song* and will visit Dalton Ranch again when the second book in the series is released. I can't wait to share the stories of twin sisters Sage and Daisy Dalton. As always, thank you for reading!

Best wishes,

Makenna Lee

The Rancher's Love Song

MAKENNA LEE

HARLEQUIN
SPECIAL
EDITION

HARLEQUIN®
SPECIAL
EDITION™

Recycling programs
for this product may
not exist in your area.

ISBN-13: 978-1-335-59452-5

The Rancher's Love Song

Copyright © 2024 by Margaret Culver

For questions and comments about the quality of this book, please contact us at CustomerService@Harlequin.com.

Harlequin Enterprises ULC
22 Adelaide St. West, 41st Floor
Toronto, Ontario M5H 4E3, Canada
www.Harlequin.com

Printed in U.S.A.

Makenna Lee is an award-winning romance author living in the Texas Hill Country with her real-life hero and their two children, one of whom has Down syndrome and inspired her first Harlequin book, *A Sheriff's Star*. She writes heartwarming contemporary romance that celebrates real-life challenges and the power of love and acceptance. She has been known to make people laugh and cry in the same book. Makenna is often drinking coffee with a cat on her lap while writing, reading or plotting a new story. Her wish is to write stories that touch your heart, making you feel, think and dream.

Books by Makenna Lee

Harlequin Special Edition

Home to Oak Hollow

A Sheriff's Star
In the Key of Family
A Child's Christmas Wish
A Marriage of Benefits
Lessons in Fatherhood
The Bookstore's Secret

The Fortunes of Texas: Hitting the Jackpot

Fortune's Fatherhood Dare

The Women of Dalton Ranch

The Rancher's Love Song

Visit the Author Profile page
at Harlequin.com for more titles.

This book is dedicated to my grandmothers. They were all amazing women who inspired me in so many different ways.

Chapter One

Stud Farm was written beside the silhouette of a stallion on the crisp white background of an oval sign swinging from an antique metal lamppost.

Elizabeth Dalton pulled her car to a stop in front of an intricate wrought-iron archway that led into Dalton Ranch. She rolled down her window just as a horse neighed. Shielding her eyes from the midafternoon sun, Elizabeth caught sight of a black horse racing across the pasture at a full gallop. The animal's dark coat glistened in the sunlight like black glitter.

The cowboy riding him had his head tucked low toward the horse's neck. He rode with such skill, moving as if he were one with the powerful animal. A shiver rippled across her skin. "Oh, my. The sign does not lie. This really is a stud farm."

He was too far away for her to make out his features, but she could tell the cowboy was tall with long limbs and a strong, muscular body. Neither of her aunts were married, but whoever he was, maybe he'd be willing to teach her to ride even half that well. She would have plenty of time to discover his identity, along with catching up on everything she had missed over the last fifteen years.

Lizzy stretched her arm out of the car window to enter the code onto a silver keypad. The iron gate swung open, and she drove her white hand-me-down Cadillac up the tree-lined driveway that led to the farmhouse. The oaks and redbuds were dressed in a thick cover of summer leaves, and a few remaining yellow flowers decorated the honeysuckle on the fence line. The weariness from her three-day drive was well worth it to once again visit Channing in the ranch lands on the outskirts of Fort Worth, Texas.

She had not been to the Dalton family ranch since she was ten years old, and there had been some changes over the years. Good ones. So many wonderful childhood memories were tied to this place. Spending time with her grandfather in the horse barn and her grandmother in the kitchen and laughing with her identical twin aunts, who were only ten years her senior. Her throat tightened, cutting off her smile.

She'd been denied access to this part of her family for far too long. Something big had made her father cut his sisters from his life. Something he wouldn't talk about. But she was done waiting for answers and intended to find out the truth of why she'd been kept away from her aunts and the ranch after her grandparents died.

The white two-story farmhouse came into view. The covered porch stretched across the front and down both sides, giving a choice of where to sit depending on the time of day. The shutters were now a soothing blue and held back with cast-iron hooks, and two dormers were perched across the front of the shiny metal roof. Huge ferns overflowed four hanging baskets suspended across the deep-set porch. Petunias and zinnias sprang up from blue ceramic pots that sat on each side of the front door.

It could be the fresh paint and pretty flowers that gave the farmhouse a calming, happy vibe. Her aunts, Sage and Daisy, were taking good care of the place. This was the opposite of her father's speculations about his younger sisters. Countless times, Lizzy had heard him predict that the twins would no doubt let the house fall into disrepair and end up losing the ranch to the bank.

Would his little sisters' success in the face of his cynicism be enough to teach him that he wasn't the authority on everyone and everything? Doubtful. Lizzy shoved down a mean-spirited urge to call her father and tell him what she'd discovered, but calling him would require talking to him. And that was not happening anytime soon.

Lizzy parked her car and got out, stretching her arms wide to relieve some of the stiffness from her long drive. After the thousand miles and sixteen hours of driving from Chicago, she was kind of glad she'd arrived before her aunts were home. It would give her a little time to look around the place on her own.

She inhaled the warm, clean air. There wasn't a hint of car exhaust or the fetid reek of public trash cans. Instead, the scent of soil that was damp from a recent rain made her think of helping her grandmother work in the garden. Filling her lungs with this sweet air might make it easier to stretch her voice, find her full range and work the wobble out of her vibrato. Maybe she could even get in her first outdoor singing session before they returned.

She groaned and pressed her fingertips to her temples. The thought of singing brought to mind memories of her recent audition with the Chicago Opera. It had not gone well. Not well at all. Her nerves had gotten the best of her, and she'd frozen up, her lungs constricting and choking off her voice. Her dream of singing with the Chicago Opera had withered like her vocals.

Afterward, one of the directors had been kind and approached her with a bit of advice. She said others had found confidence by choosing a secluded place where they could sing without the worry that someone was judging them. One of her suggestions was to do that until she felt more comfortable and then once again sing in front of people before auditioning at another opera.

Lizzy's city apartment with a roommate had definitely not been the place for that, but since she suddenly found herself with no job—*thanks a lot, Dad*—and couldn't pay her half of the rent or afford her voice coach, the only place she could think of going was to Dalton Ranch. When she'd called her aunts, they had not only asked her to come visit but suggested she stay for the whole summer. So here she was, ready to reconnect, get some answers and stretch her voice with no one to critique her.

She had to be ready for the open auditions at the famous Bass Opera House in Fort Worth. A few months was plenty of time to prepare. All she needed to do was up her confidence level enough to sing without freezing up.

"No time like the present to get started."

She cleared her throat and started a vocal warm-up exercise. Undulating *ing* sounds moved into *vo va vo*, each round growing higher in pitch. Elizabeth pushed the button to open the trunk of her car and let her voice rise in volume. Grabbing the handle of her large, overpacked duffel bag, she gave an extra heave to lift it up over the lip of the trunk and used its weight as momentum to swing it around to the ground.

But it didn't hit the ground.

Instead, her target uttered a very male grunt as the air left his lungs, followed by a muttered curse under his breath.

She dropped the bag onto the gravel and clasped her hands to her mouth. It was the cowboy she'd seen riding across the front pasture. "Oh, my gosh. I'm so sorry. I didn't hear you come up behind me."

"That's probably because you were…" He cleared his throat and rubbed the palm of one hand over his ribs. "Was that singing?"

Elizabeth bristled. Her confidence and ego had been wounded enough lately. Never mind that he was even better looking up close, the last thing she wanted was a dusty cowboy's opinion of her voice. Even if he did have moody brown eyes and the hint of a dark, ruggedly sexy beard. And especially a cowboy who probably knew zero, zip and zilch about opera.

"Those were vocal exercises to warm up. I'm an opera singer."

"Great."

That one word, spoken in a deadpan voice and accompanied by a blank expression, gave her little clue as to his true thoughts. Was he being sincere or sarcastic? She had a feeling it was the latter.

"Who are you?" she asked.

"Travis. The ranch foreman. You must be Lizzy."

"My name is Elizabeth." Almost everyone called her Lizzy, but this guy had managed to rub her the wrong way in only a few seconds.

One of his dark eyebrows raised enough to be hidden under the shade of his tan cowboy hat. "Your aunts aren't back from the auction yet."

"I know. They said if I got here before them I could use the hidden key."

"Need help with—" he circled his hand in the vicinity of her open trunk "—all that?"

His words were right, but the scowl making his eyebrows

into dark slashes gave her the impression he could think of much better ways to spend his time.

"No, thanks. You can go back to whatever it is you were doing before I got here."

"I'll unlock the house." Gravel crunched under his boots as he spun and headed for the front porch. He pulled keys from his pocket and had the door open by the time she made it onto the porch with the duffel bag.

"Thank you, Travis."

Without a word, he used two fingers on the brim to tip his hat and then walked away.

Thank goodness he didn't look back because she was staring at the way his faded jeans hugged his exceptionally nice backside and long legs that led to a pair of dirty cowboy boots. She didn't see many real cowboys in the city, and he was definitely the real thing. But he was so not her type.

Although, with her dating record, she wasn't exactly sure what her type was, or even what it should be. She'd had anything but good luck in the guy department over the past few years. Two of the men she'd liked the most had suddenly ghosted her, leaving her to wonder if there was something wrong with her. Lizzy mentally scolded herself.

There's nothing wrong with me.

That was her new mantra. The problem was just her ability to judge a guy's character, and she was working on improving that skill.

She rushed inside before he caught her gawking and lowered her bag to the narrow-plank oak floor. The walls of the wide entryway were eggshell white with an eclectic mix of artwork. Watercolor landscapes, black-and-white family photos in antique frames and a collection of McCoy pottery wall pockets holding dried flowers. The entryway led from the front door to the center of the house, where a staircase went up to the second floor.

On each side of her were identical archways. To the left was a cozy living room with a fireplace and lots of windows to let in the light. To the right was a dining room where she remembered family dinners and lively conversations with plenty of laughter. She hoped to recapture some of those happy feelings while she was here.

She walked through to the kitchen at the back of the house. As a child, it had been one of her favorite rooms because her grandmother would sing with her while she cooked and baked. Lizzy, Sage and Daisy would help her and listen to stories, some true and some made up by her grandmother's brilliant imagination.

A row of windows ran above the butcher-block counter-top with the large farmhouse sink, allowing for a great view of the backyard that was shaded by mature oak, magnolia and pecan trees. The cabinets had been painted the palest of blue, and the sturdy marble-topped island had two pendant lights above it. The same round kitchen table sat off to one side of the room with a porcelain pitcher of fresh flowers in the center.

Without anyone even being here to greet her, Elizabeth felt a sense of being home and welcomed in a way she didn't feel at her father's house. Before further exploration, she went back outside to unload her car, but the rest of her belongings were already out of her trunk and in a neat pile on the porch.

Glancing around, she saw no one, but she knew who'd done it, and it made her smile. "That was nice of him."

Travis might be a grumpy cowboy of few words, but apparently, he was also a southern gentleman. Maybe he wouldn't be so bad after all. They might have gotten off to a better start if she hadn't slugged him in the stomach with her bag.

Their second meeting would be much better. She would make sure of it.

* * *

Another diva singer was the very last thing Travis Taylor needed or wanted in his life. One was enough for a lifetime. His heart and mind could attest to that fact.

After Elizabeth *dismissed* him, he'd turned for the barn, but it was too ingrained in him to help. His grandpa and great-grandpa had instilled old-fashioned values, and even though chivalry wasn't as expected as it used to be, he continued to do what he could to make them proud. He liked to think of the grandpas giving him thumbs-up as they looked down from heaven, probably on horseback. They'd both been big on taking care of others, and Lord knew his own mom had given him plenty of chances to do just that.

Sometimes Travis thought he'd taken their looking-out-for-others lesson overboard. He'd been taken advantage of one too many times, but old habits were hard to break, and it's not like unloading Elizabeth's bags was going to make her dependent on him. Still, outside of his job as foreman, he had to start putting limits on what he was willing to do for others. He needed to focus on his own life.

His mom would ignore that fact, and no doubt show up now and then with a problem, but right now, he was only responsible for keeping himself and the animals on this ranch alive. Another human was not his responsibility.

As soon as Elizabeth had pranced up the front steps like a princess and gone inside the house, he'd unloaded her suitcases and boxes and put them on the front porch. Thankfully, she hadn't come back outside before he made his getaway.

Stepping into the shade of the horse stable gave him some relief from the midafternoon sun. He rubbed the left side of his ribs where the tiny blond had clocked him with her bag that had felt as if it contained bricks. If he had to guess, it was probably full of shoes, and judging from the ones she'd been wearing, all of them impractical for a ranch. Her high-heeled wedge sandals were begging for a turned ankle, and her white sundress would be dirty in no time.

The new black stallion, Zeus, whickered and gave a snort as Travis came close to the spot where he was tethered.

"I'm coming, big guy. I'll have that saddle off in no time and then brush you down." He patted the animal's muscular neck and took off the bridal. The feisty stallion was almost tame enough to let someone other than Travis ride him. He was glad they'd decided to keep Zeus on the ranch so he could ride him anytime. Tomorrow, he'd get started training the three horses a new client had dropped off.

He barked a laugh at the thought of the diva, Elizabeth, on horseback. Sage and Daisy had told him she'd want to ride, but she would need different attire for that and hopefully had some in one of her many suitcases.

"What do you think, Zeus? Should we start her out on a Shetland pony?"

The horse tossed his head and stomped one hoof, making Travis chuckle.

He could keep pretending Elizabeth wasn't pretty and didn't make his libido stir, but he'd never been able to lie that well, especially to himself. But she wore too much makeup, and her hair was too perfectly styled into a sleek, blond waterfall that flowed passed her bare shoulders. She'd probably refuse to put on a hat for fear of making it frizzy.

Why did she have to be a singer? Opera, of all things. She'd be even louder than Crystal was because, as he understood it, some opera singers didn't even need to use microphones. And she'd be here for the whole summer.

Travis shook his head and started unbuckling the saddle. There was no reason to worry about whether Elizabeth was attractive or too city-girl or loud or liked to climb trees and howl at the moon in the middle of the night. None of that mattered. He would not get tangled up with someone complicated who could buck his new, simple life as sure as a bronc in the rodeo arena.

Never again.

Crystal had etched that warning into his heart and mind. When you got down to the bones of the matter, she had used him, and then when he didn't do exactly what she wanted she'd put him aside for someone shiny and new. Her latest boy toy had music biz connections and enjoyed the spotlight, unlike him. Crystal had made it a point to tell him he wasn't outgoing or fun enough. She wanted a man who craved the glitzy lifestyle as much as she did. That would have been a very helpful fact to know *before* he gave up things that were important to him and joined her on a tour of sold-out country music shows.

Travis growled under his breath. He'd been a fool to believe he would be enough for a woman who sought stage lights and fame. It was easier to tame the wildest of horses than someone who had no desire to stay in one place and live a simple life.

Once Zeus was brushed down and in his stall with fresh hay, Travis drove out to check on the ranch hands who were repairing a fence in the north pasture.

In the distance, he could just make out the top of the two-story barn on the Martin Ranch next door. After Travis's father died when he was eight years old and then his mom left, he'd grown up in the bunkhouse on that ranch. Great-grandpa Roy and Grandpa Will had become his guardians and raised him.

The Grandpas—as Travis had called them—had worked the ranch for the Martin family for most of their lives. It was there that they'd taught him about horses and cattle and the value of a hard day's work. And that sometimes, being a man came with responsibilities you might not love. Because they had lived and worked on the Martin ranch for most of their lives, his dad, both grandpas and a few other family members were buried there in a small family cemetery.

His truck tires rumbled over the metal bars of a cattle guard that separated two pastures, and he made a mental note to suggest repainting it.

According to the grandchildren who now owned Martin Ranch, it would go up for sale in about a year, but even with twelve months to save, he'd have to make sacrifices to afford a down payment and secure a loan for the four-hundred-acre ranch. His mom's last fly-by visit had put a huge dent in his savings. As it stood today, he didn't have enough.

No one in his family had ever owned land, and Travis had promised his grandpa that he'd be the first, rather than only work on someone else's the way four generations of his family had done for most of their lives. Even if it couldn't be the ranch where his family had been laid to rest, someday he would have a place of his own with enough space to breed and train horses and have a little house with a view.

He parked beside the Murphy brothers' muddy black truck. Finn, Riley and Jake were working on the last section of fence where the new gate needed to be hung. He'd taken a chance hiring the brothers with a rowdy reputation, but they'd proven themselves to be hardworking and dependable, and today they'd made better progress than he'd thought they would.

There was no doubt that these three were family, with their blue eyes, mountain-man size and features so similar you might think they were triplets if it wasn't for their different hair colors ranging from blond to reddish and light brown.

Travis climbed out of his truck and raised a hand in greeting. "Need help getting the gate hung?"

"We won't turn down a fourth pair of hands," Finn said

and lifted his cowboy hat to brush back his pale blond hair. "Goes faster when you work as a team."

Travis knew this to be true from his time working with his grandpas and his father before he'd died. Now he had no male family members to team up with. A flash of jealousy tightened his chest. These three brothers had something he never would.

The word *brother* always put a lump in his throat.

Within twenty minutes the job was done, and since the Murphys had started at sunrise, he sent them home. After checking the new pump on the windmill, he stopped by his log cabin behind the new horse stable. He needed a shower and a few minutes to prepare himself before going up to the main farmhouse.

Right inside his front door, he toed off his work boots and hung his hat on a hook Great-grandpa Roy had fashioned out of a deer's antler. His cabin was blessedly quiet. Just the way he liked it. He grabbed a glass of water and headed straight for the shower.

Sage and Daisy had insisted that he come to supper this evening so he could meet their niece, but after their first encounter, he wasn't exactly looking forward to their second meeting. He'd probably walk away with a black eye or something worse. Even so, he wouldn't say no to the sisters who had welcomed him to their ranch and always treated him like family. They'd given him a peaceful place to live and work far away from the constant noise and spotlights of the last few years.

It was because of loud, booming music that he hadn't heard the shouts of warning and ended up with an injury at his last rodeo. It had been bad enough to land him in a hospital bed with broken bones and a head injury. The embarrassing part? He was a bronc rider, who'd been hurt by a runaway bull he hadn't even been trying to ride.

At the doctor's strongly worded suggestion, there would be no more rodeo life for him—which meant no more prize money to add to the savings account earmarked for purchasing land.

On the plus side, now that he was retired from rodeo life, he didn't have to travel all the time or spend a week recovering from bruises just in time to ride again.

Travis took off his dirty T-shirt and rubbed his fingers across Elizabeth's handiwork on his ribs. A bruise was already forming. So much for not having to recover from bruises. Apparently, Elizabeth Dalton had something in common with bucking broncos.

He couldn't deny that she was pretty, but pretty dangerous might be more accurate. Physical pain was something he was used to, and he could take that. The emotional part was a whole different story.

"I'm done being used by other people for their selfish gains."

Travis finished undressing, adjusted the water temperature and sighed as the spray began to wash away the day's grime. This tiny cabin suited him. It reminded him of the happy years on Martin Ranch with the grandpas.

A little over six months ago, he'd gone from rodeo arena to being right in the middle of the chaos of traveling in a tour bus. He'd earned this calm, quiet lifestyle in a place where he could hear himself think. A place to heal his body, mind and heart. It was time to know when to help and when to say no.

And to not be taken in by sexual attraction or beauty. When he did start looking for love again, it would be with a woman who would stick around and be happy living a simple life, side by side.

Forever.

Someone down to earth. He was only interested in stability and kindness and thoughtfulness. Someone who was more of a homebody than a wanderer. Dating Crystal had been all the proof he'd needed that beauty didn't guarantee a kind heart.

Getting mixed up with Elizabeth Dalton—an opera singer of all things—was not anywhere on the list of good choices.

"Why in the hell am I still thinking about Elizabeth Dalton?"

He plowed his hands through his wet hair, and then turned off the water. Yanking the shower curtain open with too much force caused two metal hooks to pop off the rod, but before he could deal with reattaching them, his cellphone rang from beside the sink. He looked at the number and swore before letting it go into the abyss of his voice mail, just like all the others.

Chapter Two

Before lugging anything upstairs, Elizabeth went up to see if she could tell which one of the five bedrooms would be hers for the summer. In the one where she had slept as a child, there were fresh wildflowers in a crystal vase on the nightstand beside a lamp and a couple of Harlequin romance novels. The double bed with an antique iron headboard sat between two tall, deep-silled windows that were framed with gauzy white curtains. A set of fluffy pink towels were artfully arranged with fancy soaps on the wedding ring quilt.

The biggest clue to this being her room was the bundle of her favorite old-fashioned candy sticks held together with a blue satin ribbon. A little paper tag read *Welcome home*. It touched her that they remembered and had welcomed her with such a thoughtful treat. And the word *home* on the tag made a nostalgic and forgotten feeling stir inside her.

She sat on the bedside and unbuckled her new silver wedge sandals—that would be the last new shoes she bought for a long while. She was eager to walk barefoot through the house and go out into the shady backyard to feel the grass beneath her feet. This was a great opportunity to test out the article she'd read about grounding. It said walking barefoot on dirt or grass was a great way to pick up free ions from the earth's surface.

She wiggled her toes on the soft throw rug and then lay back on the bed with a long, satisfied sigh. The feather mattress topper was like a cloud, and a nap would feel so good right now. Reaching to her side, she grabbed a green candy stick with tiny pink lines spiraling from one end to the other. She peeled back the cellophane wrapper and swirled her tongue around the candy. Tart sweetness tickled her taste buds.

"Yum. Watermelon. My favorite."

Maybe Travis liked this candy, too. Would he think it was ridiculous if she gave him one as a thank-you for unloading her car? Probably. She wanted to find a way to make peace, but she could not—would not—let the cranky cowboy distract her from her summer goals.

All her focus needed to be on reconnecting with family and singing. And her upcoming audition.

She was here to practice singing until it felt as comfortable as breathing. In a few months, she had to ace her audition at Bass Opera Hall. If she didn't, she wasn't sure what she was going to do. She had enough money to get through the summer and a few months more, but after that, she would have to get a job.

The thought of going back to being an office manager at her father's company, Dalton Realty, made her want to cry, but with her degree and experience, that was likely the kind of job she'd end up doing if she didn't do well at her audition.

Lizzy bit off a piece of candy and crunched it between

her back teeth. She'd prove to all the doubters—mostly her father—that her goal of being a working opera singer who traveled the world wasn't foolish or a trivial hobby. She had not made this trip to Channing, Texas, only to give up or turn around and go back to Chicago. The towns might start with the same letter, but they were like different worlds.

And most definitely not back to her old job at Dalton Realty. Not after Joshua Wayne Dalton's latest stunt. Not after the information she'd discovered right before they had their first real fight. His over-the-top interference had ruled her life for far too long, and she was proud of finally standing up for herself.

She grabbed the top book on the stack and grinned at the title: *Cowboy Nights*.

An image of Travis on horseback flashed through her mind. She was not here to get caught up in a fairy-tale romance with a cowboy who hadn't shown even the slightest interest in her.

Why am I always drawn to people and situations that I know aren't good for me?

After a good night's sleep, she would thank Travis for unloading her things. She was going to be here all summer, and there needed to be harmony between them.

Friendly terms, Lizzy. Nothing romantic.

His gruffness should make that easy enough.

She heard a soft jingle right before the bedframe creaked as something heavy landed on the mattress. With a scream lodged in her throat, she sprang into a sitting position and came face-to-face with a fluffy white cat. The animal sauntered closer and rubbed her head against Lizzy's arm.

"Hello there. You gave me quite a fright sneaking up on me like that." The animal's fur was silky soft, and a small bell jingled on a baby blue collar. The heart-shaped tag said Lady. "You sure are a beautiful girl."

Lady's meow was a soft chirp, and her fluffy feather-duster tail swished through the air.

Lizzy hadn't had a pet since she'd lived in Texas fifteen years ago. This extended trip to Channing was the fresh start she needed. It was long past time to be in charge of the direction her life took. No more doing things such as getting the college degree someone else decided was best. No more suffering daily at a job she hated.

And especially no more jumping at her father's barked orders. But ignoring his demands would be easier said than done. Years of conditioning was going to make it hard to continue standing up to him, but that was her goal.

Lady crawled onto her lap, put her front paws on Lizzy's chest and sniffed her nose, making her laugh.

"Looks like we're going to be friends." She cuddled her closer and rubbed her cheek against the top of the cat's head. It was a comfort to know there would be an animal in the house.

Before she had time to take a catnap—with an actual cat—or walk barefoot or even bring up her belongings, the sound of a diesel engine drew her attention. With Lady in her arms, she went to the window that looked out over the side of the house where the gravel driveway led to the barn and other areas of the ranch. Her aunts were getting out of a red double-cab truck with dual back wheels. A long silver horse trailer was attached to the bumper, and the words Dalton Ranch were painted along the trailer's length in fancy red letters.

The cat hopped out of her arms and rushed for the doorway as if the truck was a signal to greet her owners.

Lizzy reached the top of the stairs just as Daisy and Sage came in the front door. They were identical twins, but you could tell them apart by their styles and the one dimple in Daisy's right cheek.

Daisy's strawberry blond hair was held back in a simple, low ponytail that went halfway down her back. She wore black cowboy boots, dark jeans, and a fitted red T-shirt, and only mascara framed her green eyes. Daisy might have a flowery name, but Lizzy remembered her being a tomboy and fussing about having to wear a dress to church.

Sage's hair was the same shade of strawberry blond but was cut into a trendy bob of loose curls. She wore a full face of makeup that had been applied so perfectly that Lizzy wanted to ask her for pointers. Her chambray denim dress flowed in loose folds to her knees, and a scattering of tiny crystals dotted the red leather of her ankle boots. Sage looked more like she'd been at a party than a horse auction.

"Is that our sweet little Lizzy all grown up into a beautiful woman?" Sage asked.

"It's me."

As soon as she reached the bottom of the stairs, she was enveloped in a group hug. She hadn't had a hug like this in a really long time and it was a jolt to her system. It took a few heartbeats before she could relax into the welcoming embrace. She wasn't sure whether to laugh or cry.

Not wanting to be left out, the cat wound herself between their legs and licked Lizzy's ankle before racing back upstairs.

Daisy held her by the shoulders. "We've missed you so much."

"I've missed you, too."

"Sorry we weren't home in time to welcome you in person."

"No problem. Lady welcomed me." She didn't mention her run-in with their ranch manager. She motioned to the pile of suitcases, boxes and random bags near the foot of the stairs. "Sorry about bringing so much stuff. I gave up my half of an apartment to another roommate, and this is everything I didn't put in storage."

"The house is plenty big enough for all that and lots more."

Daisy flipped her long ponytail over her shoulder, picked up a suitcase in each hand and started up the stairs. "Let's get your things up to your room."

Sage put the duffel bag strap over one shoulder and grabbed a box.

"Thanks for helping me." Lizzy picked up as much as she could carry and followed her aunts to her bedroom. Lady was curled up directly on top of the stack of pink towels.

Sage snapped her fingers at the animal. "Get off those clean towels, you little devil."

Between the three of them, they got everything in two trips. "Just stack it all in that corner, and I'll unpack later. Can I store what I don't need in the attic?"

"Absolutely."

"I can't tell you how much it means to me that you are letting me stay here."

"This is your home," Sage and Daisy replied in that twin-like way they had of saying the same exact thing at the same exact time.

"Have you eaten?" Sage asked.

"Not since lunch. I stopped at a fast-food drive-through and got crunchy beef tacos. It's hard to get Texas-style tacos where I…" She paused before saying "live" since she wasn't sure where she was going to live. "It's hard to find them in Chicago."

"You can get plenty of tacos around here at any time of the day. For breakfast, lunch and dinner," Daisy said.

Sage started down the stairs first. "I'm glad to hear that you still eat meat because there are steaks in the refrigerator for tonight's supper. Let's cook together, just like we used to do."

"Sounds fabulous," Lizzy said.

The twins took off their boots and put them on a mat by the front door with the words *Cowgirls do it better* printed across it in turquoise letters. Apparently, they still liked to go barefoot just like she did.

Lizzy followed them toward the kitchen. "I'm ashamed it took me so long to come back to Texas and see you in person."

"Don't worry about it for a second longer. Although your father went away to school when we were very young, he came back enough for us to understand how he..." Sage bit her lower lip and shot her sister a brief glance as if she hoped her twin would fill in the rest of the information.

"Manipulates and directs people?" Lizzy finished for her.

"Yes. That's one way to put it," Sage said.

"I wish he could see how wonderful everything looks. You two have built this ranch into something really special."

"We've been busy. That's for sure." Daisy opened the refrigerator and studied its contents. "In the beginning, we had to sell the cattle, and then we started focusing on horses."

"You'll have to give me a tour around the ranch and tell me more about what happens on a stud farm."

And tell me more about the hot cowboy.

"Of course," Daisy said. "Tomorrow we can walk around or even take a horseback ride."

"The kitchen is just like in my memory." Lizzy opened the punched-tin door of the old wooden pie safe that was still next to the kitchen table. Her grandmother's collection of pie plates lined four shelves, but unfortunately, none held actual pie. Gamma had made the best pies. Tartly sweet cherry, pecan drizzled with a bit of brown sugar crumble and caramel sauce, pumpkin to die for and coconut cream that had won a blue ribbon.

Daisy came up behind and put her hands on Lizzy's shoulders. "Do you remember baking with Mama?"

"I do. Those are some of my favorite memories." Lizzy had grown up hearing her aunts, who were only ten years older than her, calling her grandmother Mama. Her version of mama combined with grandma had come out as Gamma, and the name had stuck. "She would sing with me, and I think it is thanks to her that I love it so much."

"You not only love singing, but you are so incredibly good at it," Daisy said.

Lizzy blew out a long, slow breath. "Not good enough to get a spot at the Chicago Opera. Not even in the chorus."

"They must need their hearing checked." Daisy tapped her ear. "We've seen some of the videos of you singing, and you're amazing."

"Thank you." She wanted to be as amazing as her aunts thought she was. From the pie safe, Lizzy picked up a red wooden recipe box with yellow flowers painted on it. She opened it to see Gamma's beautiful looping handwriting. "Around the holidays, this pie safe would be filled with goodies."

"Those are all of her dessert recipes. Her other recipe box is on a shelf in there." Sage pointed to a cabinet closest to the refrigerator.

Lizzy pulled out the first recipe. It was for cheerful cherry pie. She flipped over the card and on the back was a quote written in her granddad's handwriting.

"A day is never the pits if there is cherry pie."

"Oh, wow. I had forgotten about Granddad having a funny saying to go along with every kind of pie." Lizzy tucked the card back into its place between recipes for peach and apple caramel-streusel. "Can I use these recipes while I'm here?"

"Of course. We'll need to make a trip to the grocery store for baking ingredients." Daisy opened a lower cabinet and got out two enameled-metal dish pans, one orange and one yellow.

"I remember those." Lizzy said. "Gamma always used them to rinse the fresh vegetables we picked from the garden."

"That's just what we're about to do. We need to wash the potatoes and green beans."

"It's so cool that you still use her pans." She could almost hear Gamma's hearty laughter. It had always made her laugh right along with her.

"We always have, but I'm sad to say that the garden is no longer the bountiful place you probably remember. Neither of us has Mama's green thumb."

"You two have had your hands busy turning Dalton Ranch into a success. I think letting the garden go can be forgiven."

"Something sure had to give." Sage filled the orange pan with water and put it on the counter beside the sink. "Could you snap and rinse the green beans while I scrub the potatoes?"

"You bet."

Her stylish aunt added ice cubes to the water. "It will help crisp the beans." She filled her own pan and got a scrub brush from a drawer.

Lizzy began snapping the ends off the long string beans and dropping them into the ice water. "You didn't grow these?"

"No, our neighbor, Mrs. Martin, grew them. She passed away recently, and this is the last of the beans from her garden. We bought the potatoes at the grocery store."

Lady pranced into the kitchen, wove herself between everyone's legs and then meowed at the back door to be let outside.

Daisy opened the wooden door, the top half of which held a large pane of glass that looked out over the backyard. In a well-practiced move, the cat pushed against the screen door and slipped through the crack while her aunt used her foot to slide a metal doorstop into place. "Did your father give you the cards and gifts we sent to Chicago over the years?"

Lizzy flinched and snapped a bean with too much force. It flew out of her hand and across the room to land with a plunk on the kitchen table beside the pitcher of wildflowers. "No. He didn't give me any of them."

Her aunts shared one of their silent twin-speak expressions, and it wasn't hard to tell that they were unhappy with this news about their much older brother. This was one more thing to add to the list of Joshua Dalton's bad deeds.

"Let's not ruin tonight with talk of your father," Daisy suggested. "Unless you want to talk about him, Lizzy?"

The muscles tensed across her shoulders. They were the perfect—and really only—people she could talk to about her father, but tonight was for reconnecting and fun. She was still too upset with him to say much without getting really mad. "No. Not yet. I think I need a few days before I can talk about him." Lizzy scooped the cold, clean beans from the water and dropped them into a strainer in the farmhouse sink.

A cellphone rang, and Sage picked it up off the table. "I need to take this call in the office. Excuse me for a few minutes."

"Could you please toss the dirty water out onto the grass?" Daisy said. "Better there than wasting the water down the drain."

"What a good idea." Lizzy grasped the dishpan of ice

water with both hands and pushed backward through the screen door. Standing in the shade of the big oak tree, she could see her reflection in the shimmery water. Her smile lifted her spirits. A smile that made its way not only to her eyes but also warmed her heart. Being here only a few hours was already starting to ease her stress level.

As if it was a celebratory toast to her new adventure, she tipped the pan forward and tossed the water into the air. Her gaze followed the path of the water, and she gasped.

But it was too late.

Chapter Three

"Are you kidding me?" Travis growled the words in a deep, rumbly tone.

The pan slipped from Lizzy's fingers to clatter on the brick pathway, splashing the remaining water on the skirt of her white sundress. She looked into the whiskey-brown eyes of a dripping wet and rightly irritated cowboy.

Her skin prickled with a feeling she couldn't explain, and it wasn't the least bit unpleasant but more of an awareness…of him. "I'm sooo sorry. This is not at all how I saw our second meeting going."

His upper lip twitched, but not in a way that suggested he was withholding a smile. It was more like the way someone gets a twitchy eye when they're upset. And yet, he was radiating an energy that was strangely appealing. She mentally rolled her eyes at her unfortunate fascination for the bad boy type.

Water dripped from the brim of his hat and trickled down

his face and neck to disappear into the collar of his blue-and-white plaid shirt.

The sight of him had her battling between holding her stomach with laughter and running back inside. He, however, wasn't the least bit amused—if his expressionless mask was any indication. But he also wasn't intimidating. Travis was intense in a sexy kind of way. She took a few steps back, not out of fear of him, but rather a fear of her own lack of willpower.

He took off his hat and shook it, droplets of water flying into the shade-dappled light. He mumbled something about dangerous women but not quietly enough that she didn't hear him.

"Only to guys who sneak up on me."

"Walking up to the door right in front of you is hardly sneaking, but to be safe, I'll start announcing myself from now on."

"You're very quiet for such a big guy, and I was looking at my reflection in the water."

He made a noise in his throat that sounded suspiciously like a laugh he wasn't willing to share, and then he flicked the remains of a melting ice cube from his shoulder.

"It was an accident, you know. I really didn't mean to soak you with ice water."

"I know."

"At least it wasn't the potato water," Lizzy said with a shrug and grin.

His dark eyebrows drew together into a deep V. "The what?"

"The water we used to scrub the dirt off the potatoes. This was only the water I used to rinse the green beans."

"Yippee for me," he said in a deadpan voice. He reached for the collar of his shirt with both hands. It would only take one swift tug to pop open all the pearl-snap buttons, but instead, Travis started with the top snap and slowly popped it open.

She knew she should look away, and even started to drop her gaze, but she just couldn't make herself complete the movement. He continued to torture her. One…button… at…a…time. The white T-shirt beneath the plaid was disappointing, but the wet cotton molding to every curve of his torso wasn't half bad. Not bad at all.

What is wrong with me and my self-control?

Clearly, it had been way too long since she'd dated anyone, but she'd promised herself there would be no more falling for a handsome face or nice physique. There were so many things that were more important. A fondness for smiling and a sense of humor, just to name a few. Travis the grumpy cowboy was not seeing the humor in the situation.

"Do you need a towel?" Daisy asked from the open kitchen doorway, ending Lizzy's brief trip into fantasyland.

"No. Most of the ice-cold water hit me in the face. In this heat, my shirt will be dry in no time."

Her aunt was doing her best not to laugh but basically failing. "Travis, could you please turn on the gas grill so it can heat up?"

"Yes, ma'am. I'll do that."

"You know it makes me feel old when you call me ma'am," Daisy said and pointed a finger at him. "I'm only thirty-five. That's only five years older than you."

This time, he did offer up a barely there smile for her aunt. "You got it, Daisy."

He headed for the large red-brick patio that hadn't been here when Lizzy was a child. It was laid in a herringbone pattern and had a built-in grill and a polished concrete counter beside it. An outdoor dining table and six chairs were in the center and a firepit and four rocking chairs were at the other end.

He tossed his wet plaid shirt to land perfectly on the back of one of the patio chairs, making Lizzy wonder if he had some roping skills.

When they got back into the kitchen, she quietly laughed with Daisy. "I can't believe I did that. When I first arrived, I was singing while unloading my trunk and didn't hear him come up behind me. I spun around and hit him with one of my bags."

"And then you tossed water in his face?" Sage asked as she came out of the walk-in pantry with a bottle of red wine.

"Yep. I've made a fabulous first impression."

"Well, he won't forget you anytime soon." Daisy got the tray of meat out of the refrigerator and put it on the island's marble top.

"Not exactly how I want to be remembered. Is he always so grumpy or is it just because I abuse him every single time I see him?"

Sage's skirt swirled around her legs as she moved to look out the window above the sink and then took a moment to watch him. "Travis is a really good guy just like his grandfathers were, but he's been more down in the dumps than usual. He's always been a man of few words, but lately he's been even more so. He recently lost his grandpa and went through a bad breakup, and he hasn't quite gotten back to himself."

They paused their conversation when he came into the kitchen.

"The grill will be ready in a few minutes," he said.

"Perfect. The potatoes need to be put on to bake first." Daisy handed him the foil-wrapped potatoes.

Lizzy grabbed the open bottle of wine and a couple of glasses and then followed him outside to sit on the patio. Now was her chance to smooth things over so they could come to some kind of peace between them. Otherwise, it would be a long, uncomfortable summer.

"Would you like a glass of wine?"

"No, thanks. I'm more of a beer guy."

"I'll get you one. It's the least I can do to make up for my ill-treatment of you." She went back into the house, got an amber glass bottle out of the refrigerator, and then put it on the concrete counter beside him.

"Thanks."

There was an awkward moment of silence that she felt the need to fill. "This patio and grill weren't here when I was a kid, but they're really nice. Can I help you do anything with the food?"

"No," he said a bit too quickly.

"Are you afraid if I get too close to the grill that you'll get burned?"

"The thought did cross my mind." He twisted the bottlecap from his beer then flicked it to land perfectly into a small metal trashcan.

Daisy came outside with the tray of meat and her own glass of wine. "Since the weather is nice, we thought we could eat outside."

Sage joined them and, as they sat around the patio table, the conversation turned to Lizzy's singing.

Travis chose a chair at the opposite corner from Lizzy and seemed to be purposely avoiding eye contact.

Admittedly, he now had a reason—or two—to keep his distance from her, but that was a good thing because she needed to keep her heart protected when it came to her attraction to this moody cowboy.

"What are your plans and goals for the summer?" Sage asked her.

Her aunt Sage had always been the twin who set goals and made plans way in advance. "I'm feeling the need to reset my life and focus on singing. If possible, I want it to be a summer with no obligations other than helping you out here on the ranch and preparing for my audition."

"A singing audition?" Travis asked while he picked at the label on his beer bottle.

"Yes. In a few months, they're holding open auditions at the Bass Opera Hall in Fort Worth."

"She's an amazing singer," the twins said in tandem, and then started talking about the earlier phone call from a client.

Lizzy turned her attention back to the off-limits cowboy. "At this point in my career, I don't expect to get a major role. I just want to be part of an opera company and work my way up so I can sing and travel and do what I love."

"Sing *and* travel." He repeated her words with a faraway gaze as if talking more to himself than her.

While Lizzy searched for the right response, the cat climbed out of a nearby tree and bounded across the patio to hop onto her lap.

After another long sip of beer, Travis stood. "I should turn the potatoes."

"He's a tough one," she whispered to the cat who was purring on her lap.

The conversation continued as they ate and laughed and started on a second bottle of wine. Travis was loosening up in small increments and even chuckled at a story she told.

"What does your father have to say about your plans to—" Daisy clapped a hand over her mouth. "Sorry. I forgot we aren't talking about him tonight."

Lizzy waved a hand and took a healthy swallow of wine. "When I do tell you about his latest stunt, you'll understand why I'm finally here."

It wasn't difficult for Travis to pick up on the family drama and tension where her father was concerned. He had no memory of the twins' older brother, Joshua. He never came around the ranch and they never talked about him, and he didn't know why. It had to be the reason Elizabeth hadn't been here in so long.

He was tempted to ask for details, but he couldn't act too interested and encourage her to talk to him more than she already did. Even though he could sympathize with having a parent who caused stress in your life, he had enough of his own without adding her problems.

But his conscience was poking at him. He shouldn't be so gruff with Elizabeth, but she truly did pose a danger to him. Not in a physical way like he'd made her think but in an emotional way. With her fancy fashion and makeup and singing and a desire to travel with an opera, there were too many similarities to his ex. His gut cramped as if a rope had been yanked tight around his middle.

"Travis, are you still going into town tomorrow to pick up that new brand of horse feed we ordered?" Sage asked.

His empty beer bottle clinked as he set it on the metal tabletop. "Yes. Do you need me to pick up something else?"

"Daisy and I have a meeting with a prospective new client, and I'm not sure how long it will take. Would you please take Lizzy with you to pick up some groceries so she can bake?"

His skin prickled with goose bumps. Being alone with her in his truck tomorrow was one of the last things he wanted to do, but he couldn't say no to their request. He made himself answer without giving away his thoughts.

"Sure, but it might be easier if you just give me a grocery list since Li—" He'd almost said Lizzy, but apparently, he wasn't allowed to call her by that name. "Since Elizabeth probably wants to rest after her long road trip."

"I would actually like to go with you," she said. "I'm not sure what all I'll want to buy, so I need to be there in person. I also want to see how things have changed in the area since I was last here."

"Great." *Not great. Not great at all.* "I'll be leaving by nine o'clock. Can you be ready by then?"

"Absolutely. Nine works for me."

Elizabeth's sunny smile disarmed him in a way he did not want to examine too closely.

Lizzy topped off her glass of wine and then Sage's, but when she started to pour more into Daisy's glass, her aunt put a hand over the top. "No more for me."

"We have a rule," Sage said. "Never give her a third glass of wine."

Daisy giggled and shrugged. "It's true. I tend to lose my filter if I have more than two glasses. Unfortunately, I have embarrassed myself more than once."

Sage grinned at her sister. "Like the time she met Finn Murphy and his brothers."

"What happened?" Lizzy asked. "Will you tell the story?"

"I first saw Finn at a festival. I kept running into him first in one part of the festival and then another. The third time, he joked that he promised he wasn't following me. Before I thought better of it, I said, 'Would you like to?'"

Lizzy laughed along with the twins, but Travis ducked his head, and with his hat on, she couldn't even tell if he was smiling. "Sounds like something I might do. What happened then? What did he say?"

"I didn't give him a chance. I was so embarrassed that I spun away and left the area as fast as I could. Then I saw him a week later at the grocery store and managed to embarrass myself yet again."

"I've never heard this story," Travis said.

"I'm surprised Finn didn't tell you." Daisy stretched her arms above her head and yawned. "At the store, I walked right up to him and said, 'You really are following me. And you've cut your hair.' He just grinned as if he had a secret and then told me I had him confused with someone else. That I must have met one of his brothers. Not a second later, the first brother who I'd seen at the festival walked up. He was followed by a third Murphy brother."

"Triplets?" Lizzy asked.

Sage swirled her wine. "No, just brothers who are close in age and look a whole lot alike."

"Like Viking warriors," Daisy said with a dreamy expression. "Now, all three of them work for us. You'll meet them soon, Lizzy."

"I'll make sure to warn them." One half of his full mouth quirked up just the slightest as he rose from his chair.

The warmth of a blush heated Lizzy's face. "Ha-ha-ha. Funny guy. You be sure to do that." Even his barely-there grin increased her desire to see what he looked like with a full smile. The fact that he was teasing her had to be a good sign.

Somehow, they'd find a way to peacefully coexist during the hours he was at work on the ranch.

"Thanks for dinner, ladies. I should get going because morning comes early. Have a good rest of your evening."

"You know you're welcome to join us for dinner anytime. You don't have to wait for an invitation," Sage said.

"I appreciate it." He tipped his hat and walked into the shadowy night.

"I'll be ready by nine in the morning," Lizzy called after him.

He gave a thumbs-up without turning around.

They gathered the last of the dishes and went inside to finish cleaning up.

Sage swirled a short curl around her finger. "I got the feeling that our quiet Travis Taylor was a little bit jealous when we were talking about the Murphy brothers."

A feeling—much like jealousy—hit Lizzy in the pit of her stomach. Was there something romantic between Travis and one of her aunts? "Does one of you have something going on with him?"

"Definitely not," they said in unison.

Her relief was instant and spoke to the trouble she was in if she didn't get a quick handle on this little crush of hers.

Daisy covered another yawn. "He's like a little brother to us."

"But that doesn't mean you have to feel the same way. He's a good age for you to date," Sage said with a wink.

Lizzy laughed, a little too enthusiastically, and shook her head. "Not a good idea." She had to stop wasting time and energy on guys who weren't that into her.

Travis made her feel too many things all at once. Conflicting urges and emotions. Wanting to yell at him while fighting the urge to see if he was a good kisser. Being so physically attracted to him while finding him completely frustrating was confusing.

It was a good thing Travis was standoffish and on the grumpy side because it would force her not to fall for a sexy grin. But since the man didn't seem to know how to form his mouth into a true smile, that wasn't a current danger.

I've got this situation under control. No problem.

Chapter Four

The night was dark with only the sliver of a crescent moon lighting the way. Travis glanced over his shoulder at the farmhouse, and the kitchen light was like a spotlight shining on Elizabeth as she stood at the sink.

A mental image flashed through his mind. Crystal standing in the spotlights on a big stage with her fans screaming. He growled and kicked a stick with the toe of his boot, and it bounced across the ground. Elizabeth wanted the same type of in-the-spotlight lifestyle his ex-girlfriend did. The only difference was the type of stage—one with fans who danced wildly and sang along with the country music, and the other a more dignified scene with fancy clothes and appropriately timed applause.

He'd taken this job way out in the country for the peace and quiet, but he had a strong feeling that Elizabeth's arrival was going to interrupt his tranquility. He realized he'd come to a complete stop while he stared at her washing dishes. This irritated him, yet again.

What is my problem?

He turned away from the house and continued toward his cabin. Even in the dark, he'd walked this path many times and knew his way well enough. A few minutes later he was across the clearing behind the barn and at the front door of the small cabin that had become his home while working on Dalton Ranch.

He changed his alarm clock to give himself an extra thirty minutes of sleep. When your workday was as long as his and you worked as hard as he did, every minute of extra sleep was precious. He'd still have plenty of time to eat, down some coffee and tend to all the morning duties before driving into town. He hoped Elizabeth wouldn't slow him down too much because he had much to do once they returned.

Normally quick to fall asleep, he soon realized it wasn't happening. Thoughts of the new addition to the ranch kept his mind active, and when sleep finally did come, it was fitful and uneasy.

On some level, Travis knew he was dreaming, but it was a really good dream about pie, and it was too good to give up by returning to reality. Apple, cherry and peach. He took another bite of each, inhaling the amazing scents and savoring the flavors and… The sound?

Why was his apple pie making an indescribable sound?

Startling awake, Travis flipped onto his back and almost toppled out of bed but caught himself with a hand on the cedar headboard. His mind was still foggy, but it only took a few pounding heartbeats to recognize the sound. It was singing. More specifically, it had to be Elizabeth singing.

At top volume.

Why was she inside of his cabin and singing so loudly? Had he overslept and she was here to wake him up? He glanced at the window to see that it was still dark outside.

"What in the pre-dawn hell is going on?" So much for sleeping past sunrise.

Since he slept naked, he yanked the blanket off the bed and wrapped it around his waist before storming from the bedroom, but his living area was empty. She was not inside his cabin. He tossed the blanket over the couch and crossed to the living room window.

The barest hint of a golden glimmer along the horizon was only a promise of the coming sunrise, but it was enough to make out the figure of a woman in the center of the clearing between his cabin and the old barn. With her arms outstretched and her head tipped back, she looked like a goddess or warrior princess preparing for battle.

He had no idea what she was saying because she was singing in another language, but whatever the meaning, it was way too much for this hour. Maybe it was a call to battle, or maybe he hadn't been wrong when he joked to himself about her howling at the moon.

Even though his great-grandpa Roy had played opera music every weekend until the day he died, it was not Travis's go-to music. These days, no music was. Especially at zero dark thirty when everything should be blissfully quiet. One of the major reasons he lived out in the country in a cabin by the woods.

But he knew enough about opera to know that she was talented. How did someone so small produce such powerful sounds?

A shiver rippled across his skin, as his frustration began fading. Elizabeth singing in the dawning light was kind of fascinating. Unique and powerful.

And dangerously captivating.

A few hours later, Travis had finished his morning routine and started the Murphy brothers working on another section of fence. As he approached the farmhouse, he could once again hear Elizabeth singing, but this time it wasn't her big opera voice that had been his wake-up call. It was a soft, lilting voice that he had to admit was beautiful. It was a much more pleasing tone than Crystal's high-pitched twangy one.

Travis shook his head and reached for the kitchen doorknob. He'd been here often enough that he was free to come in without knocking during daylight hours. Elizabeth was once again unaware of his presence. With his thumb and pointer finger between his lips, he let out a loud whistle.

Elizabeth jumped straight into the air, spinning on him in one swift movement as she hurled a muffin his way. "Good grief, Travis."

He caught the pastry in one hand. "What?" He took a bite of the muffin to keep her from seeing how much her reaction had entertained him. He was not willing to give in to his urge to chuckle. "I was just announcing my presence. I don't have time to change my clothes before we leave."

She still had a hand to her heart. "I am so going to get you a jingly bell like the cat wears. You just wait and see. I'll slip it on you while you are asleep in your bed," she said and turned back to close the refrigerator.

The thought of her near his bed made his skin heat and his pulse race. If she was in his bedroom, sleeping would be the furthest thing from his mind.

I can never let this woman anywhere near my bedroom.

"Ready to head to the grocery store?" he asked.

"Yes. I just need to put on my shoes."

He glanced at her bare feet. They were tiny with bright pink toenails, and she was wearing another sundress almost the same shade as the nail polish.

She slipped on and buckled the same pair of impractical high-heeled shoes she'd been wearing when she arrived at the ranch, and then grabbed a small—yep, you guessed it—pink purse from the countertop.

"Lead the way, cowboy."

When they reached his truck, Travis opened the passenger side door and noticed her surprise at his action. Had she never had a man open a door for her before?

"Thanks." With her heels, she was tall enough to easily climb into his truck.

He walked around to the other side, got in and started the engine. "I have a couple of stops to make along the way. Hope you aren't in a big hurry to get to the grocery store."

"Nope. No hurry at all." She snapped her seat belt into place and then smoothed her skirt. "It's not like I have anything pressing that I need to do. I've been looking forward to seeing some of the area and how things have changed."

"We *are* on a schedule," he said, now worried that she'd want to add a bunch of unnecessary stops. "I have work to do when we get back to the ranch."

"Other than the grocery store, where are we going?"

"To get gas and to the feedstore."

"Do we have to drive all the way to Fort Worth for groceries?"

"No. There's a new grocery store here in Channing."

"That's handy. The last time I was here, the only choice was Zimmerman's General Store."

Travis glanced her way briefly before looking back at the road. "You haven't been here in how many years?"

Her whole body tensed as if she'd been scolded. What had he said to cause such a negative reaction?

Lizzy grasped the handle above the window as they drove over a bumpy section of the country road that led into the small town of Channing, Texas. "It's been fifteen years since I was here."

An icky feeling of guilt made her palms sweat. It was shameful to have waited so long to come see her aunts.

I'm an adult, for goodness' sake. I should've stood up for myself sooner.

Every time she started to chastise herself, she remembered to give herself a little bit of mercy. It was only a few weeks ago that she'd found the nerve to finally stand up to her overbearing father.

On a day at work when her patience had already been spread as thin as tissue paper, he'd pushed too far, and she'd snapped. Her plan had been to audition for the Chicago Opera without telling him and only bring up the topic if she was chosen to be part of the opera company. If not, there was no reason to set him off. A lengthy lecture about what's most important was all that would come of something like that.

Somehow, he had discovered her plan to audition and immediately discouraged her. When she'd told him she was doing it anyway, her father had laid on the lecture with a thick slab of guilt. He had actually tried to forbid her from doing it, claiming it would interfere with work at Dalton Realty.

"Elizabeth, you need to have your priorities in line and know what is really important. You're not in school any longer, and I will be disappointed if you go through with this audition."

He said he couldn't risk having her constantly taking off for rehearsals, performances and travel. What if he needed an event planned, and who would prepare the paychecks and keep everything in the office coordinated and running smoothly? He'd used his I-will-be-obeyed voice and then left the room like the matter was settled, but Lizzy had rushed after him and into his office, where she'd closed the door—none too gently.

Years of pent-up frustration had bubbled to the surface, spilling over in a burning fountain. He'd guilted her with the threat of disappointment one too many times. This final blow had toppled his control over her. She'd finally stood up for herself and said more than she ever imagined she could and quit her job at Dalton Realty right on the spot. Taking that huge step had given her even more courage to go through with the audition.

The truck bounced over another rough section of road, and she glanced at Travis as he drove with his left hand on the steering wheel and his other on the console between them. If she was alone in this truck, she would roll down the window and scream into the wind to release the exasperation she felt about being a wimp for so long.

No matter what her father or anyone else thought, she would someday make money doing what she loved.

Auditioning had been a learning experience that led her to where she was right this very moment. Lizzy tapped a fingertip against her lips. Now that she thought about it, she begrudgingly owed her father a teeny-tiny bit of thanks for his last command because it had gotten her to this moment in her life. Going after her dream. Reconnecting with her aunts. Back in a place she loved.

And riding in a truck with a cowboy who…well, that part wasn't in the plan, but she would find out how he fit into her life. Or not.

Her mind once again unwillingly flashed back to her recent audition in Chicago. While singing, her father's words had gotten in her head, and she'd messed up her song. But there had also been something odd about the audition. It wasn't the fact that she hadn't been chosen as a lead because she had not expected that at this stage of her career. Their reaction to her had been…off, and she couldn't exactly put a finger on it.

One of the women on the selection committee had caught up to Lizzy right before she'd left the building.

"Don't give up on your singing. Before your nerves got the best of you, I heard a beautiful voice that deserves to be celebrated." The woman clasped Lizzy's hands in her own. *"It will be a while before we hold another audition, but that doesn't mean you can't get in a bit of practice to help with nerves and then audition with* other *opera companies."*

Lizzy had wondered at the way she emphasized the word *other* like it had underlying meaning. But why had she bothered to tell her how good she was and give her advice if she didn't want her to come back again to audition for them?

I've got to stop spinning this around in my head over and over. I'm here to get on with my life.

"Have you been making a living singing in an opera?" Travis asked.

Her breath hitched. Had she spoken any of her thoughts aloud? The prospect of being caught talking to herself was embarrassing but preferable to Travis being a mind reader. Especially with the flood of inappropriate thoughts she'd been having about him since she arrived.

"What made you ask that?"

"Simple curiosity."

"No. I'm not. But lots of singers do." She studied the folds of her pink skirt, not ready to have a conversation about her failed audition. She was proud of herself for giving it a shot, but her father's years of training to never disappoint people was so engrained that she couldn't bring herself to tell him more.

They were thrown into silence once again, and it was making her jumpy. Without giving it any thought, she turned on the radio.

"No music," Travis snapped and turned it off.

"No music? Why in the world not?" Her hands went up in the air and then dropped to slap against her thighs.

"Because I don't like it."

She gaped at him. "You don't like music? Everybody likes music."

"I don't."

"What's the deal? Why not?"

"Drop it, princess."

He pulled the truck up to a gas pump, and she glanced out the side window. "Oh, wow. Zimmerman's General Store is still open?"

"Yep. It'll just take a minute to fill up." He got out and turned to the pump.

She got out, too. "I'm going inside."

"Wait. We have a schedule to keep. I have work to do once we get back to the ranch."

"I'll be quick," she called out and glanced back over her shoulder in time to see his scowl, but she didn't stop. Not even when he called her name in a warning fashion.

The old wooden building was no longer the lemony shade of yellow she remembered. It had been painted a soothing pale green with crisp white trim around the double-hung windows that stood like a row of soldiers on each side of the centered door. Window boxes were overflowing with colorful flowers.

A bell above the door announced her entrance into a quintessential old-fashioned grocery. Rows of wooden shelves in the center of the store were low enough to see over and an area of angled baskets held produce and bakery breads. She was further surprised to see Mr. Zimmerman behind the old-fashioned cash register with the pull-down handle. He had to be in his mid- to late-eighties, but he was still running the store.

"Sage? Is that you?" Mr. Zimmerman squinted at her.

"No, sir. I'm Lizzy Dalton. Sage's niece."

"My goodness. You're all grown up into a beautiful young lady."

She smiled. "It's so nice to see you again." She wanted to ask about his wife but feared she might have passed away.

To the right of the register sat the display of ten different flavors of candy sticks. This is where her welcome home candy had come from. The same place she'd bought it as a child, and from the same man. She loved every flavor, except root beer. The thought of it made her shiver.

Travis came inside and stopped a good foot away from her as if he feared she might throw something else at him. "Good afternoon, Mr. Z. Would you put the gas on the Dalton Ranch account, please."

"Already done," the old man said.

"Thanks." Travis turned to go but stopped and looked back when she didn't follow.

Before she could tell Travis that she needed just a few more minutes, Mrs. Zimmerman came out of the little office that was behind the counter. The old woman smiled, the creases around her brown eyes making a web of wrinkles. "I didn't hear anyone come in," she said in a voice that was a bit too loud.

"She can't hear a thing and won't wear her hearing aids." Mr. Z's comment was softened by the way he looked at his wife with so much affection.

Travis's broad chest rose and fell with a deep breath that he held in before sighing. He shifted his cowboy hat, but not in the polite way he did when saying goodbye. It was a frustrated, jerky movement that conveyed his restlessness to get going.

Or possibly to hold in the steam that was building under his hat. That thought made Lizzy want to laugh.

"You must be kin to the Dalton family," Mrs. Zimmerman said. "You look a lot like Sage and Daisy."

"They're my aunts. I'm Lizzy Dalton."

"Little Lizzy?" She came out from behind the counter, moving like she was thirty years younger than her actual age. "Aren't you a beauty. I'm so glad you've come back. Welcome home."

"Thank you." Another person welcoming her *home* lightened her anxiety another notch.

Barely holding on to his good manners, Travis started tapping one of his brown cowboy boots against the floor.

She internally rolled her eyes then turned back to the couple. "We have a schedule to keep, but I'll be back to visit with both of you very soon," she said in a voice loud enough for Mrs. Zimmerman to hear.

"Take one of these for the road as a welcome home," Mr. Z said and handed her a green apple–flavored candy stick. "Now I know why the twins bought so many of these the other day. If I remember correctly, they were your favorite."

"That's right. Thank you so much," she said and waved as she followed Travis outside. "You didn't tell me Zimmerman's was still open."

"You didn't ask."

She sighed and had to double time her steps to keep up with his long stride.

"The place looks nice with the fresh paint and all the flowers," she said as he pulled away from the gas pump. "How long ago did they repaint?"

"I did it about four months ago."

"You painted it?" This surprised her. But maybe it shouldn't. The twins had said he was a good guy.

"I had help. There has been a big push to refurbish a lot of the historic buildings around town. Mostly in Old Town on the section of Main Street near the courthouse."

"That's good to hear. Can we drive down Main Street? I want to see what's changed."

"Yes, but we don't have time to stop or get out."

"Ten-four, captain cowboy."

He almost smiled, and she'd take that reaction for now.

He stopped at the feed store, and it only took a few minutes for several young guys to load the bed of the truck with fifty pound bags of horse feed, and then they were on their way once again.

The original part of Channing was now referred to as Old Town. Buildings on both sides of Main faced one another with wide sidewalks for foot traffic. The shops were a mix of styles ranging from the early 1900s to about the 1950s. Older but well-tended houses in a variety of styles spread out from the center like legs of a spider.

In this area, Main Street traffic slowed to twenty miles per hour. You could see the work being done, but there were still a lot of shopfronts that were vacant and in varied states of repair. On one corner, the Rodeo Café had taken the place of the hardware store she'd gone to with her grandfather.

"Is there still a fountain in the big courtyard behind that row of buildings?"

"Yeah, it's being fixed up, too."

"Oh, I want to see it." She held up the candy Mr. Z had given her and grinned. "I'll share this with you."

"Are you trying to bribe me?"

"Is it working?" She wiggled the candy stick in his direction and started unwrapping it slowly, edging the cellophane down a little bit at a time like a candy striptease. His lips twitched, and she was one step closer to an actual smile.

"Tell you what." Travis tapped his thumb on the steering wheel. "If we hurry at the grocery store, we might have a few minutes to stop and take a look on the way back."

"Deal." She snapped the candy into two mostly equal pieces and gave him the end that was still wrapped.

"Thanks." He stuck the unwrapped end into the corner of his mouth like a toothpick and sucked on it.

She crunched off a little piece, chewed it and then sucked on her half all while trying not to look at his lips while he worked the candy from one side of his mouth to the other with his tongue.

Warmth swirled in her belly. Giving him candy was a mistake. Why did she find this grouchy guy so appealing? Was grumpy her new thing and she just hadn't realized it?

The scenery changed as they left Old Town and moved into a newer area of town. Unlike Zimmerman's and the historic area, the grocery store was shiny and new but without any character or charm.

Not surprisingly, Travis was quiet as they chose a shopping cart and headed into the store. She started in the produce section. It was a great time of year for fruit pies.

"What's your favorite kind of pie?"

He looked startled as if it were a shocking question. "Why are you asking me about pie?"

She cocked her head to study him. "Because I'm trying to decide what kind I want to make first. That's why we're here. To buy ingredients to make some of my grandmother's recipes. I'm a big fan of peach."

He hooked his thumbs in the front pockets of his jeans and nodded. "Me, too. But I'll pretty much eat any kind of pie."

"So, Travis Taylor is not a picky eater?" She ripped off a plastic produce bag and rubbed it between her fingers to open it.

"Not very."

She brought a peach close to her nose to inhale its sweet fragrance and then put a dozen into the bag.

He opened a second bag and held it while she loaded it with shiny green apples. "Do you only plan on making fruit pies?"

"That's what I was planning for this go around. What else would you suggest?" Had she actually found a topic that would get him talking?

"Lemon. But I guess that's still a fruit pie."

"That's debatable, but I do like lemon pie. Although, I'm not a fan of meringue. I always end up scraping it off."

"Me, too. Whipped cream is better," he said.

"Wow. We actually have something in common. What other kinds do you suggest?"

"Maybe chocolate or pecan."

"Hmm. Are you trying to get a job as my taste tester?"

"That depends." He put a twist tie on a bag of red apples. "Are you a good cook or will I be setting myself up for a bellyache?"

"I've never had any complaints. You should be safe from harm, but that's only if I decide you are qualified to be my taste tester. Got any references? I need to know if you are pie worthy."

His eyebrows disappeared into the shade of his cowboy hat. "Do I even want to know the qualifications for being pie worthy?"

"Some simple questions and maybe a reference or two," she said and stopped to let a mom with a baby and two small children pass by. One of the curly-haired toddlers waved with a big, dimpled grin, and Lizzy had the urge to rush over and hug him. She definitely wanted kids someday, but years from now after taking a shot at an opera career.

"Just ask your aunts about my eating habits," Travis said.

"I'll do that. I should work my way through Gamma's recipe box and make all of them. After all, I'll be here all summer."

"Until when...exactly?"

She tried to judge his mood or the spirit in which the question had been asked, but his expression was unsurprisingly blank. "I don't have an exact departure date. It's not like I have a flight scheduled. If you'll remember, I drove."

"I remember."

"Do you need an exact date for the investigation you're doing on me?"

He looked startled. "I'm not investigating you. Why would I?"

"I'm teasing you." She tilted her head to see him better. Under the cowboy hat and scowl there had to be a sense of humor in there somewhere.

They moved to other sections of the store for milk, cream, eggs and lots of butter. He added a few canned goods to his section of the cart and then lunchmeat, bacon and sausage, assuring her he was not a vegetarian.

At one end of the baking supply aisle, Travis added a box of waffle mix beside his other items. "I forgot something. I'll catch up to you."

"Okay. I'll be in this aisle for a while." Lizzy snuck a peek at his tall, muscular body as he walked away and instantly scolded herself as she looked around, relieved that no one had seen her staring. She chose a large bag of pecans and other baking essentials.

So far today, she hadn't splashed Travis with any cold liquid or injured him in any way. And most surprising, she was actually starting to enjoy his company or at least be entertained by him. Since they'd started shopping the day had gotten better.

Feeling more relaxed, she was smiling and humming to herself, but when she glanced up...her stomach plummeted to her toes.

No! What on earth is he doing here?

Chapter Five

Travis came around an endcap of s'mores makings and paused to watch Elizabeth. She was turned away from him as she pushed the cart down the aisle and then stopped beside the marshmallow cream. She leaned down to grab a jar with one knee bent and her foot went up in a very feminine move that made him think of a Barbie doll.

He adjusted his stack of frozen dinners as something suspiciously like butterflies kicked up inside him.

As she moved along, her hips swayed to a beat only she could hear, because it sure wasn't the announcement about free buns with the purchase of a package of hotdogs that was playing over the grocery store's sound system. Why was he so entertained by watching her choose items and put them into the cart in a neat and orderly fashion?

Naturally, she was unaware of his presence, but he shouldn't startle her in the grocery store—no matter how cute she looked when she was surprised. Especially while she was holding a can of condensed milk that was much heavier than the muffin she had thrown his way this morning.

Elizabeth glanced toward the opposite end of the aisle and her whole body stiffened.

A tall, thin man in a gray suit was walking toward her. There was recognition in his eyes, but the cocky smile on his face looked more arrogant and predatory than friendly.

The butterflies disappeared as Travis's protective instincts triggered. The same instincts that too often landed him in one difficult situation or another, and on occasion even left him bleeding or emotionally wrecked.

"Lizzy Dalton? What a surprise."

The man's annoyingly superior tone grated like broken glass on Travis's nerves.

Elizabeth stood ramrod straight and completely still, her fingers flexing on the handle of the shopping cart. "Hello, Jeff."

Her tone was curt with a sharp edge, and her body language put Travis on even higher alert. He moved close enough to hear them while pretending to check out the selection of cake mixes. He was ready to intervene at a second's notice.

"I didn't expect to see you here." Jeff raked her with his eyes and stepped close enough that his hip almost brushed the front of her shopping cart.

Elizabeth stepped farther back, pulling the cart more closely against her body. "I certainly didn't expect to see you either."

Travis barely knew her, but he'd been around her long enough to know she was friendly and talked to everyone, so the fact that she was standing in such a self-protective way spoke volumes. He moved forward, barely stopping himself from getting between them, but he didn't want to swoop in to rescue her if she didn't need it. He'd made that mistake with his last relationship.

But if this awkward interaction went on much longer or this guy threatened her in any way, he would not hesitate.

Why do I get myself involved in situations that are none of my business?

"What are you doing in hick town, Texas?" Jeff asked her.

What an ass. Travis considered taking a cue from Elizabeth and throwing one of his frozen dinners at the man's smug expression.

"I lived here when I was a child, and I'm visiting my family for the summer." Her words were right, but her tone was all fake cheerfulness.

"I heard you quit your job."

"Yes, I did." Her short laugh wasn't the musical one that had come so naturally last night while drinking wine with her aunts.

Jeff's grin widened. "You're here all alone?"

Her back straightened impressively. "No. I'm not alone. I'm here with my boyfriend. Travis. His name is Travis."

Now it was Travis's turn to stiffen. One of his frozen dinners slid off the top of the stack and landed with a loud smack against the floor.

Elizabeth spun around. Her eyes widened almost as big as the pies she planned to make. Her expression rapidly twisted into one of desperation, silently pleading with him not to out her to this man. He picked up the frozen dinner and closed the distance between them. She was either living in a fantasy world or had a good reason to lie to this guy.

"Afternoon," he said and dropped his food into the cart, but he did not offer his hand to the man who was now looking at them both suspiciously. Instead, he put an arm around Elizabeth's shoulders, squeezing just hard enough to let her know there would be a discussion about this once they were alone.

She wrapped an arm around his waist and some of the

tension released from her body. "Travis, this is Jeff. From Chicago."

"Old boyfriend," Jeff said and winked at her in a way that did not send a positive vibe.

Lizzy pressed herself more closely against Travis. "What are you doing in Texas?"

"I was at a real estate conference in Fort Worth, and now I'm visiting a cousin."

Travis looked down at the curvy woman tucked against his side. "Princess, we really need to get going or we'll be late."

She made a show of looking at her pink smart watch. "You're right, honey." She grabbed the cart and spun it away from the other man. "Take care, Jeff."

She mumbled something else under her breath, and Travis could swear she'd said, "And go leap off a cliff."

"Maybe I'll see you around town," the other man called after them. "I'll be here for a few weeks."

Her steps faltered, but she didn't turn around or say another word to her old boyfriend.

"You okay?" Travis asked once they were out of earshot. He knew what it was to dread seeing an ex. He'd been declining his ex's calls for months.

"I'm fine." She didn't slow her steps but let her eyes flick briefly up to meet his. "Thank you."

She didn't need to say more for him to know the reason for her thanks. He hadn't outed her—but only because his pesky protective instincts had kicked in. And because he was curious about why she'd invented a fake boyfriend and chosen him to be that man. Now that he'd met her ex, he had a pretty good idea.

"I've got what I need," he said. "Do you have everything on your list?"

"Yes." She went straight for the first open checkout lane and put items onto the moving belt.

Except for basic pleasantries with the young man ringing up their groceries, she didn't say another word until they'd loaded their shopping bags and were inside his truck.

"I appreciate you going along with my…" She swished her hand through the air as if searching for the right words.

"Fantasy?" he suggested.

"I was going to say spur of the moment yet temporary loss of good sense."

"That's inventive."

She sighed and tipped her head back against the headrest. "I promise I didn't come to Texas with the sole purpose of tormenting you. First, I tried to beat you up, and then I gave you an unsolicited cold shower and now… Now I've dragged you into an awkward situation."

He'd been in worse, but she didn't need to hear about any of his unfortunate history.

"I can't tell you how much I appreciate you playing along and not outing me."

"You're welcome." He stopped at a red light and waved to one of the cowboys from a neighboring ranch. "Are we going to talk about what just happened in the grocery store?"

"Do we have to? There's really no need."

He felt a need to know why he'd become a fake boyfriend to a spunky woman he barely knew. "Is there something I should know about Jeff? Does he pose a danger?"

"Can't we just pretend it never happened and forget about the whole incident?"

"Nope. If it's considered an incident, I definitely need details." Her not answering the danger question concerned him.

"Fine." Her sigh was resigned, and she gazed out the

side window at the passing scenery. "We dated… Briefly. Very briefly."

He waited to see if she'd say more. He wasn't much for sharing, so pushing too hard for someone else to spill their guts wasn't his style. He would give her some time.

But he wouldn't drop the topic entirely.

A few moments later, she turned to face him, her pretty face drawn into a frown. "It ended badly. He's not a good guy." Her voice broke, and she cleared her throat then rubbed her hands on the skirt of her dress. "I don't understand why he's in Texas. If I'd had any idea he would be staying around town, I would not have said you were my boyfriend."

"Really?" He flashed an expression that he hoped came off as playful and would ease some of her tension.

"Probably. Maybe." She grimaced. "I don't want to put you in a weird position."

"Too late."

Her fingers drummed rapidly on her thighs. "So, if we happen to see him again, I'll tell him…something. I'll tell him we broke up."

Her intake of breath and then slight curving in of her shoulders told him more than words could. The thought of telling this guy they'd broken up was really bothering her. And he knew better than anyone what it could be like to have an ex who'd left you with bad memories.

Damn. Why am I getting myself so involved in her life?

Once his protective instinct kicked on, turning it off was much harder, and distancing himself could become a challenge. He needed to find a way to lighten the mood. It might be kind of fun to tease her about owing him—in a good-natured way, of course.

"Want to make a deal?" he asked.

"Depends." She drew out the word with suspicion.

"If we see him and I keep up your charade, what will you do for me?" He slowed to go around a sharp curve in the road.

"Are you asking me…" Her voice trailed off as she bit one corner of her lip, but it didn't hide her smile.

His whole body tensed. What did she think he was asking for? Because suddenly, he had a few ideas that were making him need to crank up the air conditioner several notches, and none of them could he ever say aloud. "You bought all that stuff to bake. So…"

"Oh, pies. Yes." She pointed a finger into the air. "I can feed you all the pie you can eat."

He pretended to consider it. "Deal. But if I do have to use my acting skills again, you have to spend a whole day working with me on the ranch." The back of his neck tingled. Why in the hell had he suggested that? That would be an entire day spent together. He waved a hand in the air. "Never mind. That's a bad idea."

"What? You think I can't do manual labor?"

"I have my doubts."

She pulled the strap of her seat belt away from her body enough to shift in her seat to face him. "I'll prove it to you. Even if we don't run into Jeff again."

"You want to work a full day on the ranch?" He glanced her way. "You won't be able to wear a dress and high heels."

"I do have other clothes."

"Boots?"

She glanced at her feet and tapped the toes of her fancy shoes together. "I can borrow a pair from Sage or Daisy. We wear the same size."

"Okay then. Pies first, workday second." Maybe if he put it off, she would forget about working with him.

"Sounds like a plan. You will really pretend to be my boyfriend if we see him again?"

"Yes. I never go back on a promise."

"I'm glad to hear that."

"Are you going to tell me any more about why we are playing this game of pretend around that guy?"

When she closed her eyes and rubbed her forehead, Travis knew this was a sore topic—possibly like his time with Crystal. And he definitely did not want to talk about his ex, so he let the topic drop, again. For now. "Never mind."

Her chest moved as if she'd released a silent breath. What had this jerk done to her? Before he realized how far they'd gone, they had passed Old Town without stopping. "Sorry, I forgot to stop," he said.

"That's okay. I have plenty of time to see it. Did you suggest coming here after shopping because you knew we'd have cold food and wouldn't be able to stay long?"

"It might have crossed my mind." One corner of his mouth quirked up just enough to let her know he was teasing.

That made her smile, and she reached once more for the radio dial but stopped herself. "I can't believe you don't like music."

Now they were touching on a topic he didn't want to talk about. Elizabeth did not need to know that he was afraid he'd hear Crystal on the radio. It had been months since he'd been with her, but he still didn't want to hear her voice and be reminded of the time he'd wasted on her tour. Time he should have been making money and saving it to make his dream a reality.

"So, since you don't like music, I guess you won't be okay with me singing in the truck?"

There was no good answer to her question. The standard *no* response hung in his throat. He kind of wanted her to sing in the voice she'd used in the kitchen this morning, but he hesitated to encourage her. "As long as it's not the warm-up stuff you were doing before slugging me with your suitcase."

"That part is not meant for your listening pleasure. You also don't what me singing in full opera voice while we are closed up in the cab of the truck."

"Thanks for the warning, but after this morning… before sunrise." He made eye contact. "I figured that out for myself."

"This morning?" She tilted her head, looking cute and confused before her eyes widened. "What time do you start work?"

"Not before sunrise."

"Then why were you at the ranch so early this morning?"

"Have you seen the small log cabin at the tree line behind the old red barn?"

"The—" Her mouth formed an O before she snapped it closed and bit her lower lip. "You live in the cabin?"

"I do."

"And I was singing in full voice and woke you up?"

"Yes, ma'am." He stuck his finger in his ear and wiggled it. The gesture was his attempt at joking, which he hadn't done much of over the last few months.

The tight pinch of her lips and drawn-in brow was evidence of his failure and tugged at his heart. He'd meant to tease her, not upset her. Apparently, Crystal was right about his sense of humor, or lack thereof.

"My alarm was about to go off anyway," he said. "Doesn't hurt to get up a few minutes sooner."

She propped her elbow on the window frame and stared out her side. "I'll find another spot to practice. Someplace where I won't bother anyone."

"It's a big ranch. There are plenty of spots."

They rode in silence for a couple of minutes, which turned out to be too long for her.

"Have you always been a cowboy? Not just the hat and boots and stuff but all of it?"

"Since the day I was born. Fifth-generation cowboy."

"That's cool. Like a family business. In Chicago, I was working as the office manager at Dalton Realty. My father's company. But that is a stay-in-place job, and I really want a chance to travel, and hopefully someday tour with an opera company."

His stomach clenched. That once again made him think of Crystal and the way she had made him believe that after her latest tour she wanted to settle down in one place. But he now knew she had zero intentions of ever giving up a life of touring.

Elizabeth started talking about things they were passing and what she remembered about an event or this place or that person. Nothing she said required his answer or a comment, so he just let her talk while remaining silent.

As they neared the Martin Ranch next door to the Daltons', he saw something that should not be there, and a weight as big as a horse constricted his chest. He hit the brakes and swerved onto the roadside, gravel spraying and some of the grocery sacks sliding from the backseat onto the floorboard.

Lizzy clutched the dash. "What the heck, Travis?"

Chapter Six

A huge For Sale sign was posted next to the entry gate of the Martin Ranch. A sign Travis had not expected to see there for at least another year.

"You better hope you didn't break all my eggs with your stunt driving." Lizzy loosened her grip on the dashboard and picked up her purse that had been dumped by her feet. "Why did you stop? Are you planning to make me walk the rest of the way home because I talk too much?"

"What? No." What he'd done finally registered. "Sorry about the sudden stop." He cleared his throat and pointed to the big red-and-white sign. "Was that For Sale sign there when we drove by earlier on the way to town?"

"I don't think so. I remember looking at that huge tree beside it. After working in a real estate office for so many years, I tend to notice the signs." She smoothed back her shiny hair that had fallen over her shoulders while picking up her belongings. "Is this a good thing or a bad thing?"

"Both." The Martin family grandkids had told him they

were keeping the ranch for a year and then putting it on the market. A year was the amount of time he'd estimated needing to save enough money. Now…

If it sold quickly, he would be out of time and luck. The clock was ticking.

Travis took his foot off the brake and started driving. To earn some extra money, he could go back on the rodeo circuit—at risk to his body and brain according to doctors. And if he was injured, he'd have a hard time doing his job on the ranch. Not to mention the time away when Sage and Daisy needed him. And even though he had loved the riding and competition, he hated being in the spotlight.

Lizzy finished putting items back into her purse. "I wonder what they're asking for the place. I'll look it up online this evening."

"I wouldn't mind knowing." But he also feared it was going to be a dollar amount that would depress him even further. He pulled up to the farmhouse and parked in the gravel area behind it and closest to the kitchen door.

Daisy was sweeping the patio but put down the broom and headed over to help them. "Did you have a successful trip?"

"We did," Lizzy said.

"I picked up the new horse feed. We can try it out with Titan in the morning."

"Sounds good." Daisy took the grocery sack he held out to her and headed for the kitchen door.

Elizabeth straightened and made a very female sound of appreciation. "Oh, my. The Vikings are coming. And it's not a bad thing."

She'd said the last part under her breath, but he'd heard her and followed her gaze.

The Murphy brothers, Jake, Riley and Finn, were walking side by side. They looked like they were in some damn clothing or cologne commercial.

Travis hated the hot flash of jealousy that was tightening his gut. It was not an acceptable emotion. Totally unacceptable, in fact. He could not entertain any ideas about any sort of fling or relationship with his employers' niece. But after the incident with Jeff, he was feeling way too protective of her.

"What a thing to say in front of your boyfriend," he grumbled in a low voice, not sure why he was further exacerbating the situation.

She put her hand on her cheek and fluttered her eyelashes. "Oh, my. How rude of me. So sorry, honey bunny. I don't know what I was thinking."

Her voice was an exaggerated Southern accent that almost made him laugh. "And you're a comedian, too. Yippee for me."

The screen on the kitchen door slammed and Daisy came back outside. When she saw the brothers, she pulled the ponytail holder from her long hair and shook her head to fluff it. Travis was tempted to make a childish gagging sound.

What was it about these three boneheads that made women get all googly-eyed? He strode quickly toward the brothers and met them before they could reach the women, fully aware he was being a complete fool.

"Did y'all finish the fencing?"

"Yes," Finn said. "We saw you drive up and wanted to see what's next."

"We need to unload all the feed from the bed of my truck. I'll pull around to the barn after the groceries are unloaded." He heard footsteps on the gravel behind him and wasn't surprised when Daisy and Elizabeth came up beside him.

"Good afternoon, ladies," all three brothers said in well-practiced unison as they took off their cowboy hats for the introduction to a new woman.

Travis spun on his bootheel and headed back to his truck. He wasn't going to stand around like a chump while they introduced themselves. He started unloading the groceries, not wanting to see any more of their flirting and thoroughly irritated with himself for caring.

This was not jealousy. It couldn't be. He barely knew her. Plus, Elizabeth managed to exasperate him every time he was around her. It was only his damn protective instincts kicking in after the Jeff incident in the grocery store. That had to be all it was.

One of Grandpa Roy's sayings flashed through his mind.

"It's a fine line between loving someone and wanting to strangle them."

Lizzy shook hands with the Murphy brothers. They wore faded jeans, boots and dark T-shirts that fit tightly to their work-hardened physiques, which were covered with a layer of dirt, hinting at the kind of work they'd been doing all morning. Was this the level of grunge she'd set herself up for by stupidly suggesting she could work a day on the ranch?

I can do it. No problem.

Even dusty and sweaty, the brothers managed to pull off a hot guy vibe. And hot didn't refer to overheated in this case. They were legit head turners, but their lingering handshakes had not given her the same tingle she got just from being close to Travis.

The brothers had strikingly similar features, with big blue eyes, square jawlines and full mouths that smiled in a way she had not seen from Travis yet.

Jake's hair almost reached his shoulders and was light brown with lots of natural highlights from days spent outdoors.

Riley's close-cropped hair had a touch of red mixed in with the blond. He was slightly shorter than his brothers—but still had to be over six feet tall.

Finn was the tallest of the brothers and about as blond as you could get. Wavy strands brushed the tops of his ears, and she could understand Daisy's attraction to him.

Lizzy glanced over her shoulder to see Travis disappearing into the house with an armload of grocery bags.

"How long does it take to drive from Chicago?" one of the brothers asked her.

Lizzy turned back to them. "About sixteen hours, not counting stopping at night and the other stops for gas and food along the way."

"It's about twenty-five hours from Montana," Finn said and put his black cowboy hat back on. His mouth was pulled into the kind of full-watt smile she wanted to see on Travis's face.

"You're from Montana?" she asked.

"Yes, but with the rest of our family gone, there was nothing left for us there."

Daisy licked her lips and smiled shyly. "We're certainly glad you decided to make the move to Texas."

"Us too," Finn said and gave Daisy the kind of grin that made her blush.

The adoring expression on her aunt's face was one she recognized. Apparently, this man gave Daisy all the tingles.

As they talked for a few more minutes, she could quickly tell that all three of the Murphy brothers were big flirts. The exact opposite of Travis.

While Daisy and Finn talked with the other two men about getting guard dogs that were good around horses, she took a moment to study them. Riley seemed to be the quiet one. Jake was a jokester and smiled a lot.

The sound of Travis's truck starting interrupted their conversation.

"We need to get back to work," Jake said. "It was nice to meet you, Lizzy."

She and Daisy said goodbye and turned back toward the house. Travis drove up beside them and pulled to a stop. "All the groceries are in the kitchen, but I didn't put anything in the refrigerator."

"Thanks for that and for taking me to town today."

He nodded and made some kind of noncommittal sound.

Abandoning Travis with the groceries had been rude, and she wanted to make it up to him. "I'll probably bake the first pie tomorrow. Come by for a piece."

"Maybe I will." He did his two-fingered hat tip thing and drove toward the old red barn she remembered from her childhood.

It had a hay loft where she'd spent many hours playing, pretending it was everything from Narnia to Alice's wonderland. She'd made wonderful memories up there.

"How can one ranch have so many hot guys?" she asked her aunt Daisy as they walked back to the house.

"Right? What are the odds?"

"Is that why you have 'stud farm' in the name of the ranch?"

Daisy laughed. "No. We named the ranch long before any of them came to work for us. However, that doesn't mean it's not true." She opened the kitchen door. "Tomorrow I'm driving to Fort Worth. Do you want to come with me to the hospital to hold babies at the NICU?"

"I would love to go. Brand new babies are so magical. Is this something you do all the time?"

"When there's a need." With bags of sugar and flour in her arms, she went into the pantry.

Only two eggs had suffered from Travis slamming on

his brakes, so Lizzy scooped them out into the trash. His reaction to the For Sale sign had been a strong one, and she was very curious about why. She would look up the property and see what she could find out. "How many acres is the Martin ranch next door?"

"I'm not sure. Why do you ask?"

"It's for sale and I was just wondering."

"I didn't even know it was on the market, yet."

"The sign wasn't there when we left for town, but it's there now. Travis had quite the reaction to seeing it. And from what I could tell, not a good one. Does he know them?"

"Yes. He grew up on that ranch."

"I didn't know that. He was right there that close the whole time we were kids? How did we never meet?"

"It's likely that you did meet at some point. But he is five years older than you, and you wouldn't have gone to the same elementary school because of where you and your dad's old house was."

Lizzy moved things around in the refrigerator to fit the gallon of milk. "If we did meet, I don't remember it."

"Now that I'm thinking about it, he didn't really start coming over to our house much until after you were taken away from us." Daisy pulled Lizzy in for a hug. "I'm so glad to have you back in our lives."

The unexpected hug surprised her, and it took her a couple of seconds to return it. She wasn't used to random displays of affection because her father had discouraged it, and when she initiated it, there was always the fear of not having it returned.

Sage walked into the kitchen then came to a stop when she saw them hugging. "Is something wrong?"

"No," Daisy said and let go of Lizzy. "We're just catching up on missed hugs."

Before moving to Chicago, there had been cuddles and

hugs and goodnight kisses. Her father was more of a pat-her-on-the-head kind of dad, and she'd missed and longed for the kind of love her grandparents and aunts had shown her before they moved away. But over the years, she'd grown used to going without.

Lizzy returned to putting away the groceries, and her stomach growled. "I'm hungry. Have either of you eaten lunch?"

"No, we haven't."

"I bought a couple of options. Sandwiches would be quick or frozen pizza will take a little bit longer."

"Whatever takes longer sounds good to me. I'll gladly watch the pizza cook. Anything for an excuse to put off doing the bookkeeping. It's my least favorite job of all." Sage poured a glass of cranberry juice and then pulled her wavy chin-length hair into a clip.

Lizzy didn't care for it either, but she was good at book-keeping. It's what she had been doing for years, along with the many other jobs her father had assigned to her. Maybe she should offer to help her aunt after she'd been here for a little while longer. She wanted to feel things out a bit more before bringing up the idea of her having access to their business and finances.

Sage set the oven to preheat for the pizza. "You haven't said anything about your trip to town with Travis."

Lizzy winced and put the apples and peaches beside the sink and sighed somewhat dramatically. "I'd love to tell you it went smoothly, but that would be a lie."

"Oh no. What happened?" Daisy's voice was muffled because she was in the pantry.

"It had a few bumpy parts. At the grocery store, I ran into a guy I briefly dated in Chicago. Not someone I ever expected to or ever wanted to see again. Especially here in

Channing. Jeff is also in the real estate business, and he used me to get close to my father."

"What a jerk," the twins said.

"Why in the world is he here? Is he trying to get you back?" Daisy asked as she opened a bag of potato chips.

Lizzy made a face. "He should know there isn't a chance in hell of that happening. He said he's here for a conference and to see a cousin."

Jeff using her to get close to her father was only part of the reason she hated him. She didn't feel like getting into the night he'd become too aggressive and pinned her against a wall, and then made her feel like there was something wrong with her because she didn't want to have sex in the bathroom at a party.

"When I saw Jeff walking toward me at the grocery store, I was startled and kind of panicked. Without knowing Travis was behind me, I told Jeff that I was there with my boyfriend... Travis."

Daisy laughed. "For real?"

"Yep. I absolutely did. To my complete shock, Travis played along and didn't give me away, but now, I have to make him all the pie he wants."

"I kind of wish I'd been there to witness that," Daisy said. "It might make me feel better about the situations I seem to get myself into."

"You two have a lot in common," Sage said with a smile.

"I have a strong feeling Travis is not going to let me forget about this fake boyfriend thing. Ever."

"Probably not. You know..." Sage tapped a finger on her chin. "Maybe you're just what Travis has been needing."

"Me?" Lizzy's voice squeaked. "I don't think so."

Chapter Seven

"Wow, this is the fanciest horse stable I've ever seen," Lizzy said and turned in a circle to take it all in. It was clean and organized and smelled of fresh hay. "When did you build it?"

"About three years ago," Daisy said.

Several horses stuck their heads out of their stalls and greeted them with neighs and other horse sounds.

"We take a lot of pride in keeping things as nice as possible. When we have prospective clients visit, we like to impress." Her aunt stroked a brown horse's neck, and the animal nosed the side of her head.

"This place is certainly built to impress."

The ceiling was vaulted with timber framing. There were ceiling fans and lighting pretty enough to be in a house. The large horse stalls along one side of the barn had solid wooden walls of horizontal boards between them so the horses could not see one another. The opposite side's stalls had smooth, round metal bars on the top half of the walls so the horses could look across to see each another.

The aisle down the middle of the barn was red bricks laid in a herringbone pattern and matched the patio at the back of the farmhouse. Most stalls had a door that led to an outdoor area that was half covered by a roof so the horses could choose sun or shade while getting fresh air.

They stopped to meet each horse as they worked their way down the middle, and Daisy told her about everything they were seeing.

"This is Titan. He is our prize stud and part of the reason we were able to afford to build the stables."

"He's very handsome." Lizzy held her palm flat to give him a piece of carrot the way her aunt had shown her. His chestnut-brown coat was shiny, and his mane brushed smooth and tangle free.

At the back, there were a few rooms. The largest was the tack room. Saddles and other equipment were neatly arranged and hung on the walls. The next room had a big sliding door.

"This is the collection room."

"And by that you mean this is where the stallion makes his donation?"

Daisy laughed. "That's one way to put it."

The last and smallest room had a normal door and sleek white surfaces, stainless-steel countertops and a large deep sink. Microscopes and other equipment were lined up like a science lab. "This is where we get things ready for artificial insemination and that type of thing."

"I had no idea it's such a technical procedure. Why don't you let the horses breed the natural way?" Lizzy asked.

"Occasionally we do, but often, the mare is far away. Also, a stallion can get rough when he is excited, and we don't want him to bite or accidentally hurt an expensive horse."

They went back out into the sunshine, and Lizzy shielded her eyes as she looked at the red barn she remembered from her childhood. "What do you have in the old barn?"

"That's where we keep the bags of feed, hay and other farm equipment. Are you ready to head to the hospital?"

"You bet. I'm excited to hold a baby."

A blessedly cool waft of air hit Lizzy as the hospital's automatic sliding glass doors parted. They hurried inside but then slowed to give their eyes a minute to adjust after being in the bright midday sun.

"How often do they call you to come hold babies?" she asked her aunt.

"It varies. Sometimes it's long stretches and others it's a couple of times a week. My friend Tina is a neonatal nurse and calls me when there is a need. Today, there are two newborns who need some extra cuddling." Daisy bit her lip and gazed at the floor as they got into the elevator.

Lizzy sensed a wave of sadness from her aunt, and it made her own heart ache just as every one of her muscles tensed. She wanted to hug Daisy or at least wrap a comforting arm around her shoulders, but after so many years of being told that physical affection was unnecessary, she hesitated to be the one to initiate it. Her fear of being pushed away was still too strong.

How different would her life be if her mother had lived?

She often wondered why neither Sage nor Daisy had married or had children. She got the feeling it wasn't a simple answer. And although the three of them were quickly growing close like they'd been before her father moved her several states away, after so many years apart, she didn't feel comfortable asking such personal questions yet.

They took the elevator up to the Neonatal ICU on the third floor. Daisy stopped at the nurses' station to check in for their volunteer shifts and then they went into a narrow room with a long stainless-steel sink. They used little pre-packaged scrub brushes with the soap already in them to thoroughly clean their hands.

"Hey, Daisy. It's good to see you."

"Tina, this is my niece, Lizzy."

"I've heard a lot about you," the nurse said. "You are the opera singer, right?"

"I am."

"Maybe you can sing to the babies."

"I can do that. But I would need to tone down my opera voice."

There was a row of incubators, or what they called Isolettes, with padded rocking chairs beside them. Each chair had a metal nameplate on the back that was in memory or honor of someone. Colorful curtains hung from the ceiling and could be drawn around each infant if privacy was needed.

Lizzy smiled at parents holding their newborns and was introduced to a few more nurses and one doctor before Tina took them to their assigned babies.

"Daisy, you will be right here with this baby girl. Her dad is stationed overseas, and mom had a rough labor and then a C-section. She needs a little backup."

"She's beautiful." Her aunt stopped beside the baby's Isolette, and a different nurse began helping her.

Lizzy followed Tina a few spots down.

"This is your little one for the afternoon. Have a seat while I get a fresh diaper on him."

Lizzy sat in the rocking chair beside his Isolette that had a clear plastic top with a few places that you could open to reach in your hand. Because it was temperature controlled, he was dressed in only a diaper. He wasn't the plump baby you typically think of but was smaller than average with skinny arms and legs, but as precious as he could be.

"Is he premature?"

"He was about six weeks early. He was born yesterday and weighs a little under five pounds." Tina opened the top of the Isolette and began changing his diaper. She smiled and talked to him as she worked and then swaddled him in a white blanket with pink-and-blue stripes.

Lizzy's heart began racing, and she wasn't sure why. It wasn't a fear of holding him. She loved babies and couldn't wait to have him in her arms. "What's his name?"

"He doesn't have a name yet, but we've been calling him Angel. I'll go get a bottle ready and be right back."

Tina put him in Lizzy's arms, and she was hit with an overwhelming rush of emotions. Her whole body felt energized, and she wanted to cry and sing and kiss his sweet little cheeks. His sleepy brown eyes searched hers, and she recognized the features of Down syndrome.

"Hello, sweet angel boy. I'm so happy to meet you."

He pursed his lips and then stuck out his tongue as he stretched. That made her laugh, and she brushed the back of one finger over his velvety soft cheek. Every bit of tension she'd felt in the elevator while debating whether to hug her aunt melted away.

Was this feeling why Daisy came here to hold newborns? If Lizzy felt this strongly about the first time holding a stranger's baby, how powerful would the moment be when her own newborn was put on her chest after birth? That was an experience she didn't want to miss.

Tina returned with a preemie-sized bottle. "I'll put this right here until he's ready to eat."

"This baby has Down syndrome," Lizzy said.

"That's right. Not everyone recognizes it so quickly."

"My friend's older sister has a child with Down syndrome. I used to babysit, and what they say about them always being happy is not true. They are just like every other child. I adore her and miss taking care of her."

"It's good to know you have some experience. Do you know what kangaroo care is?"

"I've heard about it. The skin-to-skin holding?"

"That's right. Baby in only a diaper is held on your chest. It helps stabilize their heartbeat, improves breathing patterns and oxygen saturation levels and helps them increase their weight."

"Looks like he could stand to put on some weight."

"He could. We've also seen decreased crying and an earlier hospital discharge and more successful breastfeeding episodes using kangaroo care, but sadly, this little sweetie doesn't have a mom to nurse him."

"What happened?"

"She was in a car accident and tragically didn't make it."

Lizzy skin prickled and turned cold. "That's heartbreaking. I'm willing to do kangaroo care, but will his dad mind a stranger skin to skin with his newborn baby?"

Sighing sadly, Tina clasped her hands at her stomach. "Locating the father has been a bit of a challenge. The mother gave a man's name while she was in the ambulance, and someone tried to contact him only to discover he died months ago."

Lizzy gasped and held the baby a little closer. This newborn needed her to cuddle him even more than she'd first realized. "Such a tragic story."

"It gets even worse. His family said he dated the baby's mother, but their son could not be the father because he'd been dead too long for it to be possible."

"Oh, my goodness. So, who is the real father?"

"That's the million-dollar question."

"He's an orphan?" Her words were forced through a tight throat.

"At this time, yes."

Lizzy's heart was breaking for this little boy. Every baby deserved at least one person to love them. She had lost her own mother as an infant, but she'd had her grandmother and aunts to fill in that gap for her first ten years. "What about the mother's family?"

"She was estranged from her family, and they didn't even know she was pregnant. They have no idea who the father is."

"Don't his grandparents want to take him?"

"I'm afraid not."

"This just gets sadder and sadder." She gently cradled his tiny peach fuzz–coated head in the palm of her hand. Would this baby boy ever know the love of a family?

"They haven't even come to see him."

"Do they not want to take him because…" She swallowed around the lump in her throat. "Because he has Down syndrome?"

"I'm not sure." Tina looked as sad as Lizzy felt. "It does happen."

He had no mom, a mystery man dad and too many people who would look at him and see someone who was less than perfect. And they'd be wrong.

A strong need to protect him swelled inside Lizzy.

"There is hope," Tina said and began changing the bedding in his Isolette. "If we haven't found the father in three months, the mother's aunt said she would take him."

"Why three months?"

"Because she's out of the country until then."

"What will happen to him in the meantime?"

"Once he's given a clean bill of health, he will go into foster care until his father is located and given the opportunity to take him. Or until the aunt gets home."

Lizzy lifted the tiny infant closer to her face, his brown eyes speaking to her, and in a not so rare moment of impulsiveness, her inner thoughts became public.

"I'll be his foster mom."

Chapter Eight

Lizzy shielded her eyes against the afternoon sun spilling over the blacktop parking lot of the hospital. The day had taken one heck of a sharp detour off the summer path she'd planned. Who could've ever guessed that Lizzy would leave the NICU with information about how to become a foster parent, as well as the phone number of one of the foster care directors who had overheard her declaration to foster the baby?

"I didn't realize it took so long to become a foster parent." She looked at the papers in her hand, which was slightly trembling from her amped-up adrenaline. "Hours of training classes, TB test, CPR certification, interviews, home inspection, references and a background check. But I am glad to know they're thorough in the screening process."

"I know a bit about the process." Daisy hit a button on her truck's key fob. The headlights blinked, the alarm chirped and the locks opened.

"You do? How?"

"Let's get in the truck first. I'm melting in this heat." She started the truck, cranked up the AC to the highest setting and backed out of the parking spot. "I need to know how serious you are about wanting to foster the baby."

Lizzy ran the question through her mind once more and came to the same conclusion. While looking into the baby boy's precious face, he had spoken to something deep inside of her. A place she didn't often visit. A part of herself she kept closely guarded—mostly to protect herself from the memories. But something had been set in motion, and she was on a mission she didn't want to abandon.

She couldn't walk away without doing everything possible to make sure he had a good start in life. What was it about this situation that was causing her to have such a visceral reaction?

"I can't really explain why, but I am serious about fostering the baby." Lizzy directed the AC vent straight at her face. "I bet you're regretting asking me to come with you today."

"Not at all. I was going to talk to Sage before saying anything, but..." Her aunt's long, elegantly shaped fingers drummed on the tan, leather-covered steering wheel. "I think I might need your help when talking to my sister about this."

"You've piqued my curiosity."

"Sage is a registered foster parent."

"She is?" That surprised her, but at the same time, it didn't. The twins were compassionate women with lots of love to give. Lizzy once again wondered why neither one was married or had any children.

"Sage would probably need to do a few things to reactivate her status and make sure everything is up to date."

Lizzy clasped her hands together. "Are you suggesting

we ask her to be the foster mom until I can do it? That's a great idea." Hope made her wiggle in her seat.

"Wait, don't get too excited. That's *if* she will agree to do it. Sage said she would never foster again. This might take some convincing." Daisy merged into traffic on the interstate.

"What happened when she did foster?"

"The first child she took in was a three-month-old baby girl. She was with us for five months. But then she was given back to her birth parents, and it broke Sage's heart. She said she could never go through something like that again."

"That's so sad."

Daisy cleared her throat and ran a hand through her long hair. "It was really hard on me as well. We both got so attached to the little sweetie. She was crawling and eager to learn to walk. That's why I'm also a bit reluctant to take another baby into the house. A baby who is not…ours."

"Oh. I see." Lizzy nibbled at her thumbnail as hope started sinking.

There was something about babies that hit a trigger with the twins. Her aunt's expression and attitude made her almost positive. Babies were a sensitive subject.

"It was so thoughtless of me to even think about doing something this big while I'm living in someone else's house. I shouldn't have said that I would be his foster mom without first talking to you and Sage. It just came out of my mouth before I could engage my filter or take a couple of beats to think about what I was about to say. I just blurted it out like I have the filter of a four-year-old."

Daisy chuckled. "You're impulsive like me, and like Mama was. Sage is the bossy one who likes to think everything through, but I understand why you did it. After all, I am the one who took you to the hospital to share in something that I love and feel compelled to do."

"As much as you like to go hold the babies at the hospital, I'm surprised you aren't a foster parent as well. Especially since you live in the same house with someone who is."

Her aunt flexed both hands on the wheel. "I just don't feel like I can give a child the attention they deserve. Much of my work is out with the horses and around the ranch, and I travel more than my sister. Sage spends more of her time in the office doing paperwork and research and phone calls and all of the behind-the-scenes stuff."

"That makes sense." Lizzy fingered one of her dangly pearl earrings. "I'm sure the lady we talked to at the hospital will place him with a good foster family until his aunt gets back. And hopefully, when they locate the baby's father, he turns out to be a good guy who wants to raise his son."

But what if he didn't?

"I'm sure you're right. But I can tell this means a lot to you, so let's not give up on the idea just yet."

"I can't explain it. It just feels like fate or something I'm called to do."

"What are the odds of someone from the foster system being in the room when you said that and then rushing over to talk to you about it?"

"A coincidence, I guess." Lizzy watched the city land-scapes zip by and was glad they were on their way back to the country.

"Although, the baby was recently born, so I guess the chances of her being there were pretty good. Let's at least talk to Sage about it."

"I'm in agreement with that. And I promise I won't push for anything that everyone isn't comfortable with."

Daisy smiled at her niece. "The three of us are going to be just fine and get right back to the close relationship we had years ago."

Lizzy's thoughts exactly.

* * *

As they drove up the driveway, Travis was once again riding a horse in the front pasture. This time it was a tan horse. And it started bucking.

Lizzy clasped a hand to her mouth.

"Don't worry," Daisy said with a laugh. "He does this all the time. He breaks and trains horses for us and for other people as well."

She released a breath but kept an eye on Travis. After another couple of hind kicks, the horse settled and moved into a trot. "He's pretty good at that, isn't he?"

"He sure is. He has all kinds of awards for saddle bronc riding. What you just saw was pretty chill compared to the horses he had to ride while competing."

She lost sight of Travis as Daisy parked the truck beside her white car. "Why doesn't he ride in the rodeo anymore?"

"He got hurt pretty badly."

That made her frown. "Then he probably shouldn't be riding that wild horse."

"Maybe not, but getting on a horse here on the ranch that bucks every once in a while is a lot different from riding in rodeo after rodeo on horses trained to fling riders into the air."

She winced. "I haven't been to many rodeos. Actually, I've never been to one."

"We can check out some of his rides on the internet. A cowboy like Travis is not going to stop riding completely."

"I guess I can understand that." It would be like someone asking her to stop singing. Not happening. Only difference, singing wouldn't put her in the hospital. They got out of the truck, and she couldn't resist glancing around to see if she could spot Travis.

"I'm so hungry. Can we cut that peach pie you made this morning?"

"Great idea. Maybe talking to Sage about the baby will go better over pie."

They went in through the kitchen door. "Sage, are you in here?" Daisy called out to her sister.

"I'm in the office."

They found her behind the large mahogany partners desk that had belonged to Lizzy's great-grandfather. She remembered her grandparents sitting face-to-face, one on each side of the desk, talking and laughing as they worked. Sage looked up from the paperwork spread across the desktop, but Lizzy and Daisy remained silent.

She tilted her head at them. "What's up? How was your day at the hospital?"

"Good," they said in unison as if they were the twins.

"You two are acting funny."

"Do you have time to talk?" Daisy asked her more serious sister.

"Why do I get the feeling that y'all are up to something? And I know when you start a conversation this way that it's going to be something big."

"It's really more of something we need to ask you," Lizzy said and sat in the center of the leather couch under two double-hung windows.

Daisy dropped onto one end of the couch. "Keep an open mind. It's something we will all need to discuss seriously. We need to all three agree and be on board with it."

"Good grief, Sis." Sage tossed up her hands. "Stop stalling and spit it out."

Lizzy jumped in before her coconspirator could answer. "I kind of said I'd be the foster mom for an orphaned baby boy with Down syndrome." Her pulse was picking up speed while she waited for her aunt's response.

Sage's annoyed expression turned rapidly to surprise and then confusion. "Well, that's something I didn't expect. Fostering a baby?" She looked from Lizzy to her sister. "Here? At our house?"

Daisy ducked her head and swiped a hand over the side table as if checking for dust. "That's what we need to discuss."

Sage rolled a fancy silver pen between her long fingers and leaned back in her red leather office chair. It creaked with her movements, sounding extra loud in the silence as she regarded them. "And you would need *me* to be the official foster parent." It wasn't a question because Sage knew why they were coming to her.

"Yes."

"Lizzy, what happened to your summer with no obligations? Time to regroup and focus on your singing."

Lizzy chuckled and then blew out a slow breath. "That is an excellent question—that I didn't take the time to consider before speaking. Fostering a newborn baby certainly wasn't something I set out to do. It just kind of happened without me giving it any thought. A problem I seem to occasionally have...according to my father." She mumbled the last part under her breath.

Both of her aunts frowned at the mention of their estranged older brother, Joshua.

"I looked down into the baby's sweet little face." Lizzy imitated holding an infant in the crook of her arm. "I couldn't stand the thought of him not having someone to fight for him and being shown love right away. But it's only an idea at this point."

"She's more like me and Mama than we realized," Daisy said.

Sage smiled at her niece and twirled a curl around her finger. "I can see that."

"I didn't mean to come here and disrupt your lives." Her throat burned, but she would not cry. How could she even consider asking this of them when she hadn't been here in so many years? "You know what? We should just forget about this. I'm sure the foster system will find someone good to look after him until they find his father, or the aunt gets back from her trip."

She really hoped that was true, because she was worried that Down syndrome might make it more difficult to place him with a family. Unfair but sadly often true.

"You have me more than curious," Sage said. "What's this about finding the father and an aunt?"

A bit more hope found its way into her heart. "They're having a little trouble locating the father. There is also an aunt who will take him if needed, but she is out of the country for three more months. And honestly, they might find the father before the baby is even ready to leave the hospital, and then this would be a moot point. If we do this, we would all go into it knowing we are only temporarily looking after him for someone else and make sure none of us gets too attached to the baby," Lizzy said.

Sage made a noise of disagreement. "I'm afraid that is a lot easier said than done."

She knew her aunt was right, but the little angel needed her. "*If* he still needs a foster family when he is released from the hospital and we do take him, I will start the process and take over as soon as I can."

Sage sighed. "Having a baby in the house…always changes things."

The sisters shared another flash of a telling glance that suggested there was more to their fostering experience than they'd yet told her. During this discussion, several similar looks had passed between them, and Lizzy's suspicions grew. There was something they weren't saying. Something big.

"Is there something you two aren't telling me?"

"No." The twins' voices were so in sync that they sounded like one person.

Lizzy wasn't fooled, but even though she was super curious, she decided to let it go. If it was something they wanted her to know then they would tell her if and when they were ready. Twins had secrets, and she could respect that.

Sage pointed at the two of them sitting side by side on the couch. "I know y'all both have huge hearts, so you both wanting to do this isn't a big surprise."

"You have a big heart, too," Daisy said to her sister. "You just guard yours a lot more than we do."

"I'll admit that is true. I do love seeing you so happy and excited about this. Sounds like you two are in agreement about fostering the baby," Sage said. "So, it's just me who needs to get on board with this idea?"

"Or you could talk us out of it," Lizzy said. "I'm being ridiculous even asking. This is too much for me to bring into your lives. I haven't been here in years and now I'm acting like this is my house and turning your lives topsy-turvy. At this rate, you'll want me to leave before the summer is even over."

"Not true," Daisy said.

"Don't ever think such a thing. Your name might not be on the deed with ours, but this is your home, too."

"That means more to me than the two of you can know." She had family who loved her. Another layer of pain from her past started to fade.

"Tell me why this is so important to you, Lizzy."

She seriously considered Sage's question while looking around the office that was filled with so many family mementos. Old books and trinkets, antique furnishings that had been handed down and photographs ranging from the time photos were first invented to the present. Her mind kept going back to her own childhood.

"When my father abruptly took me away from you and the only life I'd ever known so soon after losing Gamma, I felt like…well, an orphan."

"Oh, honey." Daisy put an arm around her shoulders. "It breaks my heart to hear that."

Sage came out from behind the desk and sat on the other side of her niece. "I wish we'd done more to help you back then. We really should have."

"You were both young and dealing with a lot of your own stuff. You two actually were orphans."

"But we were twenty years old," Daisy said. "Not ten like you were. We were technically too old to be orphans, but it did feel that way. You were just a little kid."

"I'm sure my father didn't make any of it easy on either of you. As we all know, Joshua Dalton can make it difficult to be his daughter or sister."

"That is sadly the truth," Sage said. "I'm still convinced they mixed up the babies at the hospital when he was born. He is nothing like either of our parents."

"Since he was almost eighteen when we were born, it's not like we grew up together. But we've heard stories about how he drove Mama and Daddy crazy with some of his shenanigans."

"Please don't think I hold any of my childhood feelings against either of you."

"We know," the twins said together.

Because Daisy had initiated the physical contact, Lizzy felt comfortable resting her head on her aunt's shoulder. It felt good to receive comfort without the fear of having it snatched away.

"This is a big decision for all of us, and there is a lot to consider. Maybe we should all sleep on this idea before making any decisions. And move to the kitchen for pie," Daisy suggested.

Sage stood and took a step as if she wanted to get there first. "That's a good idea."

Lizzy followed and let herself enjoy the soothing sensation of happiness. "I can't tell you how much I appreciate you even considering this. My impulsiveness sometimes gets me into situations. Such as Travis becoming my fake boyfriend." That made all of them chuckle and lightened the mood. "Now, let's eat pie."

When Travis neared the kitchen door of the farmhouse, female laughter drifted out and made him smile. He knocked and then went inside.

"You're just in time for pie." Elizabeth held up a plate with a large slice. "It's peach."

"Good timing on my part." Her glittering smile made his stomach swirl. He accepted the plate and took a seat at the round table. "Is this supper?"

"Yes," Daisy said. "And I'm adding ice cream to the menu."

"I'm good with that." When the first bite hit his tongue, he barely resisted a moan of pleasure. "I'm glad you agreed to let me be your taste tester. I approve and give you an A-plus."

"Thanks." Elizabeth sat across from him, a rosy blush rising on her cheeks. "I saw you riding that bucking horse earlier. Did you get hurt?"

"Nope. All good." No need to mention the ache in his lower back or his shoulder.

Daisy brought over a tub of Blue Bell vanilla ice cream and put it in the middle of the table. "Dig in."

Sage wasn't shy about topping off her pie with a large scoop. "Lizzy, we haven't really discussed it in detail yet, but what do you plan to do after the summer?"

"If everything goes well at the audition with the opera

in Fort Worth, I will hopefully have a place with them. At least in the chorus. Because my father always had me stay in one spot, I have dreams of traveling around the country and maybe some of the world. Seeing new places and experiencing new things. Can the ranch be my home base if I get a spot with the opera company and get to wander around the globe for a bit?"

"Of course," Sage said.

Travis's gut clenched as the pie became a brick in his belly.

Just like my mom.

He ducked his head because he didn't want anyone to see the emotion that might show on his face.

When his mom left, his little boy heart had thought she would eventually come back home to stay. Home to be his mom. She had promised to visit frequently, but she'd rarely shown up and then her visits grew fewer and further between. Less and less over the years. And there came a time when he stopped sneaking away to cry.

Now, when he heard from her, it was usually because she needed something. One of the reasons his savings had dwindled.

This was also a strong reminder why Elizabeth Dalton was not for him.

"My opera plans are another reason why the fostering would only be temporary," she said.

That made his head snap up. "Fostering?"

"Daisy and I went to the hospital to hold babies in the NICU and there is an orphaned baby boy who needs to be fostered for at least three months."

"And you plan to do it?"

"It's still in the consideration phase," she said and looked at each of the twins.

"If we move forward with it, you will need a background

check," Sage said to Elizabeth. "Daisy and I already had ours done."

"Would I need one, too?" he asked.

"Probably. Would that be a problem?" Sage asked him.

"No. Never been arrested or in any trouble. Other than stealing cookies before supper." He liked the smile that put on Elizabeth's face. Liked it too much, so he looked down at the melting ice cream on his plate and scolded himself, again.

She is not for me. Get a grip.

The foster parent thing meant she would undoubtedly be living on the ranch longer than first planned. If he let down his guard and then she left, he'd once again be miserable because of a woman.

"The house would need to be reinspected," Sage continued. "A health inspection and a fire inspection."

Daisy grinned at her sister. "Sage won't have any trouble getting the fire inspection done in a hurry."

"Oh, really? This sounds like a story I need to hear. Do tell," Elizabeth said.

"The new fire marshal has a major crush on Sage."

Sage waved a hand as if this was not true. "It's harmless flirtation. He's way too young for me, and I'm not looking for anything serious."

Travis could agree with that statement. He wasn't in the right headspace for any kind of romantic relationship.

"Sage, why not just have some fun with the fire marshal while you can and let him know you aren't looking for anything serious?" Elizabeth flashed a bright smile his way, like she was hinting at something.

Or was it just his disobedient brain's wishful, and very risky, thinking?

Chapter Nine

The next morning Sage joined Lizzy and Daisy at the breakfast table where they were buttering toast. "I think I should go with the two of you to the hospital to meet this baby boy."

"Really?" Lizzy tried to contain her excitement, but the butter knife slipped out of her hand and clattered onto the table.

"Yes. I already called my contact and asked what I would need to do to be an active foster parent again. But by the time we get everything settled, the baby might already be with his father. So don't get too excited."

Easier said than done. Suddenly wide awake, she wanted to do a little dance. "If he does come home with us…temporarily until his family is located," Lizzy said with extra emphasis, "I'll do most of the work and care for the baby. I'll make everything as easy on the two of you as possible."

The messy morning bun on top of Daisy's head bobbed

as she nodded. "It will be easier if we all three work together as a team."

Having someone to team up with to accomplish a goal was such a new experience. She was used to being a bit of a loner. It reminded her of when she was little and the three of them had been so close, the twins more like siblings than aunts. They could be like sisters once again.

Lizzy was sweeping her bedroom floor when her phone rang. She grabbed it off the nightstand and groaned when she saw her father's number, but she took a calming breath and answered.

"Hello."

"Elizabeth, you're already dating someone in Texas?"

"What are you talking about?"

"The cowboy you went grocery shopping with."

Her jaw clenched so tightly she was surprised her teeth didn't crack. It had to be Jeff who'd told him. Who else could it be? But she wanted to make sure. "Who told you that?"

"Jeffery Smith."

I knew it! That rat.

"Why were you talking to him?"

"He brought in a big client and now works at Dalton Realty."

Her nausea was instantaneous. That was yet another reason not to ever work there again. And she'd bet Jeff wasn't in Channing to visit anyone. Had her own father sent him to spy on her? It wouldn't be a huge surprise.

"I knew letting you go to Texas was a bad idea."

Letting her? Steam built up and swirled around her insides. She had *not* asked permission, but she was still too scared of her own father to refute that fact at the moment.

"Did you send Jeff to spy on me?"

"No. I sent him to a real estate conference in Fort Worth,

and he has family near Channing. And I'm glad he does because you are acting like you're sixteen."

"Well, I'm not. I'm almost a whole decade older than that, and my dating is none of your concern." Lizzy walked in a circle at the foot of her bed, scrambling to think of something to say and highly tempted to hang up the phone. If she denied dating Travis, Jeff would find out. But thanks to the deal she'd made with a cowboy, that was an embarrassment she could avoid.

"You should listen to someone with more experience. Look how easily that artist and that construction worker you were dating just walked away," her father said.

"What do you know about my relationships with either of them?" His longer than normal pause made her skin crawl.

"I know that one day they were hanging around and the next they weren't."

She gasped softly as things clicked into place. Her own father had done something to make them ghost her. He was even more manipulative than she thought.

"And don't even get me started talking about wasting time auditioning with the opera. Singing was a fine hobby while you were still in school, but it's not real life for people like you."

"People like me? What does that mean?"

"If you can't be the very best at it then you need to move on to other things. You're good at taking care of business at Dalton Realty."

His lame compliment meant nothing and only served to ramp up her anger for immediate take off toward fury, where she'd likely say something she'd regret.

"I have somewhere I need to be. I can't talk right now. Bye." She ended the call, tossed her phone onto her bed and screamed into her fists, making the cat jump off the mattress. "Sorry, Lady. My good mood just went down the toilet."

And then…her mood took another nosedive.

"Oh. My. God. Did he do something to try to ruin my chances at the Chicago Opera?" Her fingernails dug into her palms as she pressed her fists to her thighs.

The first time she'd seen her father after her audition, he had acted as if he already knew she'd failed to get a spot and hadn't been the least bit sympathetic. He'd been pleased and told her they could now get back to business as usual. And to think she'd almost asked him to put in a good word with his golf buddy who was on the board of the Chicago Opera.

Lizzy snapped her hands to her hips. "His friend…on the board. That's got to be what happened."

It was true she hadn't sung her best, but could her audition have gotten her a chorus spot if he hadn't interfered? Suddenly sweating, she flapped her white cotton blouse away from her body.

"I need some air."

She hurried downstairs and out into the backyard. Everyone was off working, and there was no one around to vent to, but she had an idea. Lizzy headed for the corner of the ranch that backed up to a Texas state natural area. Unless there was a hiker this far into the nature preserve, no one would be close enough to hear her singing, or if they could it would be a distant sound.

When she got there, she let loose with Puccini's "O Mio Babbino Caro," which was about a feuding family. A great choice to work out her frustration. Her voice came out more powerfully than she'd ever heard from herself. And it felt fabulous. By the end of the aria, she was smiling and laughing.

"Thanks, Dad. Now, I feel even better about my chances of singing in an opera."

* * *

When Lizzy neared the stables, Travis was cursing about whatever he held in his hand. "What's wrong, cowboy? Did someone try to kick your horse?"

"Not if they want to live." He turned to her with a broken bridle, and then sighed with an apologetic expression. "I didn't mean to be so gruff. It's just that everything seems to be going wrong today, and I think I should just go back to bed."

"Want to talk about it?"

"No," he said quickly but worked his mouth as if he wanted to say more.

"I'm a good listener."

"I looked up the listing for the Martin Ranch," he said in a rush. Tension hardened his jaw, but his eyes held sadness.

"I did, too. It's a lot."

"Too much." The broken bridle clanged as he chunked it onto the top of a wooden bench.

This was another strong reaction to the sale of the place where he'd grown up. Was it only nostalgia, or... "Oh. You want to buy it."

He shrugged but remained silent.

"I'm sorry you're having a glass-half-empty kind of day. I know the feeling. But if you think of it as filling up or almost full, you will feel better."

"Sorry, little Miss Sunshine. My glass is empty at the moment."

If he only knew the mood she had just overcome. "I feel better when I sing, but I guess that won't work for you."

"You can sing if you want." He spun away from her as if he hadn't meant to say it aloud.

His statement surprised her, and because her confidence had been restored, Lizzy walked along the aisle between the horse stalls, singing a gently melodic song meant to calm both man and animals.

Several horses stuck their heads out, and one made soft whickering sounds as she drew near. Travis stayed in the area, close enough to hear, but not so close that it was obvious. Was he starting to warm up to her?

A more intriguing question, was Travis Taylor having as much trouble staying away from her as she was from him?

Chapter Ten

It was the morning of the day Travis had been dreading. The day he had to spend hours working closely with Elizabeth. It would no doubt put him behind schedule and likely cause him even more work, but they'd made a deal, and as he'd told her, he always fulfilled his promises.

Now he just had to keep a promise to himself. They could be casual friends, but he would not fall for her.

She must have seen him walking up to the house because she came out of the kitchen door and waved. "Good morning."

"Morning. Ready to get to work?"

"I sure am." She fell into step beside him.

He was surprised to see her hair curlier than normal and pulled into a high ponytail, and her face was washed clean of makeup. She wore jeans that looked too nice for ranch work, a pink T-shirt that would be stained by the end of the day and a pair of brown boots she had borrowed from one of her aunts.

"Daisy gave me a tour of the barn, but we ran out of time, and she didn't get to tell me about the areas outside." She pointed to a round pen off to one side of the stables. "Is that where you train the horses on one of those long ropes?"

"It's called longeing. I do train some horses in there, but it's also a place to exercise them."

"What is that concrete area over there?"

"That's where they're bathed when the weather is nice." He led her around the stables to the old red barn where tools were kept.

"What are we going to be doing today?"

She certainly asked a lot of questions, but he was rapidly growing used to it. As much as he'd fought it, she brought out a playfulness he'd been hiding away behind his misery over wasting time with Crystal and missing Grandpa Will. The opportunity was too good, and Travis couldn't resist messing with her.

"Since you're part of the Dalton family, you should know what makes the real money around here. You'll be doing a collection from our best stallion, Titan."

Her steps faltered and her expression went from confused to horrified in a second.

He couldn't stop a brief chuckle. "Kidding. That's not on the schedule until tomorrow."

"Good, because I don't think I'm ready for that level of…" She swirled her hand through the air in uncertainty and wrinkled her pert little nose. "Um, getting that personal with an animal as big as a horse."

He had to clear his throat to fight a full-out laugh. There were so many things he could say to that. Most of them inappropriate, so he kept quiet. Who could've guessed that being around her was going to be good for his mood? But the day wasn't over, yet.

"Working with Titan takes training and experience. And it's not for everyone."

"I would think not. What *will* you have me do? For real. I'm betting whatever is the dirtiest and worst job?"

He swung open the barn door. "There might be some dirt involved."

"Do you have the same list of chores every day?"

"There are some chores that happen daily, even on the weekends and holidays, but other things that change. It depends on the season. Or when there's a need for maintenance or repair. Today, I need to fix a broken water pipe. We'll have to do some digging and replace it."

"Well, that's certainly something I've never done."

"If you want to back out now, you can, and I'll understand."

"No way." Lizzy straightened her spine and increased her stride to keep up with him. "You can't make me give up that easily."

He was betting she'd last about an hour before making an excuse to go back to the house. She'd probably claim there was a phone call she'd forgotten she needed to make. "Could you grab those shovels over by the tractor? I'll get the rest of the supplies."

"Two of them?"

"Yes, ma'am." When she brought them over to the wheelbarrow where he'd loaded the bucket of pipe repair supplies, he got a good look at her manicured fingernails. That shiny pink polish was not going to survive the day, not even with gloves. "You can lay the shovels in here with the other supplies, and then please grab that length of PVC pipe."

He rolled the wheelbarrow to his truck and transferred the tools and supplies into the back before lifting the metal wheelbarrow and putting it in as well.

"Wow, you're strong."

Her appreciation of his strength was something he could get used to. "Ranch work will do that."

They drove out into the closest pasture, and he pulled to a stop beside the windmill. There was a muddy patch of ground where a pipe had been broken. The June morning was pleasant, with a breeze that made her long, blond ponytail dance around her back.

"Put on these leather gloves." He handed them to her and watched to see if she would balk about putting her hands into someone else's dirty work gloves, but she surprised him when she did it without one word of argument. But her nose did wrinkle slightly.

She clapped her gloved hands together. "Now what?"

"Grab a shovel. We need to dig out all the mud around the broken pipe, and then we can replace it." He demonstrated how to scoop up a shovel full and put it into the wheelbarrow.

She jabbed her shovel into the ground and made an *oof* sound when she lifted a load as if the effort was more than she had expected. "Why are we putting the mud into the wheelbarrow instead of just tossing it out of the way on the ground?"

"Because that will make it easier to put the dirt where I want it without having to use the shovels again."

"That's smart."

"It happens on occasion." He had waited long enough to find out more about the arrogant Jeff. "Tell me about why you felt the need to make up a fake boyfriend in front of that guy at the grocery store?"

"It's kind of hard to explain."

"Try." When she shot him a hurt expression, he softened his request. "Please. I got the feeling you were frightened."

She straightened, and the mud slid off her shovel to splat back into the hole. "You could tell?"

"Yes. It was in your body language."

"That figures." She wiped the back of her arm across her forehead. "I hope Jeff didn't get the satisfaction of knowing that."

"I doubt it. He seemed too arrogant to notice much about other people."

"Good call."

She had stopped working, but he didn't point that out because he wanted to keep her talking. If this jerk was a threat, he needed to know.

"Guess what I found out about him? He works for my father now. I hope the two of them are very happy together." She thrust the blade of the shovel back into the hole and then gave it such a fling that the mud sailed over the wheelbarrow and splattered on the ground.

"Does your father know how you feel about the guy?"

"Pfft. Like he cares."

"What did Jeff do to you?" The answer might piss him off, but he had to know.

"He used me to get information. And then, there was the night he got drunk at a party and…let's just say he wanted more than I was willing to give."

Mud slid from his shovel onto his boots as hot rage filled him. "He hurt you?" he said through gritted teeth.

"No. I'm fast and got away."

His body tensed like it did when he was preparing to ride in a rodeo and knowing there was danger ahead. Travis was tempted to find the guy and tell him what could happen to men who mistreat women in this part of the country.

"Honestly, when I saw him in the store, I was also being a coward. I didn't want him to know that I'm basically starting over with next to nothing because I'm not willing to ask my father for anything." She'd rushed through the sentence and paused to take a breath. "I don't have a pay-ing job, I messed up my audition with the Chicago Opera and my only prospects at this point are hopes and dreams. If my audition in a few months doesn't go well, I might end up working at Zimmerman's."

"I get it. I rodeoed for years, and I know what it's like to have hopes and dreams."

"Did you achieve your dreams?"

"Some."

"Why did you stop?"

He shrugged. "I did it until I couldn't."

"You got hurt?"

"Yes. We need to get this work done. There's more to do after this."

She rolled her eyes and scooped another half shovel full of mud. "Now who is the one who doesn't want to answer questions?"

He couldn't argue with that.

"My ultimate dream is to be part of an opera company that tours. Doesn't that sound grand? New places and people all the time."

An icy finger slithered down his spine.

Exactly like Crystal.

Why did so many of the women in his life feel the need to roam? He was thoroughly annoyed with himself for allowing Elizabeth to continually distract him from his plan to keep her at a distance. His reactions were simply a biological response to her feminine beauty. And it had been way too long since he had been with a woman. That's all it was. His heart didn't have to get involved.

"If I do well at my audition and get a place in the company, think of all the experiences out there just waiting to be explored."

"Not much for staying in one place?"

"I did enough of that in Chicago. Staying put because of

my father's wishes. Now, it's my time to see the world and choose my own path."

In other words...don't even think about asking her to stay here on the ranch.

He flinched and rubbed at tension constricting his torso.

Why in the hell am I thinking about her staying?

They stopped for a break a few minutes later. She guzzled water from her bottle and then rubbed her right shoulder. There was mud on her clothes, her arms and even a smear across her cheek. He'd never thought to see this opera diva in such a state. Travis was throwing everything he could at her—within reason. But maybe he was going too far.

Why am I testing her?

He answered his own thought honestly and winced. He wanted to know what kind of woman she was. Her work ethic and if she was cut out for ranch life. So far, she was doing better than he'd anticipated, but he doubted it would last.

There was no way she'd be coming back to work with him again tomorrow, and he'd be able to get through the day without her distracting him with her beauty, and whatever that sensation was that made him hyperaware of her presence.

Chapter Eleven

With the back of her gloved hand, Lizzy wiped a lock of hair from her face, adding another layer of filth on top of the dried bits already on her cheek. "Next time, remind me to pick a day that doesn't involve schlepping through the mud."

Travis straightened and turned to her, flinging mud off the end of his shovel to splatter across her jeans…and proving her point. "Next time?"

"You still don't think I'm cut out for this kind of work?"

He made a noncommittal sound in his throat. "Who says you get to pick the day?"

"My pie-making schedule," she said, grinning with a hip cocked out to the side and her fist braced on it.

He grumbled playfully. "Fine."

She caught the beginnings of a smile before he turned his head. They continued to work in silence for several minutes; the only sounds were those of nature and their shovels digging into the thick mud. She was determined to show him she could work as hard as her aunts. She'd prove this cow-boy wrong, but it sure wasn't going to be easy.

Lizzy scooped another shovel full of heavy, dark-brown mud filled with little chips of limestone and added it to the heap in the wheelbarrow. She was used to long workdays at Dalton Realty, but today's intense physical exertion was on a level she'd yet to do, not even during the workouts at the gym with the trainer they all secretly called The Demon.

Why do I always open my big mouth and get myself into situations like this?

She could never let Travis know that the work and this day had been way harder than she had ever thought it would be. She ached in new places that she didn't even want to think about. At least he'd given her gloves and she didn't have any blisters, but the tiny muscles in her hands and fingers were making their displeasure heard loud and clear.

"Hold the shovel like this and it will be easier." Travis said and demonstrated where to put her hands on the wooden shank.

"I've already exhausted today's usage quota for the muscles it takes to hold it that way."

He stopped shoveling and propped the blade of the tool against the ground. "Elizabeth, you can stop. Don't hurt yourself."

She inwardly cringed at the sound of him using her full name. When she'd told him to call her Elizabeth, she'd been annoyed with him. But every time he said it, she was reminded of her father calling her by her full name. He was one of the few people who did, but she did not want to think of her father right now, and certainly not in connection with Travis. A man who—despite his prick-liness—she was growing too fond of. She let her shovel fall to the ground.

He cocked his head. "What's wrong? Other than being tired."

"I don't like it when you call me Elizabeth."

He backed up a step. "Excuse me, *Ms. Dalton*, but you're the one who told me to call you Elizabeth." He abruptly turned and took a few steps before she caught up to him and hooked her finger in the back pocket of his jeans. He came to a stop but didn't turn around.

"Travis, wait. You misunderstand what I mean. I guess I wasn't very clear. I want you to call me Lizzy."

He slowly turned to face her, the only part of his face showing any emotion were his tilted eyebrows. "What brought on this change in my status?"

"I don't like it when you call me Elizabeth because that's what my father calls me."

"I see. What if calling you Lizzy feels wrong to me?"

She sighed. "I understand. I might've been a bit of a diva when we met. What do you want to call me?"

"Can I pick out my own name for you?"

"It depends on how unflattering it is." She rubbed her gloves together to knock off the dried mud while he took his sweet time thinking. "Don't leave me hanging."

"I think I'll wait for it to reveal itself." He stalked toward the truck, leaving her to follow along behind him.

"What are you going to call me until then?" she asked.

"I'm not going to call you anything at all," he said without turning around.

This man…

She took a deep breath, once again completely annoyed with him.

But also…kind of turned on. His rough edges heightened his appeal.

Once they'd finished that job, they reloaded the truck and drove back to the barn.

Travis unloaded the wheelbarrow from the bed of his truck. "The rest of the things I need to do today are things you can't help me with. You can head back to the house."

Relief was instant, but she would not let him see that. "Okay. I'll see you back out here tomorrow."

"You're actually coming back for more?"

"I told you I'm no quitter." She took two steps but then paused. "Oh wait, I can't work with you tomorrow."

"That's what I thought." He crossed his arms over his broad chest.

"We're going back to the hospital tomorrow."

"Hospital? Why?" His arms dropped to his sides as he stepped forward .

"To see the baby. Sage decided she's going to do it until I can get approved to foster, and we're starting the process to bring the baby home with us."

"You're really going to become a foster parent?"

"Yes. You sound surprised. Is taking care of a baby something else you think I can't do?"

He ignored her question. "I got the impression Sage wasn't all in on that idea. And aren't you leaving at the end of the summer?"

She shrugged. "I guess that remains to be seen. There are going to be some home inspections. Sage said you know how to do electrical work. Do you think you can repair the light in the dining room before then? It keeps flickering."

Travis leaned against the wall of the barn with one boot crossed over the other at the ankle. "Let me see if I have this right. You aren't going to come help me work, but you want me to do a favor for you?"

Her hands once again ended up on her hips. She knew he was teasing, but she was hot and tired and rather cranky at the moment. "No, actually, I don't think I want you to do anything at all for me. I'll just google directions for how to rewire a light fixture."

"That sounds safe."

His deadpan delivery was actually kind of funny, but she was too annoyed to laugh. She stalked toward the house—as fast as her sore muscles allowed, all while gritting her teeth against the aches radiating from many locations on her body. There was a hot bath and a large glass of wine singing her name. And there would be no calorie counting tonight. Not that she ever really did, but still, she'd burned enough calories to eat an entire pizza and a whole cake.

Lizzy arrived at the NICU just in time to feed the baby, and they were snuggled together in a rocking chair while a nurse prepared his bottle.

"Hello, angel boy. Did you have a good night?"

The baby yawned and stretched big enough to get one arm out of his swaddling. His fingers spread wide in chorus with a soft baby grunt.

"Oh, it was that good?" Stroking his soft, round cheek had him turning his head to mouth her finger. "Your bottle is coming, sweetie."

Right on cue, the nurse arrived with a bottle of formula. "He's such a good baby and hardly ever cries. All the other nurses have been stopping by to love on him."

"I can understand that." She rubbed the clear nipple against his lips, and he eagerly started sucking. "Is there any news on the search for his father?"

"Nothing yet, but they'll keep looking."

"How did the rest of his medical test turn out?"

"All good reports. His heart is strong with no abnormalities."

"That's excellent news. I've been reading about Down syndrome and some of the things to expect."

"You're going to make a great mom someday." The nurse patted Lizzy's shoulder and went to tend to another baby.

Someday, she'd be the kind of mother she imagined hers would've been. Loving. Great at making holidays special. And quick with a hug or words of encouragement. What would this sweet baby's dad be like? Would he want his son?

Lizzy rocked slowly while he drank his bottle and sang a lullaby her grandmother had sung to her. He burped like a champion, and when she started singing again, he stared at her, and his lips turned up at the corners.

"Was that a smile? I think it was." Lightness and joy filled her. She wasn't going to tell anyone and have them ruin it by telling her it was only gas. She would hold to her belief that he'd smiled just for her.

After a diaper change, she snuggled him skin to skin on her chest with a blanket covering them. His tiny body was warm against her breasts and his skin as soft as a velvety rose petal. One perfect little fist was against his mouth, and he made soft sucking sounds that brought a smile to her face. "That's it, sweetie, dream about eating and growing and getting strong enough to leave the hospital."

While he napped, she daydreamed about her future. Singing and reconnecting with the twins and starting a new phase of her life on her own terms. It wasn't her fault that images of a certain cowboy slipped into her thoughts a time or two. Or ten.

On the way home from the hospital, she used the time to sing. After going through a warm-up, she sang songs from several of her favorite operas. She had not been getting in the daily practice she'd intended, but she was working it in where she could and happy with her progress.

Before she got home, hunger had her stopping at Whataburger—a Texas fast-food staple. The drink that came with her cheeseburger and fries was so enormous that she still had half of it left when she got back to the ranch.

Was it a bad sign that the first thing she wanted to do was see Travis and tell him about her day?

As far as her heart was concerned, yes. Yes, it was.

Chapter Twelve

Travis led Titan into his stall and took off the lead rope. "You did good, big guy."

Even while exercising the stallion, Liz was on his mind. That's what he'd decided to call her. It was neither of the options she'd given him, and he wanted to see her reaction to his choice. Would it annoy her and help keep a safe distance between them? Would she pull one of those faces that made him grin? He didn't want to want her. But he did.

The way he'd been purposely pushing her buttons was juvenile but keeping her at a safe distance was hard. In a short amount of time, she'd worked her way into his life. Into his thoughts.

But he could not let her into his heart.

"I need a new strategy. Got any tips, Titan? All the ladies love you."

The prized horse bobbed his head and whickered softly.

He patted the animal's muscular hindquarter, closed the

door to the stall and made his way outside into the afternoon sunshine.

Liz's late model white Cadillac was back, and she was standing beside the open door. She was singing in a voice somewhere between her full opera voice and the soft one she often used indoors. The song was in English this time, but he had no idea if it was from an opera or something else.

She held a large Styrofoam cup from Whataburger in one hand and a wadded paper bag in the other.

Not wanting the drink tossed in his face if he got too close and startled her, he whistled loud enough to be heard over her singing. Her song turned into a yelp, and as she spun around the Styrofoam cup crushed in her hand, spilling amber liquid down the front of her ruffled pale blue dress.

"Travis Taylor! What is wrong with you?" She dropped the remains of her cup and threw the wadded paper bag at him.

He caught the bag and grimaced. "Sorry. I was trying to prevent your drink from being thrown at me and didn't anticipate that happening."

With her pointer finger wagging in his direction—but her smile growing—she walked his way. "Why don't I believe that? One of these times I'm going to be holding something heavy or sharp. Something dangerous for me to be hurling at you."

"Good point. I'll find a new way to get your attention." Thankfully, she wasn't furious, but he thought better of giving in to his urge to laugh.

"I would appreciate that." She held her sticky, wet dress away from her body. "I guess this is payback for the things I've done to you, so I can't be too mad. But I still might get you that bell." She glanced at his boots. "Or maybe you could wear a pair of those jangly spurs."

That made him chuckle before he could stop himself. "I don't think you'd be able to hear a bell or spurs when you're singing, but I promise not to whistle like that again. I have to make a trip to Old Town. Do you want to ride along?"

"Yes. I'd love to." She looked down at her dress, and then shot him a playful scowl. "But first, I need to change my clothes."

"I'll clean up the trash while you change." With the paper bag already in his hand, he motioned to the crushed orange and white cup on the ground beside her car.

"How thoughtful of you."

"Liz."

"Yes?"

"That's the name I'm going to call you. When I'm not calling you Princess Songbird."

"Works for me, Trav." She walked away with extra flounce in her steps.

Well, that backfired with flying colors.

She hadn't been the least bit annoyed by his choice of names. It would do nothing to keep him safe from her charm. Now it was even worse. She'd liked it *and* shortened his name, too. Like they were lovers.

He waited outside while she went to change her clothes and took the time to give himself another lecture. Maybe if he started thinking of her as someone else's girlfriend he could keep his distance. He pinched the bridge of his nose and groaned. That thought only made him feel a flash of jealousy.

I'm in so much trouble.

She returned a few minutes later dressed in a white top with big red flowers, a denim skirt that hit a few inches above her knees and her wedge heels. Although still impractical, he was starting to appreciate the way they show-cased her long legs, especially with the shorter skirt.

I'm screwed.

He opened the passenger side door for her, and then they were on their way into Channing.

"Why are we going to Old Town? Other than the fact that you owe me a trip."

He hitched his thumb toward the backseat where his toolbox was on the floorboard and a cardboard box on the seat. "I have the part that's needed to get the fountain's water pump going."

"You know how to fix a water pump?"

"I do. Great-grandpa Roy taught me when we worked together on the Martin Ranch."

"The twins said he recently died. I'm sorry."

"That was my Grandpa Will. Great-grandpa Roy died when I was seventeen. They both taught me most of what I know while we worked together."

"Three generations working together. That's so cool."

"We lived together, too." He didn't want to get too deeply into his past right now, so he changed the topic. "How did it go at the hospital?"

"It was really good. Wait until you see the baby. He is totally adorable. They still haven't found his father, but at least he has an aunt who will be his guardian."

"When did you say his aunt will be back?"

"About three months."

"That's a long trip."

"I think it's for work."

"Why do you want to be a working opera singer?"

"Because I love it. And regardless of what you think, I'm pretty good at it."

Her side-eyed glance made him internally wince. "I've never said your singing is bad."

"Not in so many words." She brushed the tips of her

fingers back and forth over the tan leather of the console between them.

"I'm sorry I made you think that. You're a good singer. Really good. I should have told you so." Her nails were a new shade of sparkly pink that suited her personality, and before he thought better of it, he covered her hand with his own. A charge zipped up his arm before he could put his hand back on the steering wheel. Lizzy appeared surprised, and he wasn't sure if she'd felt the same jolt from their touch or if it was his admission.

"Thanks for saying that. I haven't always had encouragement when it comes to my singing."

"No one can deny that you're good." Travis slowed to twenty miles per hour on Main, where businesses lined both sides of the street. He parked in front of a new coffee shop and grabbed the pump part and tools from the backseat while Lizzy waited on the sidewalk.

"Look." She pointed to a man outside on a ladder putting the final touches of yellow paint around a plate-glass window that was framed on the inside with velvety pink curtains. "It's a new boutique."

The sign read Glitz & Glam. "Looks like your kind of place."

"I hope they sell shoes."

"They'll probably have those cowgirl boots with all the rhinestones on them."

"Well, I do need a pair of my own."

He stole another quick glance at her legs. *Just when I was starting to like her fancy shoes.*

The side of Main they were on had a courtyard behind a section of it. The fountain with a rearing horse on top was in the middle of the courtyard surrounded on three sides by shops and the fourth side looked out over a little park closer to the creek where ducks swam, and people could walk over a foot bridge to the nature trails. As they entered the courtyard, he was surprised to see so many people milling around the fountain.

"Are they all here to watch you get the fountain going?"

"I have no idea. I hope not. I was only expecting to see a couple of the people from the preservation planning committee. Let's hope I can get it working."

"I know you can do it." She put a hand on his shoulder, but just like he'd done in the truck, she quickly pulled it away.

The way she'd withdrawn made him think she was feeling the same spark, and her faith in his ability to repair the fountain made his chest puff up. "Go ahead and look around while I put this final part on the pump."

"I'll do that."

While he worked, several people stopped beside him to ask questions and thank him for volunteering to do the work. He couldn't seem to stop himself from seeking Liz out. She was talking and laughing with everyone. The few people she knew and the ones she'd just met.

She threw back her head and laughed, her long hair flowing down her back and glistening in rays of sunshine. His chest tightened, and he pressed the palm of one hand against his breastbone. As much as he'd tried to find her annoying or dislike her, he could not pretend any longer.

Princess Songbird was not the diva he'd first thought. Whether she was dressed up in her fancy stuff or mud splattered from working with him, she radiated kindness and beauty. They frequently picked at each other, but he'd never known a woman quite like her and enjoyed watching her having fun.

Just as he was finishing up and they had started filling the fountain with water, Liz came over to him.

"You really do know how to fix everything." They were

facing each other, and she moved close enough to brush a leaf from his shoulder.

Her nearness made him very aware of his heartbeat. Travis glanced across to the other side of the fountain and his unusually good mood took a nosedive. Her ex-boyfriend, Jeff, was standing there staring at them with that annoyingly smug look on his face.

His protective instincts flared to a new level. This guy was begging for something he was not going to like, and if he made one wrong move, he'd find out. Travis couldn't stand the thought of her feeling like she had in the grocery store. He needed to keep her from seeing the jerk and having a similar reaction.

Jeff started heading toward them, and Travis made a quick decision. He lightly grasped her shoulders. "Liz, don't freak out. Just trust me and go with it."

"Okay." Her eyes widened, and she swayed toward him.

He surprised himself even further when he slid his arms around her shoulders, pulled her close...

And kissed her.

Chapter Thirteen

Lizzy's world shifted on its axis in a most magnificent way.

Travis was kissing her. Not a deep kiss with tongues and groping hands but a tender press of lips that she felt in every part of her body. Sparkly bubbles danced inside her as if someone had turned on a bubble machine, and she clung onto the belt loops at the back of his jeans.

When he lifted his head, there was more emotion on his face than she'd ever seen. His mouth that often frowned was relaxed and wet from their kiss. His eyes half lidded. What had made this stoic cowboy kiss her right here, right now, in public?

"Don't turn around," he whispered in a ragged voice and kept her in his arms.

She didn't even have words to answer. What was happening right now? Who was this new version of Travis? She didn't turn around, but she did look over her shoulder.

Her breath caught painfully in her lungs.

Jeff was standing there with his hands in the pockets of

his slacks and staring at them with a surprised expression. She felt several things at once. Thrilled from Trav's kiss. Shocked and most unhappy to see Jeff.

And now, an unsettling wave of disappointment eclipsed her joy. She let go of his waist but couldn't make herself step away from the protection he offered. Had Travis only kissed her because Jeff was watching? He had promised to play her boyfriend if they saw him again, and he had told her that he always keeps a promise.

"Can we leave now?" she whispered, her voice catching on the last word.

"Good idea." Travis led her quickly away from the area. He kept his arm around her waist until they were out of sight from the crowd and then dropped it to his side. "Wait in the truck while I get my tools. Lock the doors until I'm back."

Feeling strangely numb, she climbed into the truck without saying a word. She scooched down in the seat and covered her face. A mass of knots had set up residence in her stomach, and it felt like forever until the auto locks clicked and the back driver's-side door opened. His toolbox clanged as it dropped onto the floorboard.

They were silent as he got into the driver's seat and pulled onto the road. He kept flexing his right hand and one knuckle was scraped. Had he hurt it working on the fountain? The urge to take his hand and tend to it was so strong that she slid her hands under her thighs. She didn't dare touch him.

The risk of being rejected was too high.

Now that Jeff had seen her kissing Travis, she'd bet money that he was going to report back to her father. The dirty rat.

Travis cleared his throat. "I hope it's okay that I…did that."

By *that* he meant the kiss. The kiss that had rocked her

in the best way, and when she'd looked into his eyes right after, she'd thought he felt the same. But now...

What is it about me that some people shy away from?

He kept glancing away from the road to look at her, and she realized she hadn't answered. "Yes. It's okay."

"I promised I'd play your boyfriend if we saw him again, and when I did..." He shrugged. "He was coming our way, and it seemed like the thing to do."

His matter-of-fact words pressed a bruised spot on her heart. It was the best kiss of her life, but he was simply keeping a promise. "I appreciate it." Hopefully he couldn't hear the pain in her words.

In the heat of their kiss, there'd been a shift. A connection she'd thought he was a part of, too. But the kiss hadn't been real for him. It wasn't a moment of passion he couldn't contain. It wasn't that he couldn't resist her for one minute longer.

He was just a good guy keeping a promise.

They'd only been back from town for an hour, but her mood had not improved. Lizzy was stretched out on her bed with the cat on her chest. Lady's soft purring was comforting but not enough to pull her out of the self-pity spiral. So used to handling every emotional event by herself, she was hiding away.

The kiss—not a real kiss—by the fountain had completely rattled her.

What she wanted to do more than anything was go to the hospital and hold her sweet angel boy. He calmed her breathing and made her worries lighter.

Her phone rang, and she groaned before grabbing it from the bedside table. When she saw her father's number, her groan turned into a hiss.

"Already? Jeff is a big fat tattletale."

The very last thing she wanted to do right now was talk to her father. She let it go to voicemail and shifted the cat onto the bedspread so she could sit on the edge of the mattress. Her phone alerted her to a voicemail a minute later. If she didn't listen, she would drive herself crazy with wondering.

"Elizabeth, it's your father. Call me."

That was it. No hello or how are you. Just a clipped message in his brisk tone. She hadn't exactly lucked out in the father department. Once her opera career was established and she was in the right place in her life, she would have children of her own and be the best mom possible.

"I absolutely will not repeat his mistakes."

She was in no mood to jump to his demands to call him, and she couldn't keep sitting in her room feeling sorry for herself. She went downstairs and found her aunts in the living room, each of them in their wingback chair facing the blue velvet sofa. Sage's chair was pink, and Daisy's was powder blue. Their colorful furniture choices were calmed by the soft gray walls and the white fireplace mantel. The radio was playing, and they were reading horse magazines.

Lizzy sat on the sofa across from the twins and curled her feet beneath her. It wasn't the flower-patterned couch she remembered from her childhood, but the same throw pillows gave it a familiar feel. She pulled a pillow onto her lap and traced a finger over the floral needlepoint design her grandmother had lovingly stitched years ago.

"Are you okay?" they both asked.

She wasn't ready to discuss the kiss. "I just got a voice mail from daddy dearest, and I don't feel like calling him back."

A currently popular country song came on the radio, further grating on her already sour mood. "They play this song all the time, and I don't understand why it's so popular. I don't care for it at all," Lizzy said. "Sorry if it's one of your favorites."

Daisy chuckled. "Travis will like hearing that."

"Why?"

The twins exchanged a look.

"What don't I know?" Lizzy asked.

"The artist who sings that song, Crystal, is his ex-girlfriend," Sage said.

"He dated someone famous?"

"Yes, and it didn't end well." Daisy flipped her long hair over the back of her chair. "He doesn't say too much about it, but this is what we know. When his grandpa got sick, he was on tour with Crystal. She got all kinds of mad that he wanted to come home to be with his grandpa. She left him in Wyoming and went on with her tour."

The pillow dropped to the floor as she straightened. "For real? She just left him behind in another state?" Suddenly, she didn't feel the least bit bad about not liking Crystal's music.

Sage put her *Western Horsemanship* magazine on the art deco coffee table. "And that's when he started working for us here at the ranch."

"And this all happened when?"

"Less than a year ago," Daisy said. "Right when he lost his grandpa. Double whammy."

"Now I understand why Travis is so moody and closed off. He's thrown up some thick walls around himself."

"I think he should have come home from that tour sooner." Sage twirled a chin-length curl around her finger. "He hated all the traveling and bouncing from place to place. I don't think he liked traveling even when he was winning on the rodeo circuit."

Traveling and seeing new places was exactly what she

wanted to do. "Then why did Travis go? Did he love Crystal that much?"

"That I don't know," Daisy said. "At the beginning of their relationship, she was always gone, and I guess things were falling apart. I wish he had just let it crumble, but he's a good guy. To try and save their relationship, he agreed to go on her tour."

This new information went a long way to explain a few things about him. Likely the reason why he was so stand-offish. This tough guy could be as prickly as a porcupine, but she now suspected he was protecting a marshmallow center with a tender heart.

I should cut him some slack.

Maybe he just wasn't ready for another relationship yet. She would pretend the kiss never happened and not let on that it had affected her in such a deep way. Tall order, but if it made their relationship easier, she could do it. Her pulse rate spiked.

Relationship? No, no, no. Why am I thinking about a relationship with Travis?

She wasn't going to be here forever, and he wouldn't want another girlfriend who traveled for work. She flopped over on the couch and hooked her legs over the arm.

Her mind went back to the moment right before Travis had made her spill her drink down the front of her body. She'd felt a sensation like glitter across her skin, and Travis's image had popped into her thoughts. She'd instantly dismissed the sensation. There was no way it was because Travis was nearby.

But he had been. She'd sensed his presence a split second before his whistle pierced the air. Having this much awareness of Travis was dangerous. It had to have been a simple coincidence and nothing more.

Wasn't it?

Chapter Fourteen

Travis and Finn were repairing and rehanging the swing on the front porch of the farmhouse, but he couldn't concentrate on anything. A certain blond songbird was consuming his thoughts. What had he been thinking kissing her, especially in public? This is what happened when he got too protective and invested in someone. He lost his good senses and became impulsive.

He'd only kissed her to help her stick it to that jerk.

He wiped sweat from his forehead with his sleeve and cursed inwardly. That was such bull. He'd kissed her for two reasons. Because he'd promised he would pretend to be her boyfriend, but also because he had really wanted to. It had been the perfect excuse.

Travis tried for a third time to get a new bolt screwed in, and when it wouldn't, he tossed the wrench aside with a growl.

"What's got you in such a pisser of a mood?" Finn asked.

"Nothing."

"Is nothing named Lizzy Dalton?"

Travis shot him a glare. Was he being that obvious? "What makes you think that?"

Finn laughed. "For one thing, news travels fast around here, and if you don't want people talking, you shouldn't kiss a woman in public."

"It wasn't for the reason you think." The other cowboy's pale blue eyes were full of humor, but Travis thought he also saw a bit of understanding.

"Whatever you need to tell yourself. But I do understand. Dalton women have a way of getting into your head."

Travis straightened with a flash of jealousy. "You like Liz?"

"No, dude. I'm talking about Daisy."

"Oh. Yeah." What was wrong with him? He was not normally such a jealous guy. "Are you and Daisy…"

Finn held up a hand. "No. I wish, but I need this job and that seems like a good way to lose it."

Travis couldn't argue with that logic. He needed to apply some of that kind of logic to himself. "Did you hear any other rumors about me at that same event?"

"You mean the part about you scaring the slacks off that city boy?" Finn chuckled. "Yep. Riley was there, and he saw."

"Great. Liz doesn't know about that, and I was hoping to keep it that way."

"I won't say anything, and neither will my brother. He only told me and Jake. And I don't think many other people saw the confrontation because Riley said you were in the walkway between the buildings."

"I didn't even see Riley, but I was pretty focused on other things."

"What exactly did you do to the guy?"

"After I took Liz to the truck, I went back for my tools. Jeff was coming around the corner out of the courtyard as if he was following us. He immediately started backing up until his back was against the brick wall of the building. I was straightforward about him staying away from her."

"Did you hit him?"

"Only after he took a swing at me first. I got him right in the jaw, but it wasn't a full-strength punch. I knew he couldn't take it. I watched him practically run to his car, get in and drive away."

"Bet he won't be back."

"Let's hope so."

They attached the new chains to the swing and got it hung, and then Finn went to find his brothers while Travis picked up the tools.

Just as he was closing the toolbox, Liz drove up. She got out of her car and waved to him. Her jeans hugged her curves, and her green top crisscrossed in front and tied in the back. He had the inappropriate urge to pull the tie and unwrap her like a gift.

Oblivious to his thoughts, she came up onto the porch, smiling her brightest. "You got this done so fast. Thanks."

"No problem. Finn helped. Give it a try." He motioned toward the white wooden swing.

She settled onto it and gave it a gentle push with her feet. "It's perfect. Since you're so good with your hands, want to help me with something else?"

Heat pulsed through him as several options flashed in his mind, and he had the impulse to prove to her just what he was capable of doing with his hands. And mouth.

He rubbed his eyes, giving himself a moment to rein in his unruly thoughts. "What do you need done?"

"Will you have time to help us with a few more things around the house before the inspections? I want everything to be perfect with no chance of not passing."

"Besides the dining room light, what's on the list?"

"There's a drip in the upstairs bathroom sink and the screen door needs repair." She pointed to the screen with the toe of her pink sandal. "We can't leave the door open to get fresh air in the house because bugs can get in through the rip."

"I can work that into my schedule. But I might need some fuel. When are you making another pie?"

"I'll make one now. Come back after you're done with your work. Which one of my pies do you want? Cherry?"

Another flash of heat washed over him. "I'll take whatever you offer, songbird."

After her big opera audition, he would have a better feel for her future plans. Would she stay in Channing or travel from place to place?

Over the next week, Lizzy took required classes for fostering, filled out tons of paperwork and visited the baby as much as possible. He was gaining weight and growing strong enough to come home very soon. Although Sage would officially be the foster parent for now, Lizzy wanted to be able to take over as soon as possible, but she was not giving up on her singing.

As often as possible, she walked to the far corner of the ranch to sing. She kept going back to the spot that backed up to the nature preserve. It's the place she had gone after being so furious with her father. The place she had once again found the power and strength of her voice, and her confidence was returning. She could let loose and not worry about critiques.

She was still letting her father's calls go to voice mail but had sent a few texts messages asking him to give her some space. He was less than happy about her response.

When it came to Travis, they were both doing a sort of back-and-forth dance around each other. They were pleasant and friendly, but out of unsaid mutual agreement, keeping a safe distance. She wasn't sure how much longer she could do it.

Lizzy finished a singing session and found Sage in the office. Her aunt had a folder of papers clutched in her hand and was frowning at the computer screen.

"What's wrong?"

Sage put down the folder and rubbed her eyes. "I hate doing the bookkeeping. I always put it off and then have a ton of it to do all at once."

"I can help you with it," Lizzy said. "It's what I've been doing for years in Chicago at Dalton Realty." She wouldn't mention that she didn't like it either.

"If you are serious, that would be amazing."

"Of course."

Her aunt blew out a puff of air to move a curl that had fallen across her face. "Bless you, sweet Lizzy. If you're serious, I'll put you on the payroll."

"Really? That would be fantastic." This would solve one of the problems she'd been worried about, and she wouldn't have to work at Zimmerman's.

"Believe me, I'm just as happy about it as you." Sage slumped back into her chair with a smile.

"Show me what system you're using and whatever I need to know, and I'll get started." She grabbed an old cane-back chair from a corner and put it behind the desk beside her aunt. Sage took a few minutes to show her what she needed to know.

Lizzy picked up an invoice and her mouth dropped open. "Wow. That's a lot of money. What did this person buy from you? Several horses?"

Sage leaned over to look at the piece of paper. "Oh, that's Titan's stud fee."

"Holy moly. I had no idea people paid that much for Titan's…services."

Sage chuckled. "How do you think we were able to build the new stables?"

"Clearly you two know what you're doing. I kind of wish I could see my father's face when he finds out what a success you've made of the ranch that he was so sure you would lose."

"Me, too."

Daisy stuck her head into the office. "The lasagna is about to come out of the oven. Are you two ready to eat?"

"I am." Sage stood and stretched. "Lizzy, this doesn't have to be done right now. It can wait until tomorrow."

The three of them went into the kitchen and filled their plates with lasagna, salad and garlic bread. The savory scent of tomato sauce and garlic made her mouth water.

"Tell me more about how the two of you built this ranch up into the success it has become."

Sage poured a generous helping of vinaigrette dressing over her salad. "Once the ranch was safely one hundred percent ours, we started out by boarding horses, giving riding lessons and trail rides."

"And we ate a lot of Top Ramen noodles and saltine crackers," Daisy said. "But it was ours."

Ice clinked against one of Gamma's rainbow-striped glasses as Daisy swirled her lemonade. "We bought a mare who turned out to be pregnant, and the sire was a very sought-after stud. The man who sold us the pregnant horse was a friend of Mama and Daddy's."

"He knew we were struggling to get the ranch going," Sage said, picking up the story where her sister left off. "He said we could have the colt because it was his fault for selling her to us without realizing she was pregnant."

"I think he actually knew and just really wanted to help us."

Lizzy swallowed a tangy bite of lasagna and put down her fork. "He wasn't afraid of the competition?"

"He was an older man and was planning to retire soon and wanted to help us out."

"The baby foal was a boy?" she asked her aunts.

"Yes." Daisy said. "He started winning shows and awards and that led to him becoming an in-demand stud. We continued to build our bloodline from there. After sacrificing for a while, things started to go our way."

"I would say so," Lizzy said. "You two are my inspiration. I might have waited longer than I should have to explore what makes *me* happy, but it's not too late to find it."

"Absolutely. It's never too late," Sage said. "You have to go for what you want. We never thought we'd have a ranch with so many great studs."

"There are several studly humans around here, too," Lizzy said and grinned at Daisy.

Sage did the same.

"Why are you two grinning at me like a pair of preteens?" Daisy asked.

She chuckled at her aunt's attempt to be nonchalant. "I just wanted to see if you would admit to having a crush on the oldest hottie brother."

"That's ridiculous. I'm too old for crushes. Besides…" Daisy swept a hand along her body as if she were exhibit A. "Finn Murphy is not looking for an older woman who has hay in her hair more often than wearing a sexy dress or a pair of high heels."

"Now who is being silly and denying a crush," her sister said. "Just the other day I was the silly one for not going after the younger firefighter."

Daisy pointed her fork at her sister. "Isn't he the one who's coming to do the yearly fire inspection before we bring the baby home?"

"Yes." Sage stuffed a bite of salad into her mouth to try and hide her smile.

This family mealtime was exactly what Lizzy had been craving for so many years. "It would appear all three of us have crushes that we think can't or shouldn't lead to anything. Only difference is my crush is older than me."

There was a brief knock on the kitchen door, and then Travis walked in. "Evening, ladies."

Lizzy sucked in a quick breath and then coughed because of the lemonade she'd almost inhaled. Had he heard what she'd just said about studs and crushes? The way her aunts were smiling, she knew they were thinking the same thing.

"Grab a plate and eat with us," Daisy said.

"Thanks." He hung his cowboy hat on a hook by the back door and ran his hands through his thick dark hair before going to the sink to wash his hands. "I thought I'd work on the screen door this evening."

"That would be a huge help," Lizzy said. "Thank you."

"That wouldn't make us fail a fire or health inspection," Sage said.

"I know. I just want to make a good impression since I'm hoping they will fast-track my application to become the foster parent."

"I'm happy to do it." He grabbed a plate from the cabinet, filled it and sat in the empty chair beside her.

With him so close that she swore she could feel the heat of his body, she was going to have a hard time focusing on anything for the rest of the meal.

Travis hadn't expected Lizzy to come out onto the front porch while he repaired the screen, but here she was, tempting him with her scent. Something soft and floral that made him want to lean in close and inhale against her delicate collarbone.

"I've always loved this porch swing," Lizzy said. "Thanks again for fixing it."

"I had help."

"You're just being modest. You can fix so many different things."

Except his money troubles and the fact that the Martin Ranch would likely sell to someone who wouldn't appreciate it like him. He couldn't bear to think of what might happen if a real estate developer bought it. There had been a lot of them sniffing around the area.

"I wonder if the baby will like being on the swing with me?" Lizzy said.

"I'm sure he will."

This domestic scene was messing with his head. She was entertaining—if not a bit distracting. Okay, a lot distracting. Despite the struggle to keep his hands to himself, he liked her company.

"Isn't it a lovely night?" Her voice was whispery and seductive.

As she swung back and forth, a shimmery beam of moonlight moved over her face and hair, and a wave of something just as shimmery moved over his heart. "Yes, beautiful." Her big audition couldn't come soon enough. He needed answers.

Am I putting too much pressure on myself to stay away from her? She's never asked me to stay away.

Plenty of people were able to have casual relationships, knowing there was a time limit, right? Friends was all they *should* be, for both of their sakes, but could they figure out a way to have a little more?

"What are your plans once summer is over and the baby is with his aunt or his father?" Travis asked, trying to distract himself from the sight of Liz's long, tanned legs revealed by her denim shorts.

She pushed her bare feet against the smooth gray boards of the porch and then let the swing carry her back and forth. "First, I have to wait and see how I do at my audition. Wait and see if I can make my dream a reality like my aunts have."

Her dream.

A cold wave slapped against his chest. He couldn't get in the way of her dreams. This beautiful, sweet, talented woman wasn't meant for him. The screwdriver slipped, and he banged his knuckles on the doorframe. "Son of a..." He hissed and shook his hand.

"Are you okay?" She hopped off mid-swing like a kid at the playground.

"I'm fine." Travis dropped the screwdriver into the toolbox, the sharp clang of metal on metal matching his mood.

He was thoroughly annoyed with himself for entertaining the idea of any kind of romance. His reactions to her were simply physical. Biological responses to her feminine beauty.

Liar, liar, pants on fire.

It wasn't just her beauty. There was so much about her that he admired. He stood and grabbed the roll of new screen material, and she settled back on the swing.

Why did so many of the women he loved feel the need to roam?

Love?!

He flinched and tried to breathe against what felt like a metal band around his ribs. Where had that thought come from? He did not love Liz. He couldn't.

Elizabeth Dalton was a wannabe wanderer.

Just like too many other women in his life.

Chapter Fifteen

Lizzy couldn't sleep, so she finally moved the cat off her legs and got up extra early. She was too anxious about today's health and fire inspections. Everyone told her she was worrying too much, but it all had to go perfectly so she could get the baby home from the hospital.

The coffee was made, and it was a beautiful morning to sit on the porch, but she needed something to do with her hands. They said the smell of something baking was a good thing when you were trying to sell a house, so surely it would be a good thing in this case, too. She started on a batch of homemade cinnamon rolls.

She was proud of all she had accomplished to prepare for the baby to come live with them. Thanks to help from her aunts and Trav, the nursery was ready, and she had spent too much money, but everything had been so cute she hadn't been able to resist. By the end of today the inspections would be done and they could bring the baby home—officially under Sage's care.

While the cinnamon rolls were rising, she made a batch of cookies. She would have treats to offer to anyone who might want them. Totally not a bribe of any kind.

But the oven temperature had been set too high, and when she opened the oven door, smoke billowed out.

"Son of a bat!"

Burning cookies while waiting for the fire inspector was the very worst thing that could happen. She pulled out the tray of black cookies and dropped it into the sink. "Sage," she called out to her aunt right before the smoke alarm started blaring.

Sage came running into the kitchen and grabbed one of the new fire extinguishers from its hook on the wall. "Are there flames?"

"No," Lizzy yelled over the alarm and grabbed a broom to push the button on the alarm and make it stop screeching. "Open the door."

Her aunt flung open the door and grabbed a magazine to fan out the smoke. She was looking back at Lizzy when someone coughed.

The fire marshal was standing right in front of Sage.

Lizzy gasped as her heart plummeted. He'd heard the alarm and gotten a face full of smoke and now they were going to fail their inspection. And to make it even worse, Travis was standing behind him.

"Looks like I got here just in time," said the fire marshal with a smile hovering around his mouth. "At least we know the kitchen smoke detector works."

Lizzy covered her face and just wanted to crawl under the table and cry.

Sage motioned for the men to come inside. "It's just a tray of slightly overbaked cookies. Come with me, and we can start the inspection with the upstairs smoke detectors."

Travis came straight over to Lizzy and put a hand on her shoulder. "Are you okay? Are you burned?"

"No. I'm fine. But…" Her voice broke. "What if I ruined everything?"

"You didn't. You just gave him a funny story to tell." Travis pulled her into a hug.

After a moment of remaining rigid, she relaxed into his embrace. He wasn't doing this because an ex-boyfriend was watching. He wasn't pulling away just as quickly as he'd touched her, like he'd done before. This was a real hug, and she let herself enjoy it.

His big warm hands moved lazily over her back. He smelled of soap and leather, and most surprising, he was softly humming. Mr. No Music Man was soothing her with a song.

They were still standing together in the middle of the kitchen swaying to the beats of their hearts when Sage and the fire marshal returned. They stepped apart and she cut her gaze to the firefighter who could make or break their status as a foster home. It had to be a good sign that he was smiling wide enough to show dimples.

To everyone's great relief, they passed the inspection, and Sage walked him out to his truck. She expected Trav to make a fast getaway from her emotional freak-out, but he stayed. He even scrubbed the cookie tray while she sat at the table with a cup of hot herbal tea.

"Maybe baking this morning wasn't the best idea. I didn't even get the cinnamon rolls put in the oven." She pointed to a large tray on the counter covered with a cloth.

"You made homemade cinnamon rolls?" he asked, his eyes giving away his excitement.

"Yes, but now I'm scared to put them into the oven."

"I'll do it. What temperature do I set the oven on?"

His eagerness made her smile. She told him and he

started the oven preheating. "You don't have to stay and babysit me. I'm sure I'm keeping you from something important."

"It won't hurt the brothers to work without me for a little while. I've been working since sunrise and could use a coffee break." He poured himself a cup and added one spoonful of sugar.

"Can I ask you a question?"

He chuckled. "You've never had a problem with it before. Go for it."

"Do you happen to know why my aunts and my father completely ended their relationship after Gamma died? He never would tell me."

"No, I don't. Your aunts won't tell you either?"

"I haven't asked."

He sat down across from her. "Why not?"

"Talking about my father gets all of us worked up, and everything has been so good since I've been here that I guess I don't want to rock the boat. And I'm a little worried about what I'll find out."

"I think you should just ask them. It's probably not near as bad as you suspect." His phone buzzed, and he pulled it out of his pocket to read a text message. "The brothers need to show me something."

"If you get a chance, come back in a while for a cinnamon roll."

"Try and stop me. The timer is set for them to come out of the oven." He took another gulp of coffee and then went out the door.

She smiled to herself. The morning had started with an unfortunate rough patch, but because they passed the inspection, it had all been worth the tender moment in Trav's arms. She was so touched that Travis had stayed to make sure she was okay, and she felt much better. In fact, so much better that she decided to mix up icing for the rolls, and then go through Gamma's recipes for something yummy to make for dinner.

Lizzy was trying to decide between two casseroles when Travis came back into the kitchen, and the oven timer went off a second later.

"You have good timing. Could you take the cinnamon rolls out of the oven, please?"

"Sure." He grabbed the potholders, one shaped like a chicken and the other a big red flower, and took the tray of cinnamon rolls out of the oven. "These smell really good. Look good, too." He put them on the stovetop and leaned in to inhale the steam rising from the hot rolls.

"Thanks. If you'll help me ice them, you can have one. But no taste testing until the job is done."

He went to the sink to wash his hands and then took the knife she held out. The fluffy white frosting melted into the spiraled grooves of the plump cinnamon rolls.

He had a dollop of icing on his cheek, and of course she didn't just tell him like most people would or simply wipe it off with a towel. Without considering the consequences, she reached out, swiped it from his cheek and then licked her finger. "Mmm. Delicious."

His lips parted enough for her to see the tip of his tongue slide across the edge of his top front teeth.

She shivered and gripped the edge of the counter to keep from reaching for him. It's a good thing the fire marshal had gone because the sexual tension was burning her up from the inside. She was glad she hadn't just handed him a dish towel. His incredibly sexy expression was worth any embarrassment.

"Not fair." His voice was a deep rumble between them. "You said no tasting until the job was done."

The heat in his eyes made goose bumps pop up on her

skin, and she forgot all the reasons to be good and not start something she might not be able to finish. His unusually playful manner eased her smoke-detector-induced anxiety, but a different kind of tension was gathering low in her body, more delicious than the baked goods.

She grinned mischievously, and before she lost her nerve, she dipped her finger into the fluffy white icing and held out her offering.

"Want to even the score?"

Chapter Sixteen

Travis's veins swelled with a rush of hot blood as he stared at Lizzy's icing-covered finger.

He might currently be staying away from love and serious relationships, but that didn't mean he wasn't damn good at seduction. Resisting her had become the other side of impossible, and like the kiss by the fountain, this opportunity was too tempting to pass up.

Without taking his gaze from hers, he gently held her wrist and slowly sucked the icing from her finger, giving an extra swirl of his tongue around her fingertip.

Her eyes flashed with desire, or maybe it was just the overhead lights playing in her baby blues, but he had not imagined her kittenish sound of pleasure. When he let go of her hand, she swayed forward as if she'd been thrown off-balance.

Instead of saying something clever, she grabbed one of the warm cinnamon rolls and took a big bite. If she was feeling anything like him, she was turned on. He was ready to pick her up and carry her to the closest bed or other flat surface. A wall might even do.

Since that was an epically bad idea, he grabbed his own gooey cinnamon roll, letting the sweet treat melt on his tongue. As tasty as it was, it wasn't as good as the dollop he'd licked from her delicate finger.

Their flirtation was begging for trouble of one kind or another. Probably the kind that would have him kicking himself for going against his better judgment, because right now he was considering tossing good sense into the air to see where they would land—which was hopefully in a bedroom at some point in the near future.

Just when he was about to kiss the sweetness from her lips, Sage opened the kitchen door.

Liz straightened, stepping away from him. "Is he gone?"

"Yes, and you and Daisy will be happy to know that I'm having dinner with him on Friday night."

"That's great." She fumbled with the icing as if needing something to do with her hands.

"I have two pieces of good news," Sage said. "First, the health inspector called and wants to move up the inspection. He will be here in about thirty minutes."

"It will be a relief to have it done," Lizzy said and took another bite of her cinnamon roll.

"The second bit of news is even better. I talked to the case worker, and she said we can go pick up the baby today."

Liz clapped her hands like a little girl who'd been told they were going to Disneyland. "Really? That's excellent."

The pure joy on her face made him snap back to the reality of their situation. Had he almost wrecked everything? "I'll get out of your way. I really need to get back to work."

"Will you see the hot—" Lizzy cut off her words and cleared her throat. "If you will see the Murphy brothers, grab a plastic container and take cinnamon rolls to them."

What had she been about to say? Whatever it was, it had made Sage fight a laugh. He put four rolls in a container, because they didn't have to know he'd already had one, plus the frosting he'd sucked off her finger. A pleasant burn started in his belly.

"Trav, come back tonight so you can meet the baby."

"Will do." He went out the door and took a deep breath as he headed for the stable. He had a horse to train and countless other work on his to-do list. Thinking about kissing Liz was not what should be on his mind. But tell that to his brain.

That evening after Travis had taken a shower, he headed up to the farmhouse. He both looked forward to and dreaded going. He wanted to see Liz. He wanted to eat more of her baking. But it was the thought of seeing her with a baby that gave him pause.

His only personal experience with babies was when he'd been a child himself, and it had brought much heartache. More than his mother had been able to take.

As usual, he went in through the kitchen door and immediately heard a baby crying. No one was downstairs, so he followed the sound to the second floor, but the crying stopped before he made it into the bedroom they'd converted into a nursery.

"Looks like you have the knack for getting him to stop crying," he said.

She turned to him with a smile and a very tiny, swaddled baby against her shoulder. "Hey, Trav."

It made something jump in his chest when she called him Trav.

"Come meet this little angel. I need to get the bottle I left on the kitchen counter. Please hold him."

She moved forward and held the baby so close to his chest that in a natural reaction he raised his arms and took him, the protest lodging in his throat. She was gone from the room before he found his voice. The baby made a cooing sound, and Travis took a deep breath before looking down.

And the breath stalled painfully in his lungs. His adult brain wasn't sure how to process the sudden wave of confusing childhood memories. Memories that came at him hard and fast. So fast it was dizzying, and he sat in the rocking chair beside him. He hadn't been prepared to see a baby who was so much like the one he'd loved.

Why hadn't Liz told him the baby had Down syndrome? The breath he'd been holding rapidly expelled in one quick exhalation. "Davy."

Big brown eyes stared up at him, bringing a full spectrum of emotions. Love. Joy. Loss. Bone-deep pain. A child's happiness crushed by one of life's harshest lessons.

This was not the first time he'd held a baby with Down syndrome, and the experience was accessing a part of his life he'd had tucked away in a corner of his mind and hadn't visited in many years. This tiny baby boy was a reminder of a very heartbreaking time.

The baby yawned and then puckered his mouth until it looked like a cherry lifesaver.

"Hey there, tiny dude." His voice sounded gravelly with too much emotion. He unfolded the blanket. Liz had dressed him in a preemie size blue-and-white sailor suit made of super soft cotton. His tiny feet had a larger than average space between the big toes and the rest, just like his brother.

Fear gripped him. What if Down syndrome had made his heart weak like... "Davy," he whispered.

"Why did you call him Davy?" Liz asked.

His head snapped up. He hadn't heard her come in and hesitated, not sure how much he wanted to tell her, but she'd proven to be a good listener. "He reminds me of my brother, Davy."

"You have a brother?"

He stood and motioned for her to sit and then handed the baby over to her. Holding him was too emotional. "I did have a brother for three months."

"Oh, Trav. I'm so sorry. How old were you?"

"Nine."

She put the bottle to the baby's lips, and he started sucking. "What is it about him that reminds you of your brother?"

"The Down syndrome. Is this baby healthy? His heart?"

"Yes. They did extensive testing. His heart is strong and perfectly formed."

"That's good. I was so young I don't know the details, but something was wrong with my baby brother's heart."

"I'm sorry you had to go through something like that so young."

He crossed the room to look out the window and to hide his rapid blinking. There was no call for an unacceptable display of emotion. "It was rough, but they say stuff like that builds character."

For a couple of minutes, the only sound was the baby drinking his bottle. Travis studied the night sky, wishing it could give him the guidance he wanted. If only he could talk to his grandpas. They'd always had the wisdom he needed.

Should I risk my heart and take a chance on love?

A shooting star streaked across the sky, and Travis took it as a sign. He turned from the window and went to Liz. With one finger, he stroked the back of the baby's hand, and then leaned down and pressed his lips to her forehead.

She put down the bottle to cup his cheek. "Trav," she whispered then tipped up her face and softly brushed her lips against his.

"Sweet dreams, songbird." He left the nursery, wondering what tomorrow would bring.

Chapter Seventeen

Still euphoric from Trav's tenderness, Lizzy hummed a song from the opera *Carmen* and rocked slowly as the baby drifted to sleep in her arms. Davy was a good name, and it suited her little angel boy. She'd been told that sometimes the foster care system named an orphaned baby, but even if it couldn't be official, it wouldn't hurt anything if they called him Davy.

The horse-shaped nightlight cast a soft, warm glow over the polished oak floor and the fluffy blue throw rug. The baby was a soothing weight in her arms, and she had a feeling this was going to be her favorite part of their bedtime routine.

Holding him like this was a safe way to give and receive affection. He was someone she could safely cuddle. He wouldn't pat her on the head and then turn away. Today's epiphany? Holding Davy made her realize that she had an unhealthy anxiety about physical contact. She always anticipated the moment the other person would pull away to do something more important than she was or avoid contact all together.

Easing up from the rocking chair, Lizzy put her clean, fed and swaddled infant on his blue-striped sheets. Trav's reaction to him had been unexpected and heartbreaking. He'd lost so much of his family, and the more she learned about him and his past, the more she understood his stoic personality.

"You really do look like a Davy," she whispered to the sleeping infant. "I hope Trav will find it an honor and not too painful if we start calling you by his baby brother's name. Sweet dreams, angel boy."

Tiptoeing from the room, she left the door open and went downstairs to see what the twins were doing. They were in the living room watching an old movie, but Daisy turned down the volume when she came in and joined them on the couch.

"Did you know Travis had a baby brother with Down syndrome who died as an infant?"

"I remember there was a baby," Sage said. "But I had no idea about the Down syndrome. We were still kids ourselves."

"Is that why he rushed out of the house so fast earlier?" Daisy asked.

"Probably. I guess I hadn't mentioned the Down syndrome, and he was surprised. I think it brought up painful memories." Lizzy tipped her head back on the couch and stretched out her legs. It had been a long, emotional day.

The baby had been with them for five days, and they'd quickly developed a routine. When she held Davy and sang to him there was no more denying she loved him. Lizzy had never fallen in love with another human so quickly.

She'd kept busy with online classes and other foster care requirements in between taking care of Davy, and the days had flown by, but she barely saw Travis. She missed his deep voice and the way he made her laugh in between rolling her eyes.

It wasn't because he was too busy. It was because Trav was making excuses to stay away. Was it because they were calling the baby by his brother's name? He'd been the first one to call him Davy, but maybe she should've talked to him about it first.

She just hoped his avoidance didn't last long. Trav had just started to smile and talk and be close to her without acting like he'd touched a live wire, and she didn't want to lose their momentum.

One evening, Lizzy was folding laundry in her bedroom when she heard Trav's voice in the nursery. She was curious about his and Davy's interaction and didn't want to interrupt, so she peeked around the doorframe into the baby's room.

Travis lifted him until they were face-to-face. His hands were so big he could easily hold Davy up with his thumbs hooked under the baby's tiny arms and his long fingers supporting the back of his head.

The sudden urge to cry surprised her. Watching the two of them together was tapping into a place inside of her that she'd thought could wait for years until after she'd traveled and sung in the opera. Then she could have a family of her own.

Was seeing the world more important than starting a family? She was starting to question her plans. Maybe her desire to see the world was only because it was something that had been denied her.

Davy kicked his skinny little legs, one striped sock dangling and about to slip off his foot.

"Let's have a chat, tiny dude." Travis's voice made the baby start kicking again.

Lizzy couldn't wait to hear what he had to say to Davy. Maybe she'd gain some more insight into the cowboy who visited her dreams each night.

Travis stared into the baby's curious brown eyes, so much like the ones he'd looked into many years ago. He was honored that Liz had chosen to call him Davy, but it also stirred up a lot of emotions. Last night he'd pulled out the few photos he had of his baby brother. The one of his nine-year-old self holding Davy was his favorite, and he'd tucked it into the frame of his bedroom mirror. Davy Taylor deserved to be remembered.

The infant in his arms drew up his legs like a little frog and stuck out his pink tongue.

"Our Princess Songbird said you're healthy, so I'm going to need you to stay that way. You need to eat and grow and play and not get sick." He kissed Davy's forehead and then settled him in the crook of his arm.

Lizzy had said the medical tests showed his heart was fine, and he didn't need any surgeries, but things could change. He knew that all too well. It's why he'd been keeping a distance from Liz and Davy. Getting too attached wouldn't be good for any of them. It was an impossible situation because this child would soon be leaving to be with his real family.

Davy arched his back, screwed up his face and grunted. Other bodily sounds quickly followed, and Travis got the picture real quick. He once again held him out farther away from himself.

"Did you really just do that? I thought we were going to be buddies, you little stinker."

A noise from behind made him turn his head. Lizzy was standing in the doorway with a big grin on her face. "Got yourself a little problem, cowboy?"

"Oh, no. Not me. I'm not the one who signed up for this kind of natural disaster." He held the baby out to her. "Clearly, Davy wants me to go and you to stay."

She moved their way, but rather than taking the baby who was in desperate need of a diaper change, she folded her arms over her chest. "If I can dig a hole in the mud and muck out stinky horse stalls, surely you can change one tiny little diaper."

"I am not changing his diaper." Travis grimaced. "Judging from the odor wafting up into my face, I have a feeling it's going to be way worse than the horse stalls."

Lizzy laughed and thankfully took the baby from him. "You're such a wimp."

"Gotta go." He rushed from the room.

"Chicken," she called after him.

He ignored the jab and made his way down the stairs to a nontoxic airspace. He hadn't meant for Lizzy to catch him looking in on the baby. But he'd been upstairs putting things into the attic for Sage and heard the baby babbling to himself in his crib. He'd only meant to make sure he was okay and then head back downstairs for another load of boxes, but then he hadn't been able to resist picking him up.

Had she heard what he'd said to Davy?

Travis was more sensitive than anyone alive knew, and he planned to keep it that way. When he revealed too much, he often ended up hurt in one way or another. Great-grandpa Roy had told him sensitivity was an asset, but Travis didn't see it that way. It made him feel weak. Too fragile.

Liz was a new weakness. Someone he wanted in a way that scared him.

Lizzy's phone rang and because she was expecting a call from their foster care case worker, Betty, she grabbed it from the coffee table and answered without looking at the number on the caller ID.

"Hello."

"Elizabeth, it's your father."

She cringed. "Hi. How are you?" she said with fake cheerfulness that she hoped he couldn't pick up on. She caught her aunts' attention and mouthed, "It's my father."

They both grimaced.

"I've given you more than enough of an extended vacation. Enough time playing around on the ranch," he said in his most authoritative voice. The one that had always made her stiffen and get quiet. "It's time to come home and get back on track at work."

Meaning there was no one there to jump at his every command and schedule and plan and organize his life and business. She was at a loss for words. Had she not made it crystal clear when she stood in his office and yelled at him for the first time in her life? How could she tell him she was not coming back to Chicago for more than a visit or to get the rest of her belongings from his garage? She had been putting off talking to him and wasn't prepared.

"I'm not on an extended vacation. If you'll remember our conversation in your office, I resigned my position."

Her aunts had both drawn closer, and she switched the phone to speaker so they could hear both sides of the conversation.

His sigh was long and drawn out, as if she was still a child who needed scolding before being sent to her room to think about things.

Sage rolled her eyes, and Daisy opened her mouth but then pressed her knuckles against her lips as if reminding herself to stay quiet.

Lizzy could picture her father sitting in his big fancy office with a skyline view and a desk covered with a mess of papers because she wasn't there to keep him organized. "I—"

"I have let the part about you gallivanting around with some cowboy go because I know you will come to your senses, but I assumed you would have done it by now and realize where you belong."

An unpleasant cold shiver worked across her body. Her recently acquired gumption was waning, but with a hand squeeze from Daisy, she found her voice. "I don't belong in Chicago any longer."

"Elizabeth, be reasonable. I sent you to the best school. You have a business degree to manage the family business. Not to sing for other people's pleasure."

"What about *my* pleasure?"

"You can sing in the shower. There are more important things."

"Joshua, you are still a big ass," Daisy said.

"Excuse me?" he said in surprise. "Which sister is this?"

"Both of us," the twins said in synchronized harmony.

"I'm having a private conversation with my daughter."

Sage leaned closer to the phone. "Joshua, stop being a big bully. We're here to support our niece's dreams. The niece who was kept from us for way too long. She is old enough and smart enough to know what's best for her own life and happiness."

"As you so helpfully pointed out, you haven't seen her in years," Joshua said. "I am the one who knows what is best for her. I knew the Chicago Opera wasn't the right place. Even the chairman of the opera board agreed that her place is at the family company."

Lizzy gasped and felt instantly sick to her stomach. "It's true. You really did do it, didn't you? You told the Chicago Opera not to pick me."

There was a long moment of silence on the other end

of the phone line, and then he said words he rarely did. "I'm sorry about that. I was only trying to do what's best for you."

She was so angry her whole body was trembling. "You should hire my replacement."

"Elizabeth, take me off speakerphone."

"Sure thing. Goodbye," she said, and then ended the call.

All three of them just stared at one another for a few seconds.

"I'm getting a bottle of wine," Sage said. "We're going to need it for this conversation."

"Agreed." Lizzy flopped onto the couch, covered her face with a pillow and screamed. She couldn't believe he'd sabotaged her audition. Well, she could, but she didn't want to believe it. This is what the woman at the opera had been hinting at when she said to audition with a different opera.

Daisy settled into her powder blue chair and kicked off her flip-flops.

Sage breezed back into the room and put a bottle and three glasses on the coffee table, sat in her pink chair and started pouring. "I'm so sorry he did this to you, sweetie."

Daisy growled and mumbled under her breath before reaching for a glass.

Lizzy told them all about the audition in Chicago and how the woman had followed her out and talked to her about not giving up and auditioning somewhere else. Her aunts helped her realize that that was in the past and she had lots of opportunities in front of her.

"Will you tell me what happened to end your relationship with my father? I was too young at the time to understand all that was going on."

Sage stretched out her legs and flexed her toes, nails painted a shimmery lavender. "All three of us inherited the ranch equally, each owning a third. Joshua wasn't interested in having anything to do with animals or doing any ranch work and wanted to sell it."

"He wanted it to kick-start his real estate career," Daisy said. "He wanted to sell the whole ranch to a company that planned to build a fertilizer factory and huge warehouse."

Lizzy gasped. "I can't imagine this ranch being destroyed that way."

"Neither could we. Joshua said if we bought out his third, he'd drop his idea of selling the whole place. Someone he knew appraised the ranch at way higher than it was worth, but we didn't find out that little nugget of information until later," Sage said.

"By the time we found out, the old guy had died of a stroke after he lost his license for another infraction. And there was no use reporting it for his widow to be ashamed of."

Lizzy shook her head with disbelief. "I knew this story would be something bad, but wow."

"We were young and dumb and didn't realize how much he was manipulating us—although we should have. Plus, he had his buddies in on his plan. I'm sure they were promised something."

Daisy's nose wrinkled with her throaty growl. "And it sounds like he's gotten worse since then. He turned out nothing like Mama or Daddy."

"What happened next?" Something about knowing she wasn't the only one he did this type of thing to was oddly comforting.

"Joshua didn't think there was any way we could get our hands on the large sum of money by the date he'd given us."

"But you did get the money?"

"We did." Their musical voices were in sync and so was their body language. Both sitting forward with their elbows propped on their knees, they were showing her they were focused on her, and that she was important.

Lizzy imitated their posture. "How? Where?"

A look passed between the sisters. The kind of brief glance that happened so quickly most people would miss it, but Lizzy had grown up observing their twin link.

"We sold things," Daisy said.

"And rented out space," Sage quickly added.

Their answers were kind of cryptic, like they were code for something super-secret. And it probably was. She was a little jealous of their bond because she'd always wanted a sister. But as she looked at them, she realized she did have sisters.

"Joshua was so furious because he would have gotten a lot more money if we'd sold the whole place to the fertilizer company. Thankfully, we had a signed document, and even with a few buddies in high places, he wasn't able to get out of the agreement."

"But we had no idea he would completely take you out of our lives," Daisy said and moved to the sofa to put an arm around Lizzy's shoulders. "We begged him not to take you across the country, but he never was one to listen to either of us. Always thought he was smarter and knew better."

She leaned against Daisy. "He still does. He's the reason I haven't been here until now. And I'm ashamed of that."

Sage waved a hand to dismiss that way of thinking. "Don't be. I know how the fear of upsetting him can be. Knowing you'll have to deal with the guilt he'll surely lay on."

"Then we need to do something about that," Daisy suggested. "Let's make a pact to not let him have any more control over our lives ever again."

Just the mention of doing that made Lizzy feel a little stronger. "That's a great idea."

The three of them stacked their hands on top of one another to seal their pact.

"To making our own decisions." Her gumption was returning, and now she had an overwhelming urge to see Travis.

After drinking more than her fair share of the wine, Lizzy was tipsy. The twins assured her they'd look after Davy, so Lizzy walked toward the stable. The sun had set long ago and the overhead lights illuminated the round pen where Travis was longeing one of the horses. She propped her arms on the top railing.

His dark good looks and muscles bunching and flexing as he worked with the black horse was exactly the distraction she needed from her thoughts.

"Do you need me?" he asked.

That was a loaded question, and she couldn't hold back a grin. "No rush. Finish what you're doing."

"I'm just cooling Zeus down."

"Why are you working so late?"

"I needed something to occupy my hands and mind." He slowed the horse and brought him to a stop.

She could think of a few fabulous—but dangerous—ideas to occupy both of them. Heat swept through to land in her very center.

"We're done. I just need to get the horse tucked in for the night." He flashed a grin that used both sides of his mouth.

"You're so good to them. You're going to make a great dad someday."

His steps faltered, but he didn't respond.

She followed him into the stable.

"So, what's up? What brings you out here this time of night?" he asked.

"Remember when you asked me why I want to be an opera singer?"

"Yes. You said because you love it."

"True, but I've come up with a second reason why I have been so determined to sing professionally."

"Oh yeah?" He brought the horse to a stop and gave her his full attention.

"To be rebellious."

The threat of another grin trembled around his mouth, but he wiped it away with the back of his hand. "Since when is opera considered rebellious?"

"It's not. My wanting to do it is." She brushed her fingers through the horse's mane.

"You're such a little rebel, Princess Songbird."

"The rebellion is directed toward my father because he discouraged my singing after college. He said it's like being a cheerleader or on a dance team. It's something you give up after high school and college, and then you get serious about a career that has more of a chance for success in the real world. I just didn't realize until now that my resentment toward him is part of the reason I've been so determined."

He opened the stall beside them. "He really discouraged something you love?"

"Yes. Without even feeling bad about it."

Travis stroked her cheek with the back of his fingers as if they were lovers. "I'll never discourage something that you love, princess."

Every cell in her body sighed with pleasure, and she wanted to wrap her arms around him, but before she could, he led the horse into his stall.

"It will take me a few more minutes here. Why don't you go sit on the porch swing and I'll meet you there?"

"Sounds good. See you in a few." She could use a minute alone to think about all that had happened and where to go from here. Learning all this about her father was oddly freeing, like it was now even more okay that she had yelled at him in his office, quit her job and walked away from her life in Chicago. If she had stayed there, she never would've been as happy as she was now.

The front porch swing had a great view of tonight's silvery half-moon, dusted with a veil of wispy clouds. This was better than expensive therapy. The comforting night sounds of her childhood. The scent of night-blooming jasmine in a terracotta pot beside the swing. The peacefulness.

Travis came up the front steps, and even in a plain black T-shirt, worn jeans and boots, he made her inner voice sing in operatic fashion. The swing creaked with his weight and their thighs were only inches apart. She put her head on his shoulder, but remained slightly rigid, ready to sit up straight if he didn't respond in five…four…

Trav's arm slid around her shoulders, pulling her in snug against him. "Are you having a glass-half-empty kind of day?"

"I almost did but thanks to Sage and Daisy…and you, it's filling up." Lizzy startled when her phone rang from her back pocket.

"Oh, no. Please don't let it be my father again." She pulled it out and frowned. "It's Betty. I wonder why she's calling so late."

Had Davy's aunt come home early? Her stomach clenched. Had they found his biological father and he was on his way to take Davy from her? She wanted to cry at the thought of anyone taking him so soon. She needed more time with her angel boy.

"Hello, Betty."

Chapter Eighteen

Liz's rapidly changing expressions put Travis on alert. The joy he'd seen on his way up onto the porch had changed to worry before answering the call, and as she listened, her expressions spanned a wide range of emotions. She paced up and down the porch, and in between listening she said, "Oh no" and "Okay" and "Yes" and then hung up.

"What did she say?" Sage asked from the open front door.

"Davy's aunt..." She pressed her top teeth into her lower lip.

"Did something happen to her?"

Liz shook her head but didn't speak. She went into the house, and they followed her upstairs to the nursery.

Travis shared a worried look with Sage, but she only shrugged.

"Did she come home early and is coming for the baby?" Travis asked, wondering if he was about to have to pick up the pieces of her broken heart.

"No. She extended her business trip, permanently." Liz

lifted the sleeping baby from his bed and cradled him to her chest. He snuggled against her breasts and made sweet baby sounds of contentment. "His aunt is not going to take him. There is no member of the mother's family who wants…" Her voice trailed off as if she couldn't bear to finish her thought aloud. As if she didn't want the baby to hear.

"What happens now?" Travis wasn't sure what this meant or how to make it better.

"Looks like Davy only needing a place for three months just got extended. Indefinitely."

Sage pressed her knuckles against her mouth as if holding in big emotions.

"What about the father?" he asked.

Liz kissed the top of the baby's head while patting him gently. "They'll keep looking for him, but until then, Davy has no one. Just us."

"I was afraid something like this would happen." Sage left the room, probably to find her sister.

Liz continued to hold him like her life depended on it. And maybe Davy's did. This was supposed to be a long stint of babysitting. Like watching a friend's kid while they're on vacation. But Travis knew Lizzy would keep Davy as long as it took, which meant she'd be staying at the ranch longer than planned.

The thought of her staying made him dangerously close to something that resembled hope. When she started singing, the baby cooed, making her smile. A sensation like morning sunshine washed over him, and he couldn't take his eyes from the pair of them. Both of them falling in love. Bonding.

She was fiercely protective—as her clinging to Davy demonstrated—and would sacrifice her own dream for an orphaned baby boy. He'd seen her give someone else the last piece of pie when he knew she wanted it. She'd snapped in half her favorite candy stick to share with him, even when they'd first met and he'd been a grumpy asshole.

There was little doubt that she would put aside her own dreams for someone she loved, which meant she might put off her opera singing career. But could he let her give up? Could he protect her?

Liz kissed Davy's chubby cheek and whispered in his ear, and Travis's heart did a flip-flop. The longer Davy was with her, the stronger their bond would grow.

She is going to be crushed when the father shows up.

Hers was not the only heart in jeopardy. Before the phone call from Betty, there had been an end date to Davy's stay at the ranch, but now, there wasn't. Every day he spent around the baby was a struggle to keep a safe level of disconnect in their relationship, but it was proving to be easier said than done. He couldn't keep up this level of detachment indefinitely. No matter how hard he tried to change his nature, his heart got involved when he took care of someone.

If he wasn't careful, he was going to lose this battle. He was already most of the way to loving this precious baby boy. But Davy was someone else's baby. Not the one he'd lost. Not his baby brother.

Not his.

Shortly after Betty's phone call, Travis slipped away unnoticed. Lizzy finished singing another round of "All the Pretty Horses" and pulled the bottle from the sleeping baby's mouth. A dribble of milk slid from the corner of his pursed lips, and she wiped it away with the burp cloth. It was time to put him in his bed, but she couldn't stop looking at his sweet face as he slept in her arms, making soft sucking sounds as if dreaming about his next meal.

There was no relative willing to take Davy, and it was breaking Lizzy's heart. In her early childhood, she knew what it was like to be loved and wanted. Her grandparents and aunts had seen to that. But once she'd moved to Chicago, her father's idea of parenting had resembled a school's headmaster.

What would her life have been like if her mother had lived?

For years she'd been promising herself she would be a better parent than she'd had, and taking care of Davy had shown her that she could. Her father had never been abusive—unless you counted ignoring her much of the time—but he had hired nannies and put strangers in charge of her upbringing. Most of those nannies had been kind and helped her, and she wanted to do the same for her sweet angel boy. She wanted more love for Davy than she'd had after leaving Texas, because she'd felt like an orphan.

It was her childhood influencing her thinking and emotions and causing this protectiveness over Davy. When she'd been abruptly taken away from her aunts and the only home she had ever known so shortly after losing Gamma, she'd felt abandoned.

"I won't let that happen to you, sweetie."

But could she really promise that? Easing up from the rocking chair, she placed Davy back in the crib.

Who would take care of him and fight for him the way he deserved? Who would be his advocate when it came to medical issues and special education? Who was going to love Davy and kiss his scraped knees and hold him after he had a nightmare?

She leaned into the baby bed and kissed his forehead. "I love you, sweet boy."

Saying it aloud sent a tear trickling down her cheek to the corner of her mouth where she tasted its saltiness. She grabbed the empty baby bottle but stopped in the doorway and sighed.

"Well, hell. The twins are so right about getting attached."

With every day that passed, she hoped more and more that Davy's father would be found and want to give up custody. To her.

But she would keep this a secret, for now.

The next few days were busy but happy with lots of baby cuddles, diapers, bottles and less sleep than normal. Lizzy took a CPR and first aid class and completed other requirements on her road to officially becoming a foster parent.

Travis started coming around a little bit more each day. They playfully picked at each other, getting close only to dance away and start all over again. It was deliciously frustrating.

On this summer evening, the air was finally cooling off to a tolerable level, and she felt bad that Travis was having to stand at the barbeque grill, but the burgers smelled delicious. With Davy in her arms, Lizzy was walking barefoot on the grass that bordered the brick patio.

"Travis, you should take off your boots and walk barefoot for a while."

He looked over his shoulder. "Why would I do that?"

"Because grounding, or earthing as some call it, will improve immunity and increase antioxidants and red blood cells. Reduce inflammation and white blood cells. It can also improve your sleep."

"That…is a lot. I'll pass." He turned back to the grill and flipped a burger.

"You're missing out. Right, Davy?" She walked closer to Travis and sat crisscross on the ground. Holding the baby with one hand splayed on his chest and the other under his bottom, she let his legs dangle until his bare feet brushed the grass.

"Are you grounding the baby?"

"He likes it." Proving her point, Davy's little toes splayed, and he kicked his feet against the blades of grass. "Angel boy, tell the grumpy cowboy he should really try it."

Travis made a sound that was close to a chuckle. "I'm not doing it unless it will increase my height by five inches and turn my eyes blue."

"You never know. It might."

Daisy came out the kitchen door carrying the hamburger buns, and she was also barefoot.

"Are y'all doing this on purpose?" he asked.

Daisy put the buns on the polished concrete counter beside the grill. "Doing what?"

"The no shoes thing." He motioned to her feet with the spatula. "Liz is trying to get me to take off my boots and walk around."

She looked down and wiggled her toes on the patio. "You might like it. It's good to try new things."

Travis did not take off his boots, but they all four had a nice dinner on the patio before she got the baby ready for bed. She loved this sweet little boy and wanted the best for him, but before mentioning her desire to keep him permanently, she needed time to sit with the idea of possibly becoming a single mother. Most likely, she was setting herself up for major heartbreak.

I'm so far off my summer plan.

Sage and Daisy had warned her. It was next to impossible not to get attached to a baby you were caring for. And she certainly hadn't expected to come to Texas and fall for two men. One a complicated cowboy and one a helpless infant.

Slowly, she stood from the rocking chair and then eased him into his baby bed, keeping one hand on his chest as she straightened and then slowly lifted her hand. She had discovered this was the best way to put him down and keep him asleep.

"Sleep well, sweet angel," she whispered. He would likely sleep for six or seven hours. They were lucky that he was such a good sleeper for a newborn.

As she came down the stairs, she could hear her aunts' voices and the living room television playing.

"I'm just going to sell or try to give away the honeymoon tickets," Sage said from her spot in front of the window that overlooked the front yard.

"What honeymoon?" Lizzy asked as she walked into the room.

"I was engaged and then I wasn't," Sage said sighing deeply as she flopped onto the couch.

"I'm sorry. I didn't know."

"Don't be sorry. He turned out to be a total ass," Sage said.

Daisy made a sound of agreement. "That's the truth. An ass who did not deserve my sister."

Lizzy sat in the pink chair. "Can I ask what happened? But only if you are okay with talking about it."

"I broke it off months ago because I discovered he…just wasn't a good person. We had already purchased the honeymoon trip to Ireland and Scotland, and it's nonrefundable."

"I keep telling her she should take a friend and go on the vacation she has always dreamed of." Daisy walked behind the couch and massaged her sister's shoulders. "You deserve it, and you know it."

"Why don't you both go on the trip?" Lizzy suggested.

"Because we can't both be away from the ranch for three whole weeks," Sage said.

"What if I help Travis and the hottie brothers run things around here while you're gone?"

At least her use of their secret nickname for the brothers made Sage smile.

The twins flashed a glance, once again communicating without words.

"Surely you can give me and Travis a written list of instructions and prepare us enough for the two of you to have a vacation." The thought of being alone on the ranch with Travis for three weeks made her jumpy. In a good way. A way that made her tingle.

Suddenly, the two of them going was an even more appealing idea for her as well as for them. She'd given up trying to convince herself that she hadn't completely fallen for Travis, the grumpy cowboy who had learned to smile.

Would running the ranch together bring them closer?

"It's a thought," one of the twins said, pulling her from her daydream.

"When was the last time you two had a vacation together?" Lizzy asked.

"Before Mama died," they both said.

"Then I say it's well past time."

"She's right," Daisy said. "We have capable people that we trust. In addition to Travis and Lizzy, the brothers, especially Finn, are trustworthy and hardworking."

Sage sat forward and tapped her index finger against her lips. "You know what? You're right. And don't think we didn't notice what you just said about Finn," she added with a grin.

Daisy waved her off as if she hadn't said it. "It's a trip we have both wanted to take since we were teenagers and it's about time."

"And we deserve it."

"Yes, you do," Lizzy said.

Sage pressed her hands to her cheeks. "But wait… I'm

still officially Davy's foster mom. I don't think I can leave for that long."

"When is the trip?" Lizzy asked.

"In two weeks."

"Then it's no problem. With Betty's help, I'll be an official foster parent by then."

"Really?"

"Yes. I talked to Betty today. Start packing your bags, ladies. And teaching me what I need to know to keep this place running."

Lizzy was putting a lot of responsibility on her plate—an infant, running a ranch and all the emotions that came along with Travis—but she could do it. Right?

Travis was on board with the plan and assured the twins that, along with the help of the Murphy brothers, they could handle everything around the ranch. For Lizzy, the next couple of weeks were all about getting everything ready for Sage and Daisy to go on their long overdue vacation. Very soon they'd be alone on the ranch, and then what would happen?

Chapter Nineteen

The twins had only been gone for one day when bad weather blew into their area of Texas, and Travis was rushing around getting everything ready. The brothers were in the stable with the horses, and he would be the one to protect Liz and Davy.

The storm was coming faster than expected, and he went into the farmhouse through the kitchen, and when he didn't find her there, he went to the stairs. "Liz, where are you?"

"Upstairs. In the baby's room."

His boots thundered up the stairs, and he barreled around the corner into the nursery. "The weather has taken a turn and has all the makings for possible tornadoes." To prove his point, the warning siren could suddenly be heard in the distance. A chill washed over him.

Davy was strapped in the baby carrier on her chest, his big brown eyes blinking at Travis as he sucked on his fingers.

"I need formula and diapers and wipes. And we should take the travel bassinet. What am I forgetting?"

Travis grabbed the bag and started stuffing things in and then took her by the arm. "This is all we need. We have to hurry."

They rushed down the stairs, grabbing formula, bottles and the travel bassinet on their way through the kitchen and then out and around to the storm cellar. The wind was already whipping the tree branches around like paper fans and big fat raindrops made miniature explosions against the dry dirt. She shielded the baby with her hands, and he ushered her inside and down the concrete steps in front of him. He struggled to close the door against the wind and slide the large bolt into place.

"We'll be safe down here, right?" she asked.

"Yes."

In the center of the rectangular room, Liz turned in a circle. "This is way fancier than when I was a kid. Back then, it was darker, and I was sure a troll lived down here."

"I cleared out all the trolls," he said to lighten the mood. "If we lose electricity, it will get darker, but we have candles and battery-powered lighting. This whole place was reinforced and improved a few years ago when they built the new stable."

It was more than just an underground safe space to hide out during a storm. It was also a great place for storage. Floor-to-ceiling wooden shelves stretched across one end from corner to corner and were filled with neatly organized boxes, canned goods, vacuum-sealed packages and bedding in protective plastic.

At Sage's request, the concrete walls had been painted a creamy ivory and the ceiling was a barely there blue that she said would give the impression of having the sky above them. The polished concrete floor had a large outdoor carpet rolled across it. There was a tiny bathroom in one corner and a refrigerator in the fourth with a small table beside it. Centered on the long back wall was a red futon and a coffee table in front of it with neat stacks of games and books. Across from the table were two swivel chairs.

Travis sat on the red futon where the weather radio was kept on a low bookcase that acted as an end table. It crackled and buzzed as he tuned it to a clear station and then put it on low volume. Outside, the rain was now coming down hard while the wind whistled and moaned.

Lizzy cradled Davy to her chest and kissed the top of his head while she remained in the center of the room as if not knowing what to do. Something thumped hard against the door of the storm shelter, and even though there were multiple places to sit, Lizzy rushed over to sit right beside Travis. So close that her shoulder was against his arm. A loud boom of thunder shook the earth around them, and she curved her body toward Travis with the baby between them.

He put his arms around her and the baby as if his body could protect them from the storm.

She was trying to be brave, but her expression told otherwise. "You promise we're really safe down here?"

"Yes. Very safe. Nothing to worry about."

She sucked in a sharp breath. "What about the horses?"

"They're okay, too. The brothers are in the stable with them." He liked that she thought of the horses, even at a time like this. If he hadn't needed to get her and the baby down here, he would also be with the horses, but he couldn't stand the thought of leaving Liz and Davy alone during the storm.

"And the stable is safe, too?"

"Absolutely. A lot safer than the rental house they live in." To distract her further, he decided to tell her more about the construction. "Once Sage and Daisy had valuable horses, they built the new stable and updated this shelter at the same time. The company who built them stacked cinderblocks with steel rods running through them and then concrete poured down into them. The frame of the roof and the sliding doors are strong steel. It's all heavy duty to protect such valuable animals. And people."

He kissed the top of her head and then the baby's.

"That makes me feel better," she said.

"The construction or the kiss?" His stomach flipped. Why had he said that about the kiss? Tension leaving her face made the comment worth it.

"Both. Our space is safe, and we have a cowboy to protect us."

There was another loud thump, and the wind continued to howl, rattling things above them and creating eerie sounds that moaned down the vent pipes.

"Nothing to worry about," he said in her ear. Her blue eyes, lighter in the center and darker around the edges, telegraphed an ocean of feelings. Fear. Anxiety. And if he wasn't mistaken, lust.

"What will happen to the farmhouse if a tornado does come through the ranch?"

"Hopefully, nothing, because there probably won't be more than a windstorm with heavy rain. There will be some limbs down and stuff like that. Just because the conditions are right doesn't mean there will for sure be a tornado here on the ranch."

Thunder rumbled and rolled in the distance but then a loud crack once again shook the ground right above them. The baby screwed up his cherub face and started crying. Liz bent her head to kiss the top of his and started singing in a sweet, soothing voice. A voice Travis had grown to love. Hers was a pleasing tone that calmed him rather than making him wince the way Crystal's sometimes did.

Davy stopped crying and stared at her, completely mesmerized and reaching for her long hair trailing over her shoulder.

Liz kneaded the muscles of her shoulders and neck.

"You can take off the baby carrier and put him on the futon between us." That would put some much-needed space between them because her sweet floral scent was driving him wild, and it wouldn't be right to try and make out with her during a storm. Or would it take her mind off her worries?

"I feel like he is safer attached to one of us." Her protective hold on the baby backed up her claim.

"Why don't you let me wear Davy for a while and give your back a break?"

She looked Travis in the eyes, as if deciding whether he would truly protect Davy at all costs. She must have decided that he would because she started unhooking the straps.

He helped her lift the straps of the carrier over her head, and then he transferred Davy to the front of his body.

The baby stuck out his tongue and blew a raspberry, making them laugh.

He let Davy grasp his finger. "What's up, little knucklehead?"

She laughed. "Knucklehead? Is that another word you learned from your grandpas, or are you really an old man on the inside?"

He shrugged, not admitting that he did feel older than his thirty years, and glad that he could make her laugh during such a scary time. "That's what Great-grandpa Roy called me when I did something silly or made him laugh."

"Tell me more about being raised by two grandfathers."

"It was my paternal grandfather and great-grandfather." He leaned back against the futon and adjusted the sleeping baby on his chest.

"So, I'm guessing they're the ones who taught you to be a gentleman and do things like opening doors and taking off your hat when you are introduced to a woman?"

"They taught me so much more than just that."

"Hey, why didn't you take off your hat when you met me like you did when we were at the feedstore and you met that man's wife?"

"Because you hit me before I could take it off."

"Oh yeah." She giggled.

"And then I was too busy holding my broken ribs."

"You are so exaggerating. I did not break your ribs."

"No, but it's a first meeting I won't forget."

"It's kind of a good meet-cute."

"What's that?"

"It's when the couple first meets in a cute way in a book or movie." Her eyes widened. "Not that I'm saying we're a couple."

"I guess I might've found our first meeting funny if I hadn't been on the receiving end of your massive bag of shoes."

"How did you know it was full of shoes?"

"Lucky guess." More and more every day, he thought about what it would be like to be a couple, and that was almost as scary as the storm raging above. Loving her—because that's what would happen if he truly let her in—was a risk for them both. After her audition, they'd have more information about her future plans, and that would determine what came next.

Would she stay in Channing or go far away? Travel or put down roots? Love him, or not?

"Will you tell me more about your childhood?"

An extra strong gust of wind rattled the door, and something banged nearby the shelter. He jerked his gaze to the ceiling. A story would keep them occupied rather than solely focusing on what was going on outside. "What do you want to know?"

"Really? You're actually going to tell me more about yourself?"

He shrugged one shoulder. "Within reason."

"Can I ask what happened to your parents?"

Of course she would jump straight to something that difficult. "My dad died in a car accident when I was eight years old. A few months later, my brother was born. And then…"

Liz laid her hand on his arm that was cradling the baby. A layer of comfort on top of comfort.

The back of his throat burned. She was right about his reluctance to share. Who wanted to admit that their mother had left them? "Not too long after my brother died, my mom decided she needed to find herself. Whatever that means. I think losing both of them so quickly led to her leaving."

And I wasn't enough of a reason for her to stay. Old wounds still hurt way more than he wanted to admit, even to himself.

Unusually quiet for her, Liz leaned in close enough to kiss the top of Davy's head. Close enough that she pressed her body into the side of Travis's and then rested her head on his shoulder, giving more silent comfort. Which was apparently what he'd needed because his chest expanded with room to breathe.

"Within such a short span of time, you lost so much. I wish I could go back in time and hug you."

"So do I."

"And you were left with your grandfathers."

"Yep."

"I get the feeling you were close to them?"

"We were. Remind me to show you a photo of the three of us."

"I was really close to my grandparents. Especially to my grandmother, Gamma. How did you end up working for my aunts instead of remaining on the Martin ranch?"

"I was off rodeoing for years, and when I came back, they didn't need me there. The Martin ranch used to be much larger, but over the years, sections have been sold off a piece at a time. Now it's down to four hundred acres."

Acres he really wanted. He'd called one of the Martin grandkids and asked if they would divide it into a smaller piece he could afford, but they'd said no. He was once again thinking about selling the fancy truck he'd won at a championship rodeo and getting an old used one, but that still wouldn't be enough to also qualify for a loan that large.

Davy squirmed on Travis's chest, and Liz put a hand on his little back. She wasn't pushing for more of his story, but talking to her was oddly therapeutic.

"There was a time, before my father died, that four generations of Taylors worked together on that ranch. Well, as much as an eight-year-old can cowboy. Once it was just the three of us, we lived in a small bunkhouse on the edge of their property. They are buried in a family cemetery on the Martin ranch."

"And now it's for sale."

"Yep."

"What about the cemetery? What happens to it when land is sold?"

"Whoever buys it can't move or disturb or build on it. And they have to give access to family who wants to visit the graves.

Is it only your family buried there?"

"No. It's mostly the Martin family, but since my family worked on the ranch since right after the Vietnam War, they said it was only right that we should be buried there, too."

The thought of Grandpa Will's funeral caused a catch in

his throat. A row of marble headstones with his last name. Four generations laid out in a row, telling a story of lives well-lived. He looked down at Davy asleep against his chest with his thumb in his mouth, and his heart stuttered.

And those who were taken way too soon.

He was silent while adjusting the baby, giving himself a moment to make sure his voice wouldn't crack.

"You started working here right after you stopped rodeoing?"

"Not right away." She didn't need to hear about his unfortunate detour on the road with Crystal.

"Thanks for sharing so much with me."

Now he felt a bit guilty for holding back.

Hail began to beat on the door of the shelter, and Lizzy tensed again and pressed herself more closely against him. He put an arm around her shoulders. "I didn't start working here immediately after leaving the rodeo circuit because I spent a couple of months on the road."

"Touring with your ex-girlfriend?"

"You know about that?"

"Only that she's a famous country singer. And FYI, I'm not a fan of her music."

That made him smile. "Going on tour with her was a bad decision."

"We all make those from time to time."

Why stop now? He might as well finish the story. "I was on tour with Crystal when I got the call about Grandpa Will being in the hospital. As I was throwing clothes into a bag and making arrangements to get to an airport, Crystal was furious that I'd even consider leaving. The next stop on the tour included a big awards show, and she expected me to be by her side, smiling and doting on her while she was fawned over by her adoring fans." He rolled his eyes.

"That was more important to her than you being with your grandpa?"

"Sad, but true." By that point in their relationship, he'd been feeling more like her assistant than her boyfriend. When he'd told her that he was sorry but he had to go to Texas, she'd thrown things at him, and not in the teasing way Liz did when he startled her. Crystal had been aiming to hurt him. That's when he'd known for certain how truly self-centered and thoughtless she was. It was the final reality check, confirming what he'd known in his heart for a while.

"She tried everything to talk me out of going to Grandpa Will's bedside, saying he would be fine, and I could go see him after I walked the red carpet with her. When she broke a few things while hurling them at me, I told her that I would not be coming back."

Liz grimaced. "At least I only throw soft things at you. Muffins and wadded-up paper. But now I feel really bad about that."

"Don't. I was asking for it both times. And you're pretty cute when you scream and spring into the air like a bunny."

"So glad I can be your entertainment," she said with a laugh. "Crystal gives the word *diva* a bad rap. I want to be a higher level and much kinder diva."

"There are levels of diva?"

"Absolutely. Diva is the Latin word for goddess. The original definition is a very successful and famous female singer. The word *diva* was a compliment reserved for only the greatest singers in the world, but lately, it has come to describe someone who is acting entitled or holier than thou. Crystal is the-world-revolves-around-me kind of diva."

He chuckled, feeling the burden of resentment begin to lessen because he could finally laugh about his ex. "That's pretty accurate."

If only he'd realized Crystal's true nature before giving up things important to him to go on her tour.

When he'd made it back to Channing, Texas, he'd only had a few hours with his favorite person in the whole world. He often found himself thinking about some of Grandpa Will's last words.

"Make sure to find a woman who'll dance in the rain with you, just like your grandma did with me."

The baby arched and started fussing, breaking into his thoughts. "Is it time for a bottle?"

"It is." She got up and started preparing the formula with the bottled water. "I know how it feels to lose a grandparent that you're really close to."

"Yes, I guess you do." He loosened the baby carrier so they could more easily feed him.

"I was only eight when Papa died and ten when I lost Gamma. She was the only mother I ever had."

"You were so young. I was lucky to have Grandpa Will as long as I did."

Davy made cute baby sounds when she took him into her arms. "I wish I could've met your grandpa."

"Me, too. He would've loved your singing."

"Oh, yeah? Too bad you didn't inherit his love of music."

He sighed and rubbed a hand through his hair. "I don't really hate it. There's a reason I snapped at you about the radio."

"Let me guess. You don't want to hear you-know-who on the radio?"

Before he could say more, the lights flickered, and she once again pressed herself against his side and continued feeding the baby. The weather raged above, but they were dry and warm and safe, if not a bit on edge.

"It's okay, princess. Remember, we have candles and all

kinds of supplies down here. Guess we'll have to add baby supplies to the list."

"Good idea. I'm glad we grabbed what we did before you practically carried both of us down here." She smiled up at him but then sobered. "Can I ask you one more thing?"

"Go for it."

"Did your mother ever come back?" Her voice was soft and lilting, as if that might make the question easier to bear.

He appreciated the effort, but it never got easy to talk about. "She comes back off and on. I see her occasionally."

When she came around needing something from him. Like the money she'd wanted the last time she flew through town on her way to her next wandering adventure. But he didn't add that bit of information to the story. He didn't need Liz feeling any sorrier for him than she probably already did. He hated it when people did that.

Davy had finished eating and was falling asleep. He reached out to take him and put the tiny bundle to his shoulder to burp him.

"Is your mom the only family you have left?" She put her fingertips against her lips. "I'm sorry. I'm asking too many questions. Please, feel free to tell me to shut up and mind my own business. I'm just trying to focus on something other than the storm."

"It's fine. My messed-up story is a good distraction. And yes, my mother is the only family I have left, other than a few distant cousins scattered here and there around the country."

"Since you know the Martin family so well, can't you talk to them about buying at least the area with the cemetery? It couldn't be more than an acre or two, and surely, they care enough to want to help you."

He shrugged, and that jiggled the baby. Davy flinched in his sleep, and Travis cradled his tiny head while patting his bottom. "I wish. The only ones who would care enough to try and help me are buried beside my family. The grandchildren, all of whom live far away and don't have any connection to the land, just want the money. They don't want to deal with multiple buyers or split up the land and risk getting less profit."

"How rude," Lizzy said in a deep voice that made him chuckle. "That sounds like something my father would do."

"I would like to buy the whole ranch, but it will likely sell before I have a big enough down payment and can secure a loan." Why was he telling her this much detail about his financial struggles? Now she would know when he failed, while she would no doubt succeed and go off to see the world.

"I really hope it's still available when you're ready to buy it. I can imagine it means a lot to have the land where your family is buried."

"It sure would. The last thing I promised Grandpa Will was that I would own land. It would be nice if it was the land where he's laid to rest."

"I have no doubt that you'll fulfill your promise to your grandpa."

"Thanks for the vote of confidence. When I do accomplish that goal, I'll be the first in my family to be a landowner."

Things above them grew quieter, but only for a moment. The next sound made his blood chill.

Chapter Twenty

Lizzy had finally let herself relax and was enjoying being cuddled against Travis, but when the sounds of the storm changed, his whole body jerked and stiffened. Her pulse rate took off at a sprint.

"Is it a tornado?" The tremble in her voice telegraphed her alarm.

"Yes, princess. I think it is." He wrapped his arms around her and the baby, his usual hesitancy gone.

They say a tornado sounds like a train rumbling your way, and Lizzy now had proof that was true.

Deep vibrations rattled the earth, reaching her bones and making her heart slam against her ribs while Davy cried into the crook of her neck, likely picking up on her fear, but all she could do was press kisses to his head and pray.

Through all of it, Travis remained calm and continued to whisper words of comfort against her ear. "We're safe. I've got you."

The rumble began to die down, and it soon became a

distant sound, taking with it the howling wind. There was only the patter of rain against the shelter door.

Davy quieted, and her breathing returned to normal. It had only lasted a minute, maybe less, but every second had stretched with agonizing fear.

"It was close but not right on top of us," he said.

The three of them were still cuddled up like a family. And she liked it. A lot. But it ended too soon when he shifted away from them to pull out his phone.

"I need to check in with the brothers." He stood and hit a few buttons before putting it to his ear. "Finn, are y'all okay?" He listened while pacing their small space, his height making the ceiling appear even lower. "That's a relief. Yes, all good here. I'm keeping Liz and Davy down in the shelter, so call if you need me."

Her pulse jumped, but this time not out of fear but an excitement that stirred deep in her belly. "We're staying down here all night?"

"Yes. Just to be safe." He turned away from her as if hiding his expression.

"I take it they did okay in the stable?"

"Horses are jumpy but they're all safe. Finn thinks a small tornado passed between the house and stable, missing everything important."

"What a relief," she said taking the first deep breath since they'd come down here.

"I'm going to step up to the door and have a look outside."

"Don't go all the way. Just stick your head out because it might still be dangerous."

He looked as if he'd laugh but only grinned. "Yes, mother."

Before, him saying that would have irritated her, but now, it made her smile.

Davy grabbed a fistful of her hair, and Lizzy untwined

his little fingers as she scooted to the other end of the futon for a better view of Travis. He was standing at the top of the stairs with only half of his body exposed to the elements.

Rain fell softly, catching in the beam of his flashlight like a tiny meteor shower. Thunder rolled across the night sky, and a gust of wind ruffled his hair.

"How does it look out there?" she asked.

"Not bad." Once the door was resecured, he came back to sit beside them, his dark hair shimmering with misty droplets. "There are some limbs down, but from what I could see, Finn is right, and the tornado missed everything important."

"Thank goodness." If it was safe to go back to the house, she didn't want to know. This chance to remain close throughout the night was too good to give up.

He rubbed his hand across his head, flicking off tiny beads of water. "But we still need to stay down here for the night."

Her thoughts exactly. It was good to finally be on the same page.

"Let's unfold the futon and get out some of the bedding. We might as well be comfortable." he said.

Her pulse had just returned to normal but once again started to climb. Were they about to sleep beside each other? All night? That sounded…awesome.

"You can have the futon, and Davy has his little travel bed."

"What about you?"

He motioned to the shelves at one end of the room. "There's a sleeping bag."

Well, that's thoroughly disappointing.

"Trav, you can't sleep on this cold, hard concrete floor."

"I've slept on worse a time or two."

"Well, not tonight. There's room for both of us on the futon."

He worked his mouth like he was going to say something more but just turned to get the bedding.

Once she'd tucked Davy into his bassinet, they flattened the futon and covered it with sheets and a patchwork quilt. When she turned off the overhead light, they were cast into the soft glow from the lamp on the bookcase.

Travis was the perfect person to be with tonight. He made her feel safe, and she was enjoying their conversations. He was finally sharing things about himself that she suspected he rarely did. She wanted to keep him talking and get to know the real him and not just the image he projected for the rest of the world.

Would they leave this storm cellar with a new kind of relationship or would everything go back to dancing around their attraction and a shared fear of what getting too close might mean for each of them? It had been kind of fun flirting while purposely poking at the other to keep that last safe bit of distance between them, but she was ready for more.

With Davy back to sleep, she stretched out on the mattress. "I found out why my father and the twins became estranged."

"Oh, yeah? What happened?" He sat on the bedside to take off his boots. His dark green T-shirt pulled taught across the muscles of his back, and she had to clasp her hands to keep from touching him.

"When Gamma died, my dad and aunts inherited this ranch. There had always been tension between him and his little sisters, but it got worse. He fought with Sage and Daisy over what to do with the place. They wanted to keep things as is and fought hard to keep it. He wanted to sell the entire ranch to a company that planned to build a fertilizer factory and warehouse."

Stretching out beside her, he rubbed his hands over his face and sighed. "I'm glad that didn't happen."

"Right? He told them they would have enough money to buy an even bigger ranch somewhere else. But they didn't want some other place. He made a deal with them that if they could buy out his third, they could have the whole ranch. He gave them an amount so high that he thought they could never get their hands on that much money."

"But they did?" Trav rolled onto his side and propped up on an elbow.

"They sure did."

"Do you know how they got the money?" He looked so hopeful, like this would be the answer to affording the ranch next door that meant so much to him.

Lizzy sighed, hating to burst his hopes. "No. That seems to be something neither of them wants to talk about. They said it took a lot of sacrifice but weren't sharing details. All I got was that they sold things and rented space. I wonder what space they rented?"

"Maybe the barn or some of the land. That's the only thing I can think of."

"I guess. It was just weird that they wouldn't talk about it and the way they closed up and got cagey when I asked. I suppose people are entitled to some secrets."

His brow furrowed. "True. After they paid him for the ranch, you moved away?"

"We moved from Channing to Chicago. He cut off all contact with them."

"Even for you?"

"Yes. He forbade me to even talk to Sage and Daisy. I was only ten, grieving my grandmother and not brave enough to test what crossing him would mean." She sighed with a hand pressed to her cheek. "A lot of it was fear of the guilt trip that comes after disappointing him. He's good at laying it on as thick as peanut butter. The kind that gets stuck on the roof of your mouth."

"That sounds rough. I hate that he did that to you." Travis played with a thick lock of her hair, rubbing it between his fingers.

They were side by side in bed, talking like a couple, and she loved it. Having the twins to talk to was great, but having Trav listen and care was healing in a different way. The expressionless mask he'd worn when they met had slipped, and he could no longer hide the tenderness in the depths of his dark-brown eyes. It made her feel protected and valued.

"It was a time in my life that I really needed my aunts, who were more like big sisters to me. I thought he'd get over whatever it was and eventually let me see them, but he never did. I should've just come to see them the second I turned eighteen."

She had considered it after high school graduation, but if he'd found out, he wouldn't have paid for college, and she'd chickened out. Then after college graduation, she'd immediately gone to work for him at Dalton Realty. Her whole life, she'd been striving for his approval and fearful of disappointing her father. Fearful of his guilt trips. She'd been mad at him when she left Chicago, but after learning more about why he and his little sisters fought, him sending a spy to Texas, and interfering with her audition, she was even angrier.

I'm done with that. No more letting him control me.

Travis touched her face in a move so natural you'd think he did it every day. "What's wrong? Where did you go just now?"

"Just thinking about the lonely years that I spent in Chicago."

"You haven't mentioned your mom."

"My grandmother was the closest thing I've ever had to a mother. Mine died when I was a baby."

"Like Davy's mother," he said.

A charge zipped through her chest. She hadn't made that connection until now, but it was totally true. "Now that you mention it, yes. I suppose I see some of myself in him. A motherless baby."

"And you want him to have what you did not."

"Trav, you didn't tell me you're such a great therapist."

He barked a quick laugh. "Hardly. That title should go to you. You've gotten me to open up and share more than anyone else has." He smoothed back her hair and let his hand brush lightly across her cheek.

A wave of desire curled around her insides. She traced the tip of one finger over his knuckles, tanned and scarred from a life of cowboying but so gentle when he held the baby or caressed her skin.

He turned his hand to press his wide palm to hers as if comparing the size difference. Pale against tan. Strong against delicate. But fitting so perfectly when he laced their fingers.

"I wish I'd come home sooner."

"You're here now." He stroked his thumb over the cradle of her palm, and she shivered.

And with very poor timing, Davy started crying in his bed, and she reluctantly let go of Trav's hand and rolled over to pick him up. "What's the matter, my sweet angel boy?"

He stopped crying as soon as he heard her voice and stared at her.

"He sure is smitten with you," Travis said.

"Smitten?" She giggled. "Which grandpa taught you that word?"

"Great-grandpa Roy."

She changed the baby's diaper, gave him a pacifier and started rocking him back to sleep in her arms.

Travis was up and moving around the small space. He got two bottles of water out of the refrigerator and put them beside the bed before checking the weather radio and his phone. Every few seconds, he glanced their way with a curious expression. She would love to know what he was thinking.

She put the sleeping baby back in his bed, pulled a piece of candy out of her pocket, unwrapped it and popped it into her mouth. The tangy sweetness of green apple made her think of the next pie recipe she wanted to try out. She stretched out on the futon, wishing he'd return to lie beside her. "Did you know that if you put a Jolly Rancher on the right side of your tongue it tastes sweeter, and if you put it on the left side, it's more sour?" The hard candy clicked against her teeth as she moved it with her tongue to the other side as if to demonstrate the fact.

"You're making that up," Travis said.

"No, I'm not. It's totally true."

"Give me one and let me see."

She stuck her hand in the pocket of her khaki shorts, but it was empty. "Sorry, I don't have any more."

As he joined her on the bed, his lips slowly lifted into a smile that made his eyes narrow at the corners. "Then I guess you'll just have to share." Cradling the back of her head, he moved closer, but not close enough that their lips were touching.

"Share?" Her voice had grown husky, and her body was starting to sing.

"Liz, if there is even the slightest chance of us not making it through the night, I'm not willing to go without kissing you. A real kiss that isn't to fool an old boyfriend."

"I'm fully on board with that plan." She had never craved

someone's kiss this much in her whole life, and if he didn't kiss her soon, she was going to combust into a shower of glitter.

The warmth of his breath became the heat of his lips. And in the next heartbeat, he was kissing her fully, the touch of his tongue electric and his scent filling her head. When they eased apart, he had the piece of candy and wore an ear-to-ear grin.

She sighed contentedly and didn't even care that he heard. "I like sharing my candy with you."

"That's excellent news." He worked the candy around in his mouth. "Hey, you're right. It is different depending on which side of your tongue."

"I happen to know some very important facts. You should listen to me more often."

"I listen more than you think, songbird." Before she could respond, he pressed his lips to hers.

Their clothes stayed on—mostly—as they explored the way their bodies and mouths fit together. They kissed and teased and shared tender touches late into the night, a thunderstorm the soundtrack to their passion.

Lizzy woke to the sound of Davy snuffling in his bed, and a warm body spooning her from behind. If contentment and happiness were a song, this would be it. Travis's arm was around her waist with his hand resting on the mattress beside her. When she traced her fingers lightly over his forearm, he sighed and tightened his hold on her for a few heartbeats before kissing the side of her neck.

"Good morning, songbird."

She turned in his arms and had time for one quick kiss before Davy started crying, and they both sat up.

"We made it through the night," she said and gave him a tentative smile.

"I told you I would keep you safe."

"You didn't mention the extra perk of evening entertainment." She kissed him once more and then picked up Davy. "Good morning, sweetie. Let's get you a fresh diaper and then a bottle. How does that sound?"

Davy arched his back, stuck out his tongue and grunted.

"I'll make the bottle." Travis jumped off the futon like it was on fire.

"You just don't want to change his diaper."

"You are correct, and I don't deny it."

She smiled while tending to his dirty diaper and tickled Davy's little round tummy. He grasped for her hand, cooing and basically being the cutest baby ever. How could she be this happy when there was possible damage to the ranch she was supposed to be looking after while her aunts were out of the country?

Lizzy bundled the diaper into a tight little package. "Trav, catch."

He turned, and in an automatic reaction, he caught the diaper then grimaced. "Oh, man. Really?" But he was grinning as he dropped it into the trash.

Once she'd washed her hands, she cradled Davy in her arms, holding his bottle for him as she followed Travis up the concrete steps. When he swung open the door, a glow of warm colors blazed above the tree line, the air fresh and washed clean as if the morning was a brand new start to…everything. Side by side, they stood in the backyard. Not speaking. Not moving. Just taking in the beauty of the moment.

"It's a gorgeous morning," she whispered. Their gazes locked and they shared a smile.

Would things now be different between them, or was she totally setting herself up for disappointment? Fairy tales didn't usually come true.

Davy grasped her fingers as if trying to hold his own bottle, and she looked down at his sweet face. "The storm is over, angel boy."

Two blue jays chased each other around the barbecue pit, and she noticed several tree branches littering the ground, and then softly inhaled.

"Trav, the patio furniture is gone."

"I put it in the barn before the storm."

"Oh. That was smart. Thank you for staying with us all night. I know you normally would've been with the horses."

"They were tended to." He opened the kitchen door but didn't go inside. "But I do need to check on them. First, we should check for damage here. You take the inside. Look at all the ceilings to check for leaks or anything like that. I'll walk around the outside of the house."

"Okay. Come inside when you're done, and I'll make breakfast." The urge to kiss him made her sway forward but she bit her lip and forced herself to rush inside. The last thing she wanted to do was get all clingy and freak him out.

She started upstairs and found everything in order. On her way back down, she heard glass hitting the floor in the living room and stopped at a safe distance under the archway to watch Travis pull an arm-sized branch out of the broken window.

"Stay away from all the glass, and I'll clean it up with a pair of gloves," he said through the broken window.

"It could have been so much worse. I'm glad the twins won't come home to a destroyed house."

"No kidding. Looks like this is the only damage, and at least it's an easy fix. I'm going to check on the horses and my cabin, and then I'll cover the window with a piece of plywood until I can replace it."

"I'll make breakfast when you get back. If the brothers are still in the barn, tell them to come eat as well."

"Will do," he said with a smile and then turned to leave.

She grinned like a besotted teenager and watched him until he was out of sight. Her father would have expected her to get it cleaned up and call someone to repair it immediately. It felt nice to have someone looking out for her instead of expecting her to handle every little problem that cropped up like she was the hired help.

Travis didn't do that to her. He treated her like she was worth taking care of. Like she had value and should be cherished. But would it last, or would she find herself tending to a wounded heart?

Chapter Twenty-One

As Travis neared the stable, one of the big metal doors opened and Finn came outside, shielding his eyes from the sun with one hand and raised the other in greeting.

"Horses are all fine and everything is good here. Riley and Jake went to check on our rental. How's the farmhouse?"

"We need to board up one of the living room windows because a tree branch came through it. That seems to be the extent of the damage. I'm on my way to check out my cabin."

"I'll get started on feeding the animals."

When Travis rounded the old barn, his stomach dropped to his toes just as his heart leapt into his throat. The tornado had found a mark after all.

Part of the cabin's roof and the top portion of the outer wall of the kitchen were gone. He'd been so focused on Liz and the baby and knowing that the animals were safe that he hadn't even thought about his own belongings in the cabin.

He ran the rest of the way, and then walked around the outside. The damage seemed to be contained to one corner of the cabin. He quickly found part of the missing roof. It was in the kitchen where everything was waterlogged and crushed. It was hard to tell at this time what had been blown away and what was under the rubble.

He took off his cowboy hat and plowed his hands through his hair before jamming it back on, his gut twisting and his head beginning to ache.

"Damn it all to hell and back again."

Another thought made his gut twist. His coffee can full of cash had been in the top cabinet on the missing section of wall. It had been so stupid to leave thousands of dollars in cash from his last few rodeo wins in a kitchen cabinet. Another thing he did because his great-grandpa had done it that way. He'd meant to take it to the bank but kept putting it off and then he'd forgotten.

He needed every penny of that money and more for a down payment on the Martin Ranch. Time was running out much faster than planned, and he was moving in the wrong direction with his savings. Any day now someone would make an offer on the ranch he dreamed of owning. He once again considered selling the new truck he'd won at a championship rodeo. But even if he traded it for a junker, it wouldn't be enough.

This time, he threw his hat to land in the far corner of the living room and braced his hands on his knees. Just when he needed to find a way to quickly make more money, a big chunk of what he had counted on was gone with the wind. Why hadn't he taken it to the bank like a normal person would in this day and age?

There was a slim chance that the coffee can was under the rubble, but before he started digging to hopefully find the cash, he went to check the bedroom and breathed a quick sigh of relief that it was untouched. He pulled the wooden trunk from beneath his bed. It was filled with all the things that were valuable to him. His great-grandpa's pocket watch, letters his great-grandparents had written to each other while Great-grandpa Roy was overseas, his father's rodeo belt buckles, family wedding rings and photos. And photos of his baby brother and a pair of his tiny socks. Things that might not mean much to someone else, but to him they were priceless.

"Trav?" Lizzy called out. "Are you in there?"

"Yes, but don't come inside. It's too dangerous for you and the baby." He went out onto the tiny front porch carrying the trunk.

"What's that?"

"Family stuff."

She moved Davy to her shoulder and patted his bottom. "The damage looks kind of bad."

"The top half of one kitchen wall is missing along with part of the roof. More of the roof is in the kitchen and bathroom, and everything in those rooms is waterlogged and pretty much unusable."

"I'm so sorry, Trav."

"At least the bedroom is untouched." He put the trunk on the porch and walked over to them.

"You can't stay in the cabin with no kitchen or bathroom and a hole in the roof. Looks like you'll have to move into the farmhouse with us."

Davy gave an excited coo of agreement, his eyes like little drops of caramelized sugar.

She kissed the baby's cheek. "That's right, sweetie. Trav needs to come stay at the house so he can learn how to change your stinky diapers."

Even as upset as he was about this setback, his hard-set mouth lifted into a grin. These two unexpected humans were good for his mood. Good at putting things in perspective. "I guess you're right. About the staying at the house part, not the diapers."

One night with her in the storm shelter had tested the limits of his willpower. He had resisted stripping her bare, but how long was a man expected to keep that up? Especially when the woman beside him was Liz. Sleeping down the hallway from her would be a slow kind of torture.

Why can't that opera audition happen already! Then he'd have a better idea of her future plans.

"Want some help gathering your clothes and other important things? I can help you move them up to the house."

"It's not safe in here. You have the baby to look after, and I don't want to risk either of you getting hurt inside this disaster zone."

"You're right, but if it was just me, I would be helping. I'm the kind of diva that doesn't mind getting my hands dirty."

"After watching you shovel mud until your hands wouldn't work, I have no doubt, princess." Her sweet smile did something unexpected to his insides. Just a minute ago he'd been upset enough to smash something with his bare hands, but now there was an easing of tension in his chest.

They heard a vehicle approaching. The Murphy brothers' black truck pulled up and Riley got out.

"How is your house?" Travis asked him.

"It's fine. Just some yard cleanup. Morning, Lizzy."

"Good morning, Riley. I'm going back to the house to make breakfast for everyone. It should be ready in about thirty minutes or so. You'll all need some energy before you start working on cleanup."

"Thanks," Riley said. "That would be great, and much better than the protein bar in the truck."

"I'll see all of you in a little while." Liz flashed her smile toward Travis and then turned for the house.

Both men were quiet until she was out of earshot, but

then Riley chuckled. "I'm going to safely bet that your night was way more fun than mine was in the stable with my brothers and the horses?"

"Why do you think that?"

"Dude, the way she just smiled at you only means one thing."

Travis shook his head. "She smiles at everyone."

"I didn't get that kind of smile from her." Riley seemed to recognize the warning on Travis's face and dropped the teasing. "Looks like your cabin took some damage."

"It was the hardest hit thing on the ranch." Travis hitched a thumb at the cabin. "After we eat, can you help me haul out some of the waterlogged debris and cover the hole in the roof as best we can?"

"Of course. We'll all help."

"We have enough plywood to cover the one window that was broken at the farmhouse, but I'll need more wood and some tarps for this mess." His mood took another hit. Making repairs to the cabin was going to take time. He lifted his wooden trunk of mementos and carried it to the black truck.

Riley started the motor and headed toward the farmhouse. "I'll drive into town after we eat and get some supplies. Did you see how much they are asking for the Martin Ranch?"

"Yep. A hell of a lot higher than I'd hoped."

"Are you still looking to buy a place?"

He took a deep breath before answering. "Yes, but that dream keeps getting sidelined by one thing after another." Things like injuries and no more rodeo cash prizes, his own mother getting into his bank account, and now a freaking act of nature combined with his own stupidity of leaving cash lying around was highly likely to result in never seeing that chunk of money again.

"We're saving to buy something of our own, too. But with property prices going up, it's depressing," Riley said.

"I hear that." At least there were three of them working together, just like he and his grandpas used to do.

After breakfast, and with the brothers' help, they cleaned up the broken glass and boarded up the living room window. The four of them moved down to his cabin, hauled out everything that was ruined and got the roof covered as best they could.

He'd told them to look for the old metal coffee can, but he had not told them how much cash was in it. The last thing he needed was for them to know what a fool he was. There was no sign of the coffee can or anything else that had been in the cabinet above the refrigerator. It was gone with the wind.

Later, he'd walk the property in search of any blown-away debris, but he was not holding out much hope. The cash he'd won by giving his body a beating every weekend was probably lining an animal's nest by now.

He gathered what he needed from his bedroom and took it up to the farmhouse where he would be sleeping under the same roof with Liz. There were five bedrooms, and he wasn't sure which one he would be using. Every time his brain drifted into thoughts about sharing a room with Liz, he reined in that dangerous idea.

Spending a stormy night together out of necessity was one thing, but jumping right into sharing a bedroom was definitely on the not-yet list. If not ever.

When he started hauling his things into the house, Liz came out to help.

"The baby is napping, so we need to be kind of quiet while taking your things upstairs. Especially since your room is right next door to the nursery."

"Got it." It turned out that the baby's room was between hers and the one he would be using. The distance was a small barrier, but not enough to curb his desire for her.

"Did you lose anything valuable?" She folded his Houston Rodeo T-shirts, smoothed them, then put them into an empty dresser drawer.

"Some cash," he said without censoring himself. He was too focused on the intimate way her delicate hands touched his belongings. She really did have a way of getting him to spill his secrets and inner thoughts. In the future, he'd have to be more careful.

"Oh no. Was it a lot of money?"

"Enough to hurt." He hung up another shirt in the small closet.

Liz wrapped her arms around him from behind and rested her head on his back. "I'm sorry. I know you've been working hard to save up."

He turned in her arms and held her close, letting her sweetness soak in. Seeking this level of comfort was exactly what he should not be doing. If her dream came true, she'd move on to sing her way around the world.

She lifted her head from his chest. "Is it possible it's just mixed in with all the roof pieces and stuff that fell into your kitchen?"

"We looked but didn't find it."

"Was the money loose or inside of something?"

He hesitated but was too tired and couldn't find a reason to lie. "It was in an old metal coffee can in a kitchen cabinet." He waited for her to scold him, but she didn't.

"Since you don't see metal coffee cans anymore, I'm going to guess that it belonged to one of your grandpas?"

"Yep."

"I'll keep an eye out for it when I take my daily walks to sing. I'm pretty good at finding things."

He decided not to burst her bubble and tell her how unlikely that was. "Thanks, princess."

When she smiled up at him, she chipped away at his willpower, and he kissed her, slipping his tongue between her soft lips and capturing her moan.

It suddenly felt suspiciously like they were becoming a couple.

Travis stood at the window of his temporary bedroom that looked out over the front yard and the curving driveway that led to the front gate of the ranch. His cabin was wrecked, but everyone was safe. He hadn't wanted to be in charge of taking care of anyone, but here he was doing just that in a way bigger than he'd ever thought. And he liked it.

On this first night in the farmhouse, Travis couldn't decipher his feelings. If the twins were here, it would have been an extra layer of protection, but as it stood, there was no one to overhear or catch them kissing. No one to tell them it was a bad idea.

His songbird was singing the Journey song "Open Arms" in the bathroom down the hall as she prepared the baby's bath in a blue plastic tub that she'd set on the counter. The lyrics about hearts beating together, soft whispers and holding one another in the dark called to something inside him that made him crave more than the solitary life he'd been living.

Davy's newborn cry joined in with her sweet voice.

"Trav, would you please go pick up the baby and bring him to me in the bathroom?"

"Be right there." He walked into the nursery and looked down at the baby boy. "Hey, tiny dude. What's all this fussing about?" He picked him up and put a fingertip on his quivering chin. Davy gave another squawk before taking a shuddering breath and stopped crying. "I think you're putting on some weight."

He carried him to the changing table to undress him. He didn't want to change a diaper, but the resistance he'd been putting up was more to tease Liz than an actual aversion. The least he could do was help get him ready for his bath. With an abundance of caution, he peeled back the tabs on the diaper and let out a sigh of relief that it was only wet. With the naked baby against his chest, he left the nursery, but as he entered the bathroom, he felt a warmth spread on his T-shirt and looked down to see a wet spot.

"Oh, man. He peed on me."

Liz giggled. "At least it wasn't in his bathwater. Thanks for bringing him to me." She took the squirming baby and lowered him into the warm water.

Davy's little mouth rounded as his arms flailed out, but then he settled in and seemed to enjoy the warm water.

Travis peeled off his wet shirt and dropped it into the sink. "Now I need a bath, too."

"You'll have to wait your turn, cowboy." Her gaze roamed his bare chest, and she bit her lip. "I can only tend to one man at a time," she said in a voice that had grown husky.

Her saying things like that was not helping with the fit of his jeans, but he liked it when she flirted with him. The light she'd brought into his life was making some of the sorrow, humiliation and anger start to fade.

"Look how his arms and legs are filling out. I'm anxious to see how much he weighs at his next visit to the pediatrician."

"At his last exam, did he get a good report?"

"Yes. He's still on the small side but healthy and growing."

Travis released a breath. "That's good."

Life didn't have to repeat itself. This was a different baby. A healthy baby.

Chapter Twenty-Two

Davy had had an unusually cranky night, and Lizzy was bleary-eyed and exhausted. It hadn't helped that between tending to the baby, she'd lain awake wishing she could sleep in Trav's arms like she'd done the night before, but the only storm tonight was the one swirling in her own mind. With several self-lectures, she'd forced herself to remain in her own bedroom. But she was starting to wonder why.

The baby was still asleep—or rather back to sleep—and she needed coffee in the most desperate sort of way. She went downstairs and walked into the kitchen still rubbing the sleep from her eyes but then stopped short.

Travis was standing on the other side of the island beside the coffeepot. His hair was wet and brushed back with one thick wave falling over his forehead, a bare chest and...

Is he naked?

She was suddenly wide awake. With the island blocking her view of him from the belly button down, she had no idea what, if anything, he was wearing.

"Morning," he said with a mischievous grin.

"Are…are you wearing any clothes?"

His grin grew, making his eyes crinkle at the corners and changing his face from broodingly handsome to drop-dead gorgeous. Like a whole different person than the grumpy cowboy she'd first met.

"No, ma'am. I'm not wearing any clothes." He started to step out from behind the island.

She covered her eyes but peeked through her fingers. A green towel was wrapped around his waist, riding low on his hips, and she was simultaneously relieved and extremely disappointed.

He chuckled "You're peeking, Princess Songbird. What were you hoping to see?"

"Nothing. Not a single thing." She went around the island on the opposite side from him and grabbed a coffee mug that said *Cowgirls Do It Better*.

"Whatever you say."

His deep chuckle made her shiver.

"I'm going to go get dressed." A second before he rounded the corner into the other room, he pulled off the towel, giving her a brief but very nice glimpse of his firm butt.

She set down her coffee and pressed her fingertips to her smile.

Who was this flirty, sexy, bad-boy version of her quiet cowboy? Sage and Daisy had said he was getting back to the happier guy they remembered. Had she made it through his layers and found the real Travis?

Living here, without any other adults around, was like playing house, and with the baby, they were like a family. This was going to make it harder to resist him. Harder to stay on track with her summer plans and future goals.

Her audition was drawing closer, and thanks to the extra punch of gumption her father had unknowingly given her, she felt ready to sing for them. If things went well, she could sing opera at Bass Opera Hall and lullabies at home.

She stirred cream into her coffee, took a sip and stared out the kitchen window. It was a beautiful day. Perfect for getting outside and enjoying the simple pleasures of being on the ranch where she'd been so happy—and was once again. Would it be so terrible if she altered her plans a bit?

No one person or thing was to blame for her reconsidering her plans. It wasn't only a man who was enticing her enough to veer off course. Davy needed her, and she needed him.

Did Travis need her, too?

The afternoon was sunny, but Davy was napping in the shade of the front porch in the travel bassinet. An overhead fan added to the breeze that had picked up in the last few minutes. Lizzy snipped another stem off the azalea bush she was pruning while music played from her phone on the railing. She'd only made it halfway down the row of flowering bushes along the front of the house, and she was melting in the heat.

To prove that point, sweat trickled into the top of her yellow cotton sundress and down her forehead, and she straightened to wipe her brow. Raising up on her toes, she assured herself that Davy was all right. Lady was curled up on the swing, and a black-capped chickadee landed on the railing and cocked his head to inspect the sleeping cat. It was such a peaceful, domestic scene.

This temporary life she was living was more than she could have imagined. The ranch was a place where she felt at home and safe. And loved.

This is the happiest I've been since...

The pruning shears slid from her fingers. She couldn't think of a time or event to finish that thought. Not since she was a small child and here in this very spot. Surely, she could figure out how to have opera *and* family. She didn't want this way of life to be only a temporary stop before starting a career. Not anymore.

A cloud shaded the bright sun, and a minute later, a soft rain began to fall. She turned her face up to smile at the sky just as the song changed to "Desperado" by the Eagles, and she raised her arms and swayed to the beat. Dancing in the rain.

She was the diva in charge of her own life.

Following the sound of the music, Travis came around to the front of the house and slowed his steps, no longer caring that he'd been caught out in the rain.

His entire body tingled in the best way possible.

Liz was dancing in the rain like a nature goddess, all beauty and grace. Sweetness and sass. With a smile on his face and something shiny and new in his heart, he closed the distance between them.

She turned to him with a smile that didn't falter at being caught dancing alone. Instead, she held out her arms. "Dance with me, cowboy."

They moved into an embrace and swayed together.

This was the feeling Grandpa Will had told him to search for. It had to be.

As he held Liz in his arms, he stopped fighting. The fear he'd been clinging to started melting away with each raindrop.

"You're so beautiful. Are you real or in my imagination?"

"It feels real to me." Her fingers played with the hair curling at the back of his neck.

There was still risk. There always was and always would be, and even if she left to sing in the opera, she would come back to Channing to visit the twins. And she had asked them if the ranch could be her home base. Wasn't being with her, whenever they could be, worth the time they might have to spend apart?

Screw it. He'd been through heartache before and could do it again if necessary. If he missed taking a chance with her, he would forever wonder.

He traced the back of his knuckles along her jaw, her graceful neck, and then across to her collarbone. When she made a kittenish sound of desire, it revved him up further, and he kissed her. Fully, deeply and filled with all the things he hadn't been able to say.

She shivered under his touch, grasping the wet fabric of his T-shirt as if she feared he would end the kiss. "Don't stop."

The very thing he'd been trying to avoid since she'd slugged him in the stomach with her bag of shoes had happened anyway.

He was in love with his songbird.

Chapter Twenty-Three

Travis was holding her and kissing her like he couldn't get enough. Lizzy couldn't have asked for a bigger or better sign that her newly adjusted life plan was the right choice. The tough outer shell he showed to most of the world was only there to protect his sweet marshmallow center. One he was revealing only to her.

She had ignored every bit of common sense and everything she had been telling herself over and over. And she didn't care.

She had fallen completely in love with Travis Taylor.

He cradled both of her cheeks and kissed her once more. Softly and oh so sweetly. "Where's the baby?"

"He's asleep on the porch. Let's take him inside and see if he stays asleep."

"Good plan." He went up onto the porch, lifted the bassinet by the handles and carried it into the house. He slowly climbed the stairs, and Davy continued to sleep as he set the bassinet in the center of the nursery.

With his hand in hers, she led him back out into the hallway.

When he slipped the thin straps of her sundress off both of her shoulders, her hands went to his trim waist. His rodeo belt buckle was cool in the palm of her hand as she slid the leather of his belt from its hook.

Between kisses, their clothes disappeared and ended up in a wet trail across the floor, leading to her bed. On a rainy summer afternoon, they made love for the first time.

And a second.

The next day, after chores were done, the three of them went to Old Town. Since they hadn't stayed long enough on the day that he'd repaired the pump, because of Jeff showing up, they hadn't seen it working. Thankfully, there'd been no sign of the tattletale spy since that afternoon.

This morning, when she'd ask Travis to hand her a pair of flip-flops to wear with her favorite denim skirt and a pink blouse, he'd brought her silver wedges, dangling from his long fingers and not even trying to hide his smile. She'd had a suspicion he liked the shoes he'd first scoffed at, and she'd been right.

Davy slept as Lizzy pushed his baby stroller around to the courtyard. Travis was by her side, and he was no longer wearing the scowl that had been his go-to expression. In a cowboy hat, a pair of jeans that hadn't been faded by hard work and a tan button-up that made his chocolate eyes pop, he was making it hard for her to keep her eyes off him.

"Oh, look how pretty the fountain is. I'm so glad you fixed it."

Travis shrugged. "I only got the pump working. Other people cleaned it up."

Lizzy admired the way he never tried to take all the credit. He was the most honest, hardworking man she'd ever known. "It's just like I remember from my childhood. Sage and Daisy would bring me to this courtyard and then we'd go down to the creek to feed the ducks while Gamma shopped."

"Grandpa Will said I jumped into the fountain for a swim when I was about three. It's so weird how some of our memories are in the same places, yet we never really knew one another."

"I'm glad our new memories are shared." They paused for a quick kiss then moved closer to the fountain.

The water flowed as it should, splashing across the rearing horse's body and into the pool at the base. The three of them were getting plenty of curious stares and whispers behind the hands of Channing residents. Almost everyone knew him, especially since he was a star bronc rider with his photos hanging in the Rodeo Café on the corner, and she was the long-lost Dalton granddaughter who'd returned home. She didn't mind their curiosity and hoped he didn't either.

"Did you young folks know there is a legend about this fountain?" said an elderly man with bushy gray eyebrows and a craggy face, weathered by years of working outdoors.

"I didn't," Lizzy said. "But I would be disappointed if there wasn't."

"Good afternoon, Mr. Williams," Travis said, and they shook hands. "Have you met Lizzy Dalton?"

"Many years ago. Nice to see you again, young lady."

"You as well. I remember visiting your peach orchard with my grandmother."

"You liked to climb my trees." He chuckled.

"I sure did."

"But this little fella is someone new," Mr. Williams leaned down to smile at the baby who was stretching as he woke.

"This is our foster baby, Davy. Will you tell us the legend about the fountain?"

The old man straightened, and his grin revealed dimples hidden in the lines of his face. "You don't even have to throw in a coin to make this one work. All you have to do is have your first kiss here and your love will last forever."

Lizzy looked at Travis, and they shared a smile before she turned back to Mr. Williams. "Thanks for sharing that with us."

"We've got to keep the legend and the love alive. I'll let y'all get back to your outing. I gotta find my wife before she spends all my money," he said with a wink and walked away.

"Trav, technically, our first kiss was here, but do you think it counts if it wasn't…real?"

"It was real for me, songbird." Travis put an arm around her waist.

"It wasn't just for Jeff's benefit?"

"That was only the excuse for me to do what I'd been wanting to do for a while."

She rose up on her toes and planted a kiss on his lips. "It was real for me, too. Do you want the naked truth?"

He groaned and glanced around them. "Did you have to use the word *naked* when we're in public?"

"Consider it foreplay." She giggled when he gave her a look that said that was not helping.

"If it comes with you being naked at some point, then absolutely. Tell me," he said.

"When you kissed me that day, I thought I saw it in your eyes. That it was real. But I thought it was just wishful thinking on my part."

"I guess some wishes do come true."

They shared another kiss beside the fountain that would forever hold new meaning.

* * *

Travis thanked the young girl at the ice cream shop and walked back toward Liz and Davy with a dish of chocolate to share. She was sitting on a bench near the fountain talking to the baby in the stroller. Her smile radiated love. And he'd never seen anything so beautiful.

How did a guy like me get so lucky?

His phone rang, and he paused to pull it out of his back pocket. A growl rose in his throat. It was Crystal. Again. He hadn't responded to a single one of her calls or texts. Could she not take a hint? And what had happened to the music biz guy she'd dated right after him?

He set the ice cream on the rim of the fountain, declined the call and blocked her number, just as he should've done from the very start. It felt freeing, like a weight he'd been forcing on himself had been lifted.

"Yum. That looks delicious?" Liz said as he settled beside her. "What are you grinning about?"

"Just thinking how delicious you are." He held out a spoonful of ice cream for her, and then quickly regretted his mistake when she grasped his wrist and sucked it from the spoon with a mischievous glint in her eyes. "You keep that up and I'm about to cut this trip short."

She giggled. "Where are we going next?"

"To bed."

Over the next couple of weeks, they grew closer and Travis was finally allowing himself to be happy. They spent their nights talking and laughing and making love. He spent his days thinking of her while he worked around the ranch, but he ate lunch with her every day. Instead of lonely evenings watching TV, he had someone to share it with, and a baby who made him smile. And he'd become pretty handy at changing diapers and liked sitting on the floor with Davy while he had tummy time and making silly faces to see if he could make him smile like he did for Liz.

Whatever the future held, he'd either enjoy it, or get through it like he'd done several times before. And even if he was setting himself up for heartache he couldn't come back from, his goal was to grab happiness when and where he could. Liz and the baby were making that an easy task.

Focus on now, Travis told himself as he led two saddled horses from the stable to the shade of a tree near the back patio. Zeus was twitchy and ready to run, but the sweet palomino mare Misty was the perfect mount for his songbird. Their calm personalities suited.

"I'm ready to ride," Liz said as she came out the kitchen door, but she immediately turned to walk backward while talking to Finn. "Are you sure you got this?"

"Yes, mama bear. Between the three of us we can look after one tiny pip-squeak for a couple of hours."

"Davy has just eaten and should nap for a while."

Finn held up a piece of paper. "I read that on your very detailed note."

Travis chuckled. Davy's nap would be over before they even started their ride.

"Call if you need us," she said to Finn and then turned to face Travis and the horses. "I think I'm actually ready this time."

After stealing a quick kiss, he laced his fingers and gave her a leg up onto Misty's back. She'd ridden horses with her aunts several times before they went on their trip, but this would be their first ride together. There was something intimate about a ride with a woman just for the fun of it.

"Any particular direction you want to go?" he asked.

From her seat in the saddle, she stroked her thumb over his cheek and the beard she'd suggested he grow because she thought it was sexy. "Show me your favorite part of the ranch."

He kissed the palm of her hand and then swung into his saddle. "I know just the place."

She glanced back at the farmhouse with a smile. "I think the brothers and Davy are going to be fine. Let's take the long way around."

Just what he wanted to hear.

The late afternoon was alive with birds and the scent of dried grass kicked up by the horses' hooves. They didn't talk much as they rode toward the big pond. Sunsets were especially nice glinting over the water, and he wanted to share one with her. First, they stopped by her singing spot, and she sang just for him. Her soprano voice was beautiful, and when she hit clear powerful notes, tingles rippled through him.

Once they were dismounted and on the small dock that stuck out over the pond, he sat behind her as she leaned back against his chest. The sun was going down and the nightly show was just beginning to paint the sky.

"Trav?"

"What's on your mind?"

She tipped up her face, her smile sweet and a little bit shy. "I love you."

Lightness filled his chest and spread with the warmth of what could be a lifetime of sunsets and sunrises. "And I love you, songbird."

He kissed her lips, welcoming her contented sigh.

Having the farmhouse to themselves had been great, but the twins would be home soon. Too soon. How much would things change when Sage and Daisy got home?

Chapter Twenty-Four

One overcast morning, Lizzy kissed Travis at the kitchen door before he went to work with the horses and then put the baby in the carrier on her chest for a walk while it was still somewhat cool. She chose a different direction from her usual path because the dappled light of the wooded area still had misty fog swirling at her feet this time of the morning. It felt like a place you might catch a glimpse of a wood sprite or fairy.

In a spot with more than a normal amount of downed tree branches, she kept passing pieces of shingles and other debris from the storm. "Look, angel boy. I think these are bits and pieces from Trav's cabin."

Davy's soft cooing reminded her of an owl. She started looking harder with the hope of possibly finding Trav's money. There were a few chunks of what looked like a kitchen cabinet at the base of a tree. She walked in a circle around it, scanning the ground, but it wasn't until she looked up that she smiled.

"Davy, you'll never guess what I see."

Wedged against the trunk and stuck in the V of two branches was a red-and-yellow, rusted and dented coffee can. What were the chances that it was Trav's missing can of money?

Standing on her tiptoes, she was able to reach it and had to give an extra tug to pull it down. The top of the can was bent almost closed as if someone had stepped on it. Something sloshed inside and when she tipped it, water ran out onto the leaf-covered ground. She peered into the crushed opening and smiled. There was a large wad of wet cash inside.

"Woo-hoo. We've found the buried treasure, angel boy. I told him I was good at finding things."

She kissed the top of his head, and Davy gave her a gummy baby smile.

"Let's go find him and tell him the good news."

When she got back to the house, Finn told her Travis had made a trip to the feedstore and would be back soon. He didn't ask her why she was carrying a dented-up old can, and she did not offer any explanation.

In the kitchen, she pried open the can enough to dump the wet cash into the kitchen sink.

"Oh my gosh. This is a lot of money. More than I imagined and all large bills. No wonder he was so upset."

She was separating the last of the wet cash and laying it out on towels to dry when she heard Trav's truck pull up. She lifted Davy into her arms, and they went outside to meet him.

"Davy and I have something for you."

"Oh, yeah? What is it?"

"I'll give you a clue. We found it in the woods."

"Another plant you want me to dig up and put in a pot?" he guessed.

"Nope, so much better, and it doesn't require any work on your part. Come inside and see."

He kissed her and tickled the baby's tummy. "What's up, tiny dude?" Davy grasped Trav's fingers and tried to pull them to his mouth.

"You're going to be so happy with my powers of observation that you might even give me a backrub tonight." Lizzy took his hand and hurried him along to the kitchen.

"Princess, a backrub is a treat for both of us."

The second Travis stepped through the kitchen door, he sucked in a breath so fast that he coughed. Towels were laid out across the counters, island and the table, all covered with wet cash. "Is this mine?"

"I think so. It was in this." Lizzy pointed at the crumpled can in the sink.

"I can't believe this. How in the world did you find it? Where?"

She told him about their morning adventure in the woods.

"You really are good at finding things." He'd given up hope that his money would ever be found and had been trying to forget about his loss. Over the last couple of days, he'd realized that there was a lot more to life than money. When his dream of owning land was meant to happen, it would. And getting this cash back put him closer to the amount he needed.

Once the money was dry, he put it in a large manila envelope and headed for the bank before anything else could happen to it.

When Travis arrived at the bank, he went straight to the manager's office and knocked on the frame of the open door. "Afternoon, Mr. Thomas."

"Howdy, Travis," the older man said. His gray hair was combed over in an attempt to hide some of his bald head and dark-rimmed glasses were perched on the end of his thin nose. "Come in and sit down. What can I do for you today?"

He held up the fat manila envelope. "I have a large amount of cash and I didn't want to stand at the counter for everyone to see. I've put off bringing it for way too long. I also want to get a safe deposit box for some of my valuables."

"I can certainly help you with that. But rather than get a new one, why don't you just take over the use of your grandfather's box? It's paid up until the end of the year and you are the sole beneficiary, right?"

"Yes, sir, I am. I didn't realize he had a box here."

Because I keep putting the papers aside and saying that I will get to reading all of them later, and then I never do it.

All kinds of things went swirling through his mind. Mainly, what was inside of Grandpa Will's box. Knowing how sentimental the old man was, it was probably more photographs and old letters or something like that. What were the chances of it being something valuable?

"Do you have the key?" Mr. Thomas asked. "If you have it, you can start using it today."

"I don't. But there are some random keys with his belongings. I sure hope it's one of them."

Mr. Thomas opened a drawer and pulled out a key. "It will look something like this."

"I'll go home and see what I can find."

"Great. Let's get your cash counted and put into your savings account, and then I'll see you back here in a while with the key."

Travis drove straight back to the ranch without stopping to do his other errands. He was too eager to see what his grandpa thought was valuable enough to put in a safe deposit box.

In the upstairs bedroom he'd begun sharing with Liz, he pulled the wooden trunk holding his grandpa's belongings out from under the bed. On top of the flat boxes that held belt buckles from his father's rodeo days, there was a large circle ring with a variety of keys in all sizes, shapes and colors, some old and some new. There was an unusual flat key he thought was likely the one, but to be safe, he took the whole ring.

Back at the bank, he was taken into the vault where they used his key in one slot and the bank's in the second slot. The box was way heavier than he'd expected, and he opened it the second he was alone in a private room. The source of the weight was a dark blue plastic case. Unfortunately, it was too heavy to be filled with cash.

He flipped up the latch, raised the lid and his jaw dropped. "Holy cow, Grandpa."

It wasn't cash. It was even better. The box was filled with small gold and silver bars about the size of packs of chewing gum and some gold coins.

There was a note in his grandpa's handwriting.

Travis, this should help you with the down payment to buy that piece of land you've dreamed about. I am so proud of you and always have been.
I love you, son.
Grandpa Will

He sat back in the hard plastic chair with his mouth still hanging open. How had Grandpa Will managed to acquire this much gold and silver, and why had he kept it a secret? Maybe Travis should have actually read the last will and testament all the way through. He'd been too sad after the funeral and set it aside intending to go back to it later.

He had no idea how much the gold was worth, but it was hopefully enough for a down payment.

Travis called Mr. Thomas into the small room and asked him about how and where to sell the gold and silver and then started a loan application. Fingers crossed, he would qualify for the amount needed to buy the Martin Ranch.

He drove home with renewed hope. He was in love and things were starting to go his way.

Travis really needed to get some ranch work done, but he was too excited for that and needed to tell Liz about his discovery. He found her in the farmhouse office doing the bookkeeping while the baby napped.

"What are you grinning so big about, cowboy?"

"I found something in my grandpa's safe deposit box at the bank." From his pocket he pulled out the one gold bar he'd brought home, while the rest stayed safely at the bank.

She gasped and sprang to her feet. "Is that gold?"

"It is. And this is only one of many." He handed it across the desk.

Her smile was as shiny as the precious metal in her hand. "This is wonderful. Will it be enough to buy the ranch?"

"Hopefully enough for a big down payment that will make monthly payments affordable. I filled out a loan application."

He clenched his jaw. He hadn't meant to tell her about the application, because if he was denied, he'd have to admit his failure.

Chapter Twenty-Five

"What's been going on while we were gone?" Sage asked.

"Let's sit in the living room and I'll tell you all about it, and then I want to hear everything about your trip."

She started with details about the storm and the damage to the cabin and then about Travis moving into the house.

Daisy chuckled as she pulled the ponytail holder from her long hair. "The way you're glowing and grinning, I'm wondering what bedroom you put Travis in."

"Originally, the empty one beside the nursery." Lizzy couldn't hold back her smile and might have blushed the same shade as the dark pink dress she was wearing.

"I saw this coming a mile away," Daisy said.

"On our trip, we talked about the possibility of you two being together by the time we got home. You look very happy," Sage said.

"I really am." Lizzy shifted on the couch to tuck one foot beneath her. This next topic was going to be a harder discussion. "There's one other thing I want to talk about. I've made a decision. Since they still haven't found Davy's father, I plan to tell them that I'm interested in adopting him."

The twins stared at her with matching expressions. This time, surprise mixed with a healthy dose of worry.

Lizzy shrugged. "I know you both warned me, but I've fallen in love with two men."

"What does Travis think about your desire to adopt?" Sage asked.

"I haven't told him yet. It was only an hour ago that I talked to Betty on the phone, and when she told me there was no word on Davy's father, it got me thinking."

"And it led you straight to adoption," Daisy said. It wasn't a question because her aunt knew they thought alike.

Sage worried her hands together. "Without the biological father's identity, it will not be an easy adoption. What happens if he's found a year from now and wants his son?"

Her stomach bottomed out. She didn't want to think about that possibility. "I don't know. I realize I'm putting my heart on a very precarious line."

"Have you thought about the added challenges Davy will have?" Daisy asked.

"What about your opera singing?" Sage asked.

"I'm still going to the audition. I'm not giving up on that dream. Now I just have more than one thing that makes me happy."

After the baby was asleep, Lizzy moved around the bedroom, tidying up and feeling restless, while Travis sat on the bedside examining the new lasso that had come in today's mail.

"Looks like it will be a good one. I'll try roping while riding Zeus tomorrow." He tossed the coil of rope to land perfectly on the reading chair in the corner.

She stopped in front of him. "I need to tell you something, and I don't think it's going to come as a shock. I want to adopt Davy."

He ran both hands through his thick hair. "No, it doesn't. But..." He caught hold of her hand. "Honey, he has a father who'll be found at some point."

She plopped down beside him and rested her head on his shoulder. "I know. I'm getting ahead of myself. I just needed you to know where my thinking is."

"I'm glad you're being open with me, but it worries me that you could end up getting hurt. This was supposed to be a temporary situation. You have an opera career to chase before you become a mother."

She tensed and sat up straight. Would Travis still want to be with her if she adopted, or would it be too much for him too fast? "I'm still planning to go to my audition. I haven't given up anything."

"They aren't going to let you adopt until his father is found and then he would have to give up parental rights, and if they can't find him, I think you have to wait years to legally adopt."

"I know all this, Trav." She lay back on the bed with her knees hanging over the edge. "What if Davy's father is never found? Or he is found and wants to keep him? What if I have to wait years to adopt him and I've fallen in love with him and then—"

"Liz, you're getting all worked up for nothing."

She gasped and sat straight up. "For nothing? You think me wanting to adopt him is nothing?"

"No. That's not how I meant it, but you need to calm down."

"Do not tell me to calm down."

It was his turn to flop onto his back. "What do you want me to say?"

She wanted him to say that he supported her and wanted to be Davy's father, but she couldn't say any of that. Her insecurities were still too strong. He might not be physically pushing her away, but he could hurt her just as badly with words.

"Don't tell me to calm down unless you have a way to fix this. I'm going to take a bath."

When she reached for the doorknob, the new lasso landed around her body. She gasped and stopped, slowly turning to face him with her arms trapped loosely against her sides. It would take no more than raising her arms to free herself, but she didn't because there was something strangely comforting about him not letting her walk away to feel sorry for herself.

With every step he took in her direction, he coiled the rope, drawing her closer and closer until they were toe to toe.

"Travis Taylor, are you trying to earn a free trip to Hades?" Her lips trembled with a smile she couldn't hold back. The heat of anger was shifting into the warmth and tingle of wanting him.

He used a finger to stroke her cheek. "You're a strong woman. A fighter. We'll get it figured out."

She lifted her arms and the rope, looping it over his head to encircle both of them. "You really think that about me? That I'm strong and a fighter?"

"I know it." He kissed her and then pulled her into a hug. They swayed together until her heart rate calmed.

"Are you still going to take a bath?"

"I am, and there will be bubbles. Do you want to join me?" His slow grin made her shiver.

"I'm not sure we'll both fit in the tub, but I'm willing to give it my best cowboy try."

* * *

Travis was sitting on the living room floor with the baby on a blanket in front of him. He once again covered his face then pulled his hands away. "There's my good boy."

Davy kicked and excitedly cooed in a way that sounded like it would soon turn into baby laughter. Who knew a game of peekaboo could be so much fun. He couldn't imagine Davy not being here with them. He couldn't admit it to Liz, but he was scared to death that someone would come and take him away.

Liz came into the room with a bottle. "Looks like you two are having fun."

"We are. He finds me very entertaining." He covered his face again, and Davy waved his arms and blew bubbles. "But it's time for me to get dressed and get to work." He stood, kissed Liz and headed upstairs.

Sitting on the bedside, he pulled on one boot and was reaching for the other when Lizzy ran into the bedroom.

"Trav, they found him."

"Who?"

"Davy's father. They found him. His name is John. He's twenty-two, and he just got out of the army." She paused for a shuttering breath. "He's coming to the ranch."

The air crystalized in his lungs. Was he about to lose a second baby boy, both of them named Davy? "Does he want to take him?"

Her long ponytail swished from side to side as she shook her head. "I don't know. I only know that John wants to come and meet him."

"You're trembling." He stood from the bed and pulled her into his arms. "Take a deep breath."

She rested her head over his heart, and sighed when he rubbed her back. "I'm both excited and terrified."

"I know, princess."

"On the one hand, he might say he's giving up the baby. On the other, he might want to take him right away. What if he is mad at us for calling him Davy?" Her grip jerked on his belt loops, as if she held on tight enough, everything would be okay.

But he couldn't promise everything would work out the way she hoped. He wanted to protect her and wasn't sure how, but a good start would be talking to this young father. "We'll take it one step at a time. Together."

"Together?"

"Yes, songbird. Together."

Chapter Twenty-Six

Within hours, Lizzy stood under the shade of the front porch, pacing the length. She'd thought about having Davy in her arms when his father arrived so he could immediately see his son, but Davy was napping upstairs.

Travis, her aunts and their case worker, Betty, were in the kitchen, and she was too nervous to sit with them and make small talk. She was both excited and nervous about meeting Davy's father. Every minute closer to his arrival, her nerves pulled more tightly into a knot that felt like a ball of barbed wire in her belly.

Would he be anything like the guy she pictured in her mind? They'd told her he played on the army football team, so she expected a jock who was into sports and girls and had partying on his mind. He would likely have no idea how to even hold a baby. With no interest in and ill-equipped to handle the demands of fatherhood.

At least that's what she hoped.

The sound of a vehicle coming up the drive made her

heart race. "Please let this meeting go well." Which selfishly meant *her* way.

An old blue truck pulled to a stop in the front circular driveway. The young man stepping out was tall and leanly muscled, but not the burly jock she'd imagined. He had dark hair and eyes like Travis. And he looked as nervous as she felt.

Lizzy smiled and waved, wanting to make him feel welcome and at ease—even though she was anything but calm and wished he had given up his parental rights without coming to fall in love with the most precious baby ever. The what-ifs hanging over their heads were making her spiral.

Get a grip, Lizzy. Find your gumption.

No matter her wishes, John was here, and she would deal with whatever she needed to. With Trav's help. He'd promised they would do this together.

She met him halfway up the walk. "Welcome to Dalton Ranch. I'm Lizzy…" She hesitated, not sure what to call the baby. "His foster mom." The slight tremble in his handshake matched her own.

"Nice to meet you. I'm John."

She gave his fingers an extra squeeze. "Everything is going to be okay."

But she didn't know that at all and wasn't sure which one of them she was trying to reassure.

"I don't really know how this is supposed to go," he said.

"I'm new to this as well."

He took a deep breath and looked her in the eyes. "You must think I'm a horrible person for not knowing I have a son, but I didn't even know she was pregnant. We met when I was home on leave from the army and only dated a very short time and then lost touch."

"I don't think you're horrible. Not at all." She hooked her arm through his and started leading him toward the door.

"You didn't have to come meet him today, but you have. That tells me you want the best for him."

Please see that I am the best one to raise your son.

He nodded. "I do want what's best for him. I just have no idea what that is at the moment."

"Are you ready to meet…the baby?" She had almost said *your son* but didn't want to project that and encourage him to take Davy away from her.

"Yes. I'm ready." They walked toward the wide front steps.

"I should probably tell you that we have been calling him Davy, but it's not official."

"I like that name. My middle name is David. John David Smith."

"Really? What a coincidence."

She introduced him to Travis, Betty and her aunts and then took him upstairs to the nursery where Davy was napping.

"Wow. This is really nice," John said as they entered the large, sunny room. He took a deep breath and approached the baby bed then looked down. The tension on his face smoothed into a smile. "He's so little. And so cute."

Davy was sleeping with one hand tucked against his rosy cheek.

"Have you ever held a baby?" she asked.

"Yes, I have three younger brothers. We have a busy single mom, so I had to help out a lot."

Would his experience with younger siblings help or hurt her chances of becoming Davy's mom?

He reached out like he would touch the baby but stopped and looked at her. "Can I pick him up or should I let him keep sleeping?"

"You can pick him up." It was too early to wake him, and Davy would likely get cranky. But…maybe the baby being cranky would be a good thing. It would show this young man how hard it could be to parent a newborn. She internally winced, ashamed of her behavior, but she couldn't seem to stop herself.

John reached into the bed, lifted the sleeping baby with skill and then sat in the rocking chair. His hands were big yet tender as he cradled his son. "Is Travis your husband?"

"He's my boyfriend." A plan began to form in her mind. It was a good opportunity to show him that they were a loving family. "Can you stay and have dinner with us?"

He adjusted the baby in his arms. "That would be great. I haven't eaten since breakfast because I was so nervous, and I'm pretty hungry."

Betty came into the nursery. "Mr. Smith, do you have any questions for me?"

"No, ma'am. I read through all the information you sent to me. I also did some research of my own about Down syndrome. I didn't realize young parents could have a baby with Down syndrome."

Lizzy's hopes took a hit. *Great. He's not only capable, he's also smart.*

"That is a common misconception," Betty said.

John put the baby to his chest and kissed the top of his bald head. "They can have a lot of challenges, and it looks like it can be more difficult for them to be adopted."

"Not this time," Lizzy said quickly.

Betty cleared her throat. "As you know, Ms. Dalton would like to adopt him if you decide to go that route."

"Yes, I know."

Betty made sure he knew all of his rights and the options. He had some time to make his decision about whether to keep Davy or sign over his parental rights. Everyone was comfortable with her leaving so she could get to another appointment. At the moment, John was not giving away which way he was leaning, and it was making Lizzy very jumpy.

She couldn't shake the guilt that her true motive for the dinner invitation wasn't to feed a hungry young man who'd had his world rocked. But the responsible thing to do was to show him how much work a baby could be.

At the long dinner table in the dining room, she sat beside Travis with John on her other side. Davy was in the portable bassinet behind her. It was past time for him to eat, and he would be getting fussy at any moment. Normally she would've fed him before they sat down to eat, but not this evening. Sure enough, only a couple of minutes later, he scrunched up his face and began fussing.

Lizzy pushed back from the table. "It never fails that he needs attention while I'm eating or in the middle of something, but I don't mind a bit." She picked up the baby and put him in John's arms. "Could you please hold him while I get a bottle?"

She didn't wait for a response from the young man, and she didn't dare make eye contact with Travis or either of the twins as she left the room. They knew this wasn't the normal routine. John might know some of the challenges because of his younger siblings, but a reminder wouldn't hurt.

When she came back into the dining room, she held out the bottle. "Would you like to feed him, or should I?"

He hesitated but reached for the bottle.

"That's okay. I'll do it. You're our guest." She took her fussy little darling into her arms and kissed his forehead. "There, there, sweetie. I've got you."

He eagerly started sucking on the bottle, and she ate one-handed.

"Tell us about what you have planned since getting out of the army," Sage said.

"Well, my plan has always been to go to college at the

University of North Texas on a GI bill. I'd like to get a degree in business."

"That's wonderful," Lizzy said. "Where will you be living while you're at school? Do they have dorms on campus?" She ignored Travis's nudge to her foot under the table.

"I haven't decided yet," John said. "Right now, I'm living with my mom and three younger brothers." He told them more about his family and his time in the military.

Once Davy finished his bottle, she put him on her shoulder to burp him, and she did not cover her clothes with a burp cloth as she normally would. Sure enough, he spit up on her red blouse. "Oops. This always happens."

She got three different versions of a disapproving glance from Trav and the twins.

After dinner, Lizzy made sure to have John change a diaper while she happened to mention the cost of them and formula. So many times, she had to bite her tongue and not ask about which way he was leaning with his decision.

Davy was now asleep in his crib once again, and they were looking down at him. There was something so magical about watching a baby sleep. A peacefulness that made her smile.

"You have a very nice family," John said.

"Thank you. I have to agree. They are the best and very supportive. I want you to know that I truly do want to be his mother. I love Davy. So do my aunts and Travis."

"Are you and Travis getting married? I didn't really have a dad, but wish I had."

Panic started to resurface, but she would not do what she'd done in the grocery store when she'd called Travis her boyfriend. This was too important. "I hope so."

He reached into the crib and touched the baby's little round tummy. "I should get home. Thank you for letting me stay so long."

"Of course. Anytime"

"I'll call you after I talk things over with my mom. I have a lot to think about."

Lizzy wrung her hands. "I know you do. Thinking about Davy's future and your own is a big decision. I'll wait to hear from you. Before you leave, let me get you some of those cookies you liked. You can take them home to your brothers."

"Thanks. They'll like that."

Lizzy almost bumped into Travis when she turned around.

He steadied her with an arm around her shoulders. "Is everything okay up here?"

"Yes. Just perfect. I'm going to pack up some cookies for John." She raised onto her tiptoes and kissed Trav's cheek and then left them in the baby's room. If she gave them a few minutes to talk, John would have more time to see what a good guy Travis was.

In the kitchen, the twins were putting away leftovers, but instead of helping, she leaned her hip against the counter and finished the last sip of wine in her glass.

"I think that went pretty well," Sage said.

"I hope you're right. He said I have a very nice family. He also asked if Travis and I are getting married," she said in a hushed tone.

The twins stopped to look at her, Sage with a dripping soapy dish in her hand and Daisy holding open the refrigerator. "What did you say?" they asked.

"I said I hope so." She didn't mention her worry that her being single might be a deal breaker for John letting her adopt Davy.

Travis stood beside the young man who had a huge life-changing decision to make.

"I'm the oldest of four kids, and I had a dad and a stepdad who didn't stick around. Our mom lives paycheck to paycheck. That's why I joined the army. To help her out."

"You're a good son. I know what it's like to have a parent leave," Travis said.

"When you were a kid?"

"Yes. My mom left when I was nine." Saying it aloud dredged up a flicker of the old hurt. He tried to block it, but a tiny flash of memory got through. He'd lived his life feeling like he wasn't quite enough for her to stick around and raise him.

Travis couldn't stand the thought of Davy going through anything like that. The question of who would be his parents needed to be established with certainty.

John reached into the crib and stroked the baby's cheek. "If I give him up now, he won't ever know me or miss me, right?"

"That's true."

"I didn't expect to become a parent for many more years. I just don't know how I can go to college and make it all work without a partner. From what I've been told, a child with special needs could require specialized health care and other therapies. And being a single dad, I don't know how to juggle doctor's appointments and college classes. It seems almost impossible."

Travis put a hand on the young man's shoulder. "I know it's overwhelming, but you don't have to figure everything out tonight. Take a few days to think things over."

"I can do that."

"Give yourself a chance to sit with it a while before you make your decision. Make sure it's really what you want before you sign over your parental rights, because once you do, it's forever. You don't want to have regrets," Travis said.

Lizzy came to a sudden halt in the hallway outside of the baby's nursery. Travis's words made ice form in her veins.

"Think long and hard about it before you give up your child. Make sure it's the right decision," Travis said to John for a second time, as if the first time wasn't enough.

Why is Travis encouraging him to keep the baby? My baby.

She'd thought he'd be talking about what a good home this would be for Davy and highlighting the positives. If there had been any doubt in her mind about wanting to adopt Davy, there was zero doubt now. She wanted to be his mother. She already loved him more than anyone else in the whole world.

Her insides turned to mush as her heart began cracking. What happened to her and Travis doing this *together*? Why was the man she'd thought was on her side trying to sabotage everything she wanted?

If Travis didn't want her to have Davy, then she could not be with him, and that idea was crushing. If she lost the baby, it would be partly his fault.

The cookies rattled in the plastic container, and she felt wetness on her other hand. She was trembling so hard that her glass of water was sloshing over her fingers and dripping onto the floor. The gutted way she was feeling, it might as well be her blood seeping into the grooves between the old floorboards.

Lizzy took a shuddering deep breath, gathered herself and entered the nursery. The fake smile she'd plastered on her face seemed to fool the young dad, but she could tell it wasn't fooling Travis—the backstabber.

When John looked down at the baby in the crib, she shot Travis a thunderous glower.

He raised both eyebrows but remained quiet.

"Here are the cookies," she said to John.

"Thank you." He looked once more at his son, took the cookies and then she walked him out.

Travis didn't follow them out onto the front porch, and she was glad. She didn't want to risk yelling at him in front of John. "You call me anytime with any questions. I'm happy to talk over whatever is on your mind or just listen."

"I will. And thank you for taking such good care of my son."

His son.

Chapter Twenty-Seven

Travis stood in the hallway outside the bedroom, watching Liz open drawers to grab things and then slam them shut. "That was quite an award-winning performance you put on tonight. Were you hoping to influence his decision?"

She glared at him, but there were tears in her eyes. "You're really asking me that question? Are you serious? I could ask you the same thing."

"I know this is hard."

"No one loves Davy like I do. I loved him first!" Her voice broke, and she rushed past him and went into the bathroom, closed the door and clicked the lock before he could say more.

This isn't going to go well.

He hated seeing her so upset, but she had to think logically about the situation. He was doing all this for her own good, even if she couldn't and wouldn't recognize it at the moment. With the back of two knuckles, he knocked on the door. "Liz, talk to me, please."

"Can't hear you," she yelled.

Water began to run into the tub, which meant she was taking a bubble bath and would be in there for a while. Usually, she let him in and they would talk while he sat on the lid of the toilet, but he was currently in the doghouse with the woman he loved. His songbird was such an emotional woman and so passionate about the things and people she loved that this reaction wasn't a huge surprise. But that didn't mean it wasn't frustrating.

He leaned his back against the wall and plowed his hands through his hair. When she'd first arrived, he'd told himself not to get involved in her life and had done it anyway. He'd let himself get pulled into the dramatic world of Elizabeth Dalton. Her charisma and charm had been too much for a man to resist. And now, he loved her, and he was trying to make sure she didn't get her heart crushed, because his heart was also in danger.

"I'm trying to help you," he called to her through the door.

Her bark of laughter was filled with pain. "I've had more than enough of your brand of help for the night. I thought you were on my side, but I was so wrong."

"I am on your side, honey."

"You said we would get through this *together*, but it sure doesn't seem that way. It seems like you are trying to ruin everything for me."

"Liz—"

"I'm done talking."

"You have to come out of the bathroom at some point."

A cabinet door banged. "You forget that there's a window in here."

He turned to face the closed door and braced both hands on it. "Don't even think about climbing out that window. We're on the second floor."

"If you'll give me some time alone, I promise not to climb out the window and down the trellis."

"Fine. We can talk after your bath."

"We can talk in the morning. I'm too upset and don't want to say something I can't take back."

He dropped his forehead against the bathroom door. "Remember, I'm leaving early in the morning for Houston to deliver the horse, and I'll be gone overnight."

"Then we'll talk when you get home."

"So, I'm sleeping alone tonight?"

"Good idea. I wouldn't want to make a *decision* or say anything I'll regret later," she said, using some of the words he'd said to John. And her tone suggested he should take that under advisement.

With a heavy heart, he walked away from the bathroom door. He'd learned that she needed space and time to process and make decisions. She was high strung about John coming to meet his son and worried about him taking Davy, and he could understand that. Her aunts had warned her not to get too attached, but she had not listened, and she'd fallen in love with the baby.

And as much as he had resisted, so had he.

Travis slipped quietly into Davy's room and watched him sleeping. How could he explain to Lizzy that what he said to the baby's father was his way of trying to protect her? Protect all of them.

Rushing John to a decision to give up his parental rights and then having him change his mind before legal paperwork was signed would be so much worse than the pain they would go through if they had to say goodbye to him right now. Keeping Davy longer only to have him taken away later would be even more heartbreaking.

He'd give Lizzy the time she needed to process everything, but not too much time.

* * *

It was still dark early the next morning when Travis slipped into Davy's room. It had been a long, lonely night in the guestroom without Liz beside him, and he wanted to see her but settled for looking in on the baby before leaving for Houston. His next conversation with her might go better if he waited until he got home, when they weren't rushed and they had time to really talk. Now that he thought about it, this trip to Houston was perfect timing. It would give her time to think. And time to miss him.

Davy was stretching and waking up.

"Good morning, little fella." He picked him up and took him directly to the changing table, put a pacifier in his mouth, just like Liz did until she could get his bottle ready, and started changing his wet diaper. Davy spit out the pacifier and cooed, making him smile. "I have to go out of town today, but your…"

The words *your mother* flashed through his mind. And heart. This was the exact reason he needed to make sure John really thought things through before making his decision. The right decision for all of them. There were so many people and emotions involved, and he wanted the least hurt for all of them.

"Our songbird is none too happy with me right now, so be an extra good boy for her while I'm gone." He snapped the baby's yellow-and-green sleeper over the fresh diaper, put the pacifier back in his mouth and him back in his bed and then turned on the horse mobile that hung above the crib.

"I'll see you tomorrow, sweet boy."

Please let him still be here when I get home.

Lizzy threw back the covers and sat on the side of her bed. Trav's side. She lifted his pillow and inhaled. She'd missed him so much last night, but the sleeping apart idea had been hers. Listening to him talk to Davy just now was making her want to cry, again. He'd been trying to whisper, but his deep voice carried, and she was hyperaware of the soothing rumble.

She felt horrible about pushing Travis away last night. She'd been acting childish and wished she'd talked to him. If she hurried, they could talk this morning before he left. He would have to load the horse into the trailer, so she had time. She got out of bed and made a quick morning stop in the bathroom to brush her teeth. She wanted to kiss him goodbye with fresh breath.

Her foot was on the top stair when Davy started crying. "I'm coming, sweetie."

After morning kisses and cuddles, they went downstairs, but the kitchen was empty. The coffeepot timer had done its job, but the carafe wasn't full as it usually was this time of the morning, and his travel coffee mug and bag of snacks were gone. Then she heard the diesel engine of the red ranch truck.

"He couldn't have the horse loaded already." With Davy in her arms, she ran out the door but when she made it into the backyard, the Dalton Ranch truck and trailer were pulling away down the long driveway. She waved, but he didn't see her. Or if he did, he didn't stop.

Her heart sank a little more.

Davy blew a raspberry and flapped his arms.

"You're right, angel boy. I was such a diva last night. And not the good kind." She hated the way she'd acted and would make things right when he got home. She saw movement down by the stable. It was Finn. That was the reason the horse had been loaded and ready to go. "Thanks for nothing," she mumbled to the oldest hottie brother, even though he couldn't hear her.

Once she was settled in the pink living room chair and Davy was drinking his bottle, she sent Travis a text message.

Have a safe trip. Sorry about last night. XOXO

It took about five minutes and then his response was a thumbs-up and heart emoji. She wasn't sure how to take that. Did the thumbs-up mean they were cool and the heart that he loved her? Or had they switched places, and now he wasn't talking to her?

It was true that he hated texting, and he wouldn't text and drive, especially with such expensive cargo. So, that brief message had probably been all he had time to send while at a stop sign or red light.

Please don't let it be that I've pushed him too far.

When she'd lain awake last night, she'd calmed down enough to admit that she'd been selfish from the moment John had arrived. If only they could have a do-over of the day.

"Ugh. I need to stop overthinking it."

"What are you overthinking?" Daisy asked as she came into the living room with a cup of coffee and sat in her blue chair.

"I got too worked up and emotional last night." Lizzy put the baby to her shoulder to burp him. "I need to apologize to everyone."

"Remember, I'm the one who is emotional like you. So, I understand where you were coming from. It's a tough situation."

"A whole lot tougher than I thought. You and Sage were so right."

"I usually love being right, but not this time."

Chapter Twenty-Eight

Travis had tried to get out of making this trip to deliver the horse to the buyer, but the man's kids were big rodeo fans and wanted to meet him, which was why Sage and Daisy asked him to go instead of them. The buyer had invited him to join them in a private skybox at the evening rodeo, and he couldn't refuse. That meant not going straight home after unloading the horse.

If I'm lucky, it will give Liz a chance to miss me as much as I'm missing her.

Missing would be something he might have to deal with if she did well at her opera audition and had to travel. Now that he thought about it, she hadn't mentioned her upcoming audition in a while. Was she still planning on going? Had her considering adoption changed her goals and dreams? That was another thing they should discuss.

Since he was already going to be in Houston for the day, he decided to turn it into a positive, like Liz had taught him. First, he'd taken the gold and silver to a recommended dealer in Houston and was very pleased with the amount he got for it, and when he got back home with the check, he'd hopefully know if his loan application was approved.

In the afternoon, he got to see some old rodeo buddies and gave a riding clinic for a group of children. The extra money it paid wasn't much, but every little bit helped. The sights, sounds and smells of Travis's old rodeo life gave him mixed feelings. He missed some of it, but there were parts he did not.

Before agreeing to be at tonight's rodeo, he had not realized that Crystal was playing the concert. If he had, he would've found an excuse not to accept the invitation to stay for the rodeo and performance as a guest of Three Rivers Ranch. It was too late for regrets now. He'd made the commitment to Sage and Daisy to represent Dalton Ranch and make a good connection with Three Rivers Ranch.

He shook his head and made his way toward the rodeo arena. He was worrying too much about the possibility of seeing her. Just because he knew Crystal was here, she had no way of knowing that he was.

Travis just wanted to get in and out of this evening's events, crash in his hotel room, and then after making an appearance at a breakfast, he could be back to the ranch well before lunchtime.

He'd thought about calling Liz several times throughout the day, but wanted to talk in person to further explain why he'd said what he did to John. She needed to see his face and he needed to see hers when they worked through their first disagreement.

He made his way to the will-call window and got the ticket that had been left for him and then he found the private skybox. He was greeted with enthusiasm by the man's children and a few ladies as well. The buffet of food was huge, and the open bar was top shelf. He was given food and drink and made conversation with everyone, finally relaxing and beginning to enjoy himself.

He was standing at the front of the private box with one of the little boys when someone shone a spotlight on him.

"Cowboys and cowgirls, we have a rodeo legend in the house this evening. Retired bronc rider Travis Taylor is up in the Three Rivers Ranch box. Give him a shout-out and make him feel welcome."

Every muscle in Travis's body tensed. This was the exact opposite of tonight's plan to get in and out unnoticed. On the inside he was swearing up a blue streak, but he dutifully stepped closer to the railing of the skybox and gave his fans a smile and wave. If he had any luck at all, Crystal would be too busy preparing for her performance to hear the announcer say his name. Likely, she was being her usual self-centered self—too busy primping and letting people fawn over her to bother with him. Since he'd declined her calls and ignored her texts for months before finally blocking her number, hopefully she'd finally moved on.

"Maybe if we cheer loud enough, we can convince him to get back on the rodeo circuit," the announcer said.

Not happening.

He waved one more time and then backed up enough to be out of the spotlight. Everything in him was telling him to get the hell out of the arena, but Sage and Daisy had entrusted him to represent Dalton Ranch. It was considered an honor to even be invited to watch from a private box, and it would be rude if he suddenly left. He couldn't take the risk of offending anyone important.

They were setting up the stage in the arena and the concert was starting soon. He hoped that meant Crystal would not have time to find him, but of course not five minutes later, she breezed into the skybox with her entourage. Ignoring her completely, Travis turned away from her and went back to the railing to look out over the arena. He could hear her talking and signing autographs and taking photos.

There weren't that many people in the box, and it was only so big, and he had nowhere to hide. Maybe leaving was his only option. Before he could move around the edge of the room and slip out, she threw her arms around him from behind, and then slithered herself around to the front of his body.

Damn it!

Cameras started snapping and he knew she'd planned this. He had little doubt she'd set up this photo op for publicity purposes. And she was once again using him to get it.

"What the hell are you doing?" he growled under his breath and pried her arms away from him without making too much of a scene.

"You left me no choice." She pouted her lacquered red lips, and then she smiled in a way that made him even more nervous. "Actually, this is good fortune. You saved me a trip. On Sunday, I was planning on going to Dalton Ranch to find you."

His skin went cold. That was the very last thing he wanted or needed. What he wanted was to get home to talk to Liz and see if John had made a decision. Crystal showing up would not help that process. Not to mention, whatever media story Crystal tried to spin might look bad to the foster and adoption people. He needed to make it more than abundantly clear that there was nothing and never would be anything between them ever again.

Out of desperation, an idea struck. This was out of character, but it was called for under the circumstances. "I don't think my fiancée would like you showing up at her home." He had the pleasure of watching her momentarily speechless.

Her eyes flashed. "I don't believe you."

"Believe it." If Lizzy could use him to fool her old boyfriend, then so could he.

"Travis, my tour ends after this show, and I won't be traveling for a very long time. What's between us is not done," she said in a hissed whisper that only he could hear and wrapped her fingers around his forearm.

He gently tugged free from her grasp. "We are done," he said between clenched teeth. "Don't let me keep you from your concert. I wouldn't want you to be late for the spotlight."

Barely veiled anger simmered behind her fake laugh and smile before she turned to the rest of the guests in the box. "Nice to see everyone. Hope y'all stay for the show."

Travis was not. He'd be thanking people and saying his goodbyes as fast as he could.

Lizzy was sitting on the porch swing because she wanted to catch Travis the second he drove up. She needed to apologize in person, and then they could talk like adults. Not like the childish diva she'd been on the night of John's visit.

The fear of losing Davy had engulfed her, and she had acted selfishly.

It was past time she listened to why Travis had said what he did to John.

Sage and Daisy were in town, Davy was sleeping in his bassinet beside her, and the cat was curled up on her lap, so she started scrolling through social media on her phone. It was nothing more than to keep her mind occupied while she waited rather impatiently for her cowboy. Why was it taking so long for him to get home?

A gossip site headline caught her eye, and she jerked up straight, dislodging the cat on her lap.

What will rodeo cowboy Travis Taylor's fiancée think about his reunion with ex-girlfriend and country music star Crystal?

Her skin chilled and prickled as if thousands of needles were poking her at once. The largest ones directly into her heart. "What the fudge?"

The photo below the headline only made it fifty times worse.

Crystal was smiling up at Travis and had her arms wrapped around his waist. His arms were up as if he'd been caught right before returning the hug.

Lizzy's whole body went cold and then numb. The thought of Trav with another woman made her want to retch up her breakfast. Had she been such a brat that she'd pushed Trav right into another woman's arms?

If so, he wasn't the man she thought.

She rubbed her eyes and refocused on her phone. There was photographic evidence, yet she just couldn't believe he would do something like this. Was she just that naïve? She sighed. She'd been exactly that in the past.

Lizzy was upset on several levels and for several reasons. First, there was the obvious jealousy. And then…a new worry slammed into her mind. What would this look like to everyone around them? To John. To the foster care system. Her chances of adopting when they thought she was in the middle of some Hollywood type scandal.

She was so confused and slipping into panic mode, but then she noticed a word she'd missed the first time reading the headline.

"Fiancée."

Why would this gossip site think Travis had a fiancée? Unless…

Some of the pressure eased from her chest. Had Trav taken a cue from the grocery store incident and claimed a fake fiancée?

She remembered John talking about his single mother and wishing he'd had two parents. Could this be the way to…

"Nope. I need to stop right there with that idea."

She studied the photo a little harder. The expression on his face was not one of happiness and certainly not lust. She'd experienced nights of passion in his arms. She'd seen his bedroom eyes, half-hooded and intense, and this wasn't it.

In the photo with his ex, his eyebrows were harsh slashes. There was tension around his mouth. This was his annoyed expression. His body was angled away from the other woman. Not curving closer.

The rumble of the truck and the rattle of the empty horse trailer pulled her attention from scrutinizing the photo. She prepared for a conversation that would be interesting, to say the least.

She'd planned to run to him and throw her arms around him as soon as he got home, but now… With the worry that she'd hurt her relationship with Travis and now this gossip story, she wasn't sure what to do.

When Travis drove up the long driveway of Dalton Ranch, Lizzy was on the front porch, so he stopped the truck before pulling all the way around to park near the barn. He was so happy to be home and even happier to see her, but the frown on her face was not the welcoming smile he'd expected.

Crap. Is she still just as mad?

The motor's clatter died down, and in the quiet of the cab he took a few slow breaths before getting out and heading her way.

"What's wrong, princess? Is the baby okay? Are you okay?" *Had someone come and taken Davy away?*

"We're fine." She motioned to the porch. "He's napping."

"Then what's wrong?"

She glanced back and forth between him and her phone, and he got a bad feeling in the pit of his stomach. Did this have something to do with Crystal? He hadn't checked social media, but maybe he should've.

"I'm worried that I messed things up between us and that John thinks I'm manic and that nothing is going to work out and—"

"Princess, take a breath. Everything will work out like it should for everyone."

"You don't know that. You can't promise it will be okay."

"True, but..." He jabbed a finger into the air in an I-just-thought-of-something gesture. "I can't believe this. When did we switch places?"

She cocked her head. "What are you talking about?"

"One day, this slip of a woman blew into my life like a pink tornado. She was all, 'Look at my fancy sparkly glass. It's overflowing with positive-energy champagne,'" Travis said in a comically bad attempt to imitate her voice.

Her lips trembled with a smile.

"Now *I'm* the one who's all positive and crap, and you're knocking over your own glass and watching it soak into the dirt."

"Did you just compare me to a natural disaster?"

"A pink one, all full of glitter and shiny things."

She smiled. "I guess you're right."

"It occasionally happens."

"There is something else. Have you seen this?" She held out her cell phone.

He took it to look at the screen and growled deep in his throat. Crystal really had done it on purpose. She'd planned it, brought the people with cameras and leaked it to the press. It had to be her because she was the only one who he had told he had a fiancée. She'd set up the whole thing.

"Liz, this is not what it appears."

"Which part? The reunion with Crystal or the fiancée part?"

He took a second or two to analyze her expression. She didn't look furious, and her eyes weren't red as if she'd been crying. "It was definitely not a happy reunion on my part. And the other part... I borrowed the idea from you, and although it's not true at this moment, I hope you'll still consider a future that could lead to that?"

There was the smile he'd been wanting to see. It was like a deep cleansing breath for his heart.

"I definitely see you in my future." She wrapped her arms around his waist.

After slipping her phone into his back pocket, he pulled her in close.

"Will you tell me about the photo that I think is not what it first appears?" she said into the fabric of his T-shirt.

He tipped up her chin. "You can tell the picture isn't what Crystal wants it to seem like?"

"I think I can. It's in the expression on your face and your body language."

A huge wave of relief washed over him. This was a much better reaction than he'd expected, but then again, everything about Liz was unexpected. She could get worked up, as she'd done during and after John's visit, but she was also seriously protective of those she loved, and logical and smart when it really mattered.

"I love you, songbird." He cradled her cheeks and kissed her, and she kissed him back with all the passion and fire he needed to know it would all be okay. Even if Davy wasn't part of their lives, they could find a way to console each other and be happy.

"I love you, too, cowboy. Let's go sit on the porch while you tell me about the rest of your trip."

He kept her hand in his as they walked to the swing and then cuddled together while the baby continued sleeping.

"I had no idea until I got there that Crystal was the

headliner at the rodeo. She found me in the Three Rivers skybox and said she was going to come to the ranch to find me, and I told her my fiancée would not like that." He looked at the photo again. "This was the moment when I was about to peel her hands off me. It's just like her to do something so devious just for publicity. I'm sorry it worried you."

"Trav, I'm so ashamed of my behavior the day John was here, and I owe you an apology. I was being so selfish trying to show him how hard and expensive it can be to have a baby."

He kissed the top of her head. He knew why she had done it, but did she? "Why did you do it?"

"Because I want to keep him. Like I said, selfish."

He laced his fingers with hers. "What other reasons?"

"Because I want him to be loved and safe."

"See? You didn't freak out just for yourself. You were thinking of him, too."

She relaxed against him and exhaled deeply. "I suppose you're right. But there is one person I wasn't thinking of. John. But you thought of him, and instead of talking to you about it or doing the same, I…" She swirled her hand in the air. "Did what I did."

He chuckled. "Do you feel better now?"

"I do. You really are a good therapist. Maybe you should become one."

He laughed while shaking his head. "Hell, no. Can you imagine me having to talk to that many strangers all the time?" He gave a pretend shiver. "You're my one and only patient."

She smirked. "Knowing me, I might keep you very busy, Dr. Travis."

"If you're willing to put up with a crusty cowboy, I'll take my chances."

* * *

Travis took a seat to wait in Mr. Thomas's office at the bank, his anxiety level ramping up to epic proportions. He pressed the palm of his hand on his knee to keep it from bouncing. He hadn't told Liz why he was going into town today because he wanted to get an answer and be able to sit with it for a bit before talking about it. He hated the idea of her feeling sorry for him.

He wanted to be able to go home with good news. He wanted to fulfill his promise to Grandpa Will and have something of his own so he could ask Lizzy to marry him. So he could hopefully adopt Davy with her and officially name him after the baby brother he lost. It felt meant to be. It had to be, because why else would this baby have come into his life?

Mr. Thomas came into his office smoothing down his wispy hair. "Sorry to keep you waiting, Travis."

"No problem."

The desk chair squeaked as the man sat down. "Your loan application was approved."

His relief was so huge he wanted to jump up and pump his fist. "That's great."

Mr. Thomas turned a piece of paper around for Travis to see. "Here are the details. This is the amount of down payment you will need and what the monthly payments will probably look like."

Travis saw the amount of the monthly payment and his heart sank.

Crap.

Travis could feel his dream slipping through his fingers. His chest felt as if it had been bound by strands of wire, and the prickle behind his eyes was dangerously close to the threat of tears.

He thumped the palm of one hand on the steering wheel. "Damn it. I'm sorry, Grandpa. I tried."

He couldn't see a way to make his dream a reality. Even with his salary from Dalton Ranch and training on the side, his own place would need start-up money and take time to turn a profit. He'd managed to get the deposit needed but didn't see a way he could make the kind of monthly payments required.

He had visions of asking Liz to marry him and having something of his own to give and share with her. A home to take her to that was right next door to her family. He hated this feeling of failure. Now he was the one whose glass was draining toward empty.

What he needed was time with his songbird and a baby boy who had him wrapped around his teeny-tiny finger. He wanted the world for both of them and to be the one who could give it to them.

There was opera music coming from the living room stereo when Travis went in through the kitchen. He followed it and stopped in the archway and took in the domestic scene. Sage was sitting on the floor by the coffee table going through a box of old photos, Daisy was swaying side to side with Davy in her arms and Liz was looking out the window.

"I'm thinking about not going to the audition," Liz said.

"Lizzy Dalton," Sage said in a parental tone that meant she wasn't messing around. "You better get your butt to that audition tomorrow, young lady."

"I agree," Travis said. Even if he had to give up his dream of owning Martin Ranch, she didn't have to completely give up hers.

All three women turned to look at him, and Liz crossed the room to hug him.

"I agree with them. Why in the world are you even considering not going?" Daisy asked.

"Why do I really need to do it anymore? I no longer feel the need to prove anything to my father. I have a job working in the family business. I have a baby to take care of and…will hopefully get to adopt him."

He kissed the top of her head. "Do it for yourself, princess. Not for anyone else." Her dream was still within reach, and he would not let her give up without trying.

"If I get even a small part in the chorus, I'll need help taking care of Davy."

"You've got it," the twins echoed each other.

"They're right," he said. "You've practiced and prepared and you are going to that audition, even if we have to tie you up with a pink bow and take you there ourselves."

She chuckled. "Okay. I'm convinced. I'll go to the audition tomorrow morning."

Sage held up one of the old photographs from the box and waved it. "Check out what I just found."

They all drew close and looked at the photo of two children beside a Christmas tree. A little blond girl and a dark-haired boy wearing a cowboy hat.

"That's me," Liz said.

Travis grinned. "And that's me."

"I told you you'd likely met at some point," Daisy said.

Liz took the photo and flipped it over. "I was five years old. I remember the Christmas party and that red dress. It was one of my favorites. It had a full skirt of red shiny fabric and a row of tiny, silver jingle bells encircling the hem."

"Even back then, you were into fashion," he said, and then took the baby from Daisy and held him up to kiss his forehead.

"If I remember correctly, you ate most of the cookies."

"Sounds like something I would do."

Liz brushed a finger over the faded image of a smiling boy. "You were a cute little stinker."

Sage pulled out another holiday photo. "This was the Old Town Christmas festival that Mama used to be in charge of."

"Why did they stop having it?" Lizzy asked.

"The church where it was held burned down. I wish we could find a new place and start it up again."

"What about the abandoned grist mill in Old Town?" he suggested. "It would need some fixing up, but it has plenty of space."

"That's true," Sage said. "The city owns it and might have the funds to get it in good repair since it will bring a lot of tourists to town."

While the three women went through the box of pictures and giggled, he sat on the couch with the baby on his lap. "Look at them, Davy. They're having so much fun right now."

He wanted to be a part of this family. Officially.

Was there something he could do to turn things around before the Martin Ranch sold to another buyer?

He needed an out-of-the-box idea.

Chapter Twenty-Nine

In their moonlit bedroom, Lizzy lay across Trav's bare chest, breathing in the scent of his skin. His fingers traced slowly across the bumps of her spine. No one else had ever been so tender with her. So loving.

"When I met you, I thought you were a tough cowboy."

"And now you don't?" He lightly swatted her bottom, and she giggled.

"Oh, I still do. Big, tough and sexy. It's the inside that surprised me. You try to hide it, but you can't hide it from me. Do you know how sweet you are?"

"Nope."

She kissed her way across his chest. "Like a big toasty marshmallow."

He chuckled. "Now I'm a marshmallow?"

"You are *my* marshmallow cowboy."

He rolled her onto her back and braced himself above her. "I'll show you sweet, but first, sing for me, songbird," he whispered into the hollow of her throat.

In an operatic voice—that was not loud enough to wake up the household—she sang a made-up song about her marshmallow cowboy until they were laughing so hard that tears were running down her cheeks.

This was exactly the kind of night she needed before her big audition. Loving and talking and laughing.

Travis and the twins were not asking her to give up anything because it suited them. They were encouraging her to go for it.

His trip to the bank had been a setback, but now Travis was determined to go after his dream, just as he'd told Liz to do for herself. He was not giving up on his promise or his dream or his future with the woman he loved and the family they could have together. He would have to swallow his pride and ask for help because he had an idea that could help more than just himself. First, he needed to have a serious conversation with a few people.

On horseback, he found the brothers doing some Saturday morning fishing at the pond near the back of Dalton Ranch.

"Please tell me you don't need us to work today," Riley said and cast his line back out into the water.

"Nope. Not today, but we might have some hard work in our future." He dismounted beside their truck and loosened the reins to let Zeus graze.

Finn closed his tackle box. "Do we want to hear this?"

"I hope so. I have a problem I need help with."

"Girl trouble?" Jake asked.

Travis propped an arm on the frame of the truck bed. "Not this time. I have a business proposition to discuss with you. I know y'all want to buy some land, and since I do, too, and it would be a struggle to do on our own, what do you think about the four of us buying the Martin Ranch together?"

Jake punched Finn in the shoulder. "I told you he'd be on board with the idea."

Hope resurfaced inside Travis. "Y'all have already been talking about this idea?"

"We have," Finn said with a big smile and put down his fishing pole. "Let's talk details."

A huge weight lifted from Travis's shoulders.

For a couple hours, the four of them talked out their ideas and expectations. A surprising number of them matched up. They hashed out the few that didn't and made notes on the back of a large manila envelope they found in the truck. Divided into four equal parts, Travis would get the section that bordered Dalton Ranch and had the family cemetery and the big barn with attached stables. The brothers would get the main ranch house to share. They would breed and train horses and run a small herd of cattle. Where Dalton ranch had stud horses, they would have the mamas and babies on their ranch.

They each signed their name at the bottom of the envelope, and it became their agreement to start what would probably be called Four Points Ranch.

Jake called the real estate agent he'd just started dating and asked her to make an offer as soon as possible, and she promised to write up the offer immediately because there was other interest in the ranch. And one of them was a developer.

With his chest expanding enough to breathe deeply and his heart full, Travis rode Zeus at a gallop. The wind pulled at his hat, and hope of landing his dream was closer than it had ever been.

He'd wait to hear if their offer was accepted and hoped the answer came soon, but first, he'd wait for Liz to get home from her audition. If she had good news, they would celebrate. If the news was bad, he would comfort her. And either way, he would love her.

* * *

Lizzy was dressed up, warmed up and waiting for her turn to sing the aria she had practiced for weeks. The nerves from her Chicago audition had been conquered over the last few months, and she had not wanted anyone to come with her today. This was something she wanted to do all on her own. One of the most freeing parts of all was no longer needing her father's approval.

She'd found her gumption and was the diva in charge of her own life.

She was reunited with Sage and Daisy, in love with her marshmallow cowboy and, if everything else fell into place, she would get to be Davy's mother.

This time, Lizzy was excited instead of scared, because this time she had more confidence in her singing and in herself. She felt more powerful, her breath control had improved and her vibrato didn't wobble. She was ready to do this.

She waited just offstage for her turn to sing. Some of the other singers were good. Really good. It was doubtful she'd get a lead role, but the thought didn't bother her. She was here without wanting to faint or throw up.

"Next up is Elizabeth Dalton."

She smoothed the front of her champagne-colored dress and made her way out to center stage. The warmth of the spotlight made her nerves kick up, but she reminded herself it was excitement. When the pianist began playing her music, her voice flowed out with confidence. She was singing because her family had encouraged her to come today. She was singing for herself. Singing because she loved it.

Joy infused her voice, and she sang with all the passion she felt for the man she loved. Not to prove anything to anyone. It felt natural and free and absolutely amazing.

Lizzy left the stage smiling and feeling like a winner. She no longer felt the need to be the star of the show or center stage in the main spotlight with all eyes on her, but she still really, really hoped she would be chosen to be part of the chorus.

Now all there was to do was wait to see if she was chosen.

Chapter Thirty

When Lizzy drove around to the back of the house to park, the whole family was sitting in the shade on the backyard patio. It made her heart full to see all of them waiting for her to get home, ready to support her whether the news was good or bad.

Before coming back to Texas, singing with an opera company had been at the top of her list, but in a short time, her life and priorities had changed. She no longer felt the need to prove herself to anyone.

There were questions on everyone's faces, but she only smiled, leaving them in suspense.

"Tell us what happened at the audition." Daisy said, unable to hold it in for a second longer.

"What does your future hold?" Sage asked.

She smiled and held out a hand to Travis. "I'll be singing in the chorus at Bass Opera Hall."

Everyone started cheering and hugging, and Trav picked

her up to spin her around. She giggled and gave him a smacking kiss.

Her new opera gig was the icing on top, rather than the whole cake. Maybe even just the sprinkles on top of her new life, but some really special sprinkles that fulfilled her joy of singing.

Travis waved as the Murphy brothers drove up and all got out of their truck.

"Come join the celebration," Daisy called to them. "Lizzy rocked her audition and will be singing with the opera."

The brothers all added their congratulations, and then Finn motioned with his head for Travis to step over to the side. They knew he hadn't told anyone else yet. He didn't want to get his hopes up too high, but the way all three brothers were grinning, he was expecting good news.

"I thought it would take days, but our offer was already accepted. We got it," Finn said quietly enough for only Travis to hear.

"Hell, yes!" Travis said loudly enough for *everyone* to hear. Now all eyes were on him. "I have some good news, too. You are looking at the four new partners and soon-to-be owners of Martin Ranch."

Liz ran and jumped onto him with her legs wrapped around his waist, and he had to take a step back to keep them upright, but he was laughing.

"We can't decide if we should name our ranch four corners or four points or four star," Jake said.

"We thought about calling it hottie brothers plus one ranch," Finn said and winked at Daisy. "But it's too long to fit on a sign."

Daisy gasped. "How do you know about...that?"

"I'll never reveal my sources," Finn said.

All three women were blushing and giggling.

"This calls for champagne," Sage said. "Good thing I thought ahead and put some in the refrigerator."

Now all that was left was to see if Davy would get to stay with them.

A couple of days later, Lizzy ran into the stable so fast that she almost zipped right past Travis but skidded to a halt, her skirt swirling around her legs.

"And there is my pink tornado. What's the rush?"

"John called." She held up a finger in the universal sign for give me a minute, caught her breath and continued. "He's on his way here. He asked to talk to both of us."

His humor faded. "Both of us?"

She nodded and threw her arms around his waist. "Trav, I'm scared."

So was he.

Chapter Thirty-One

When John arrived an hour later, Lizzy was in the kitchen making snacks that they could munch on while they talked. She wasn't sure she could stomach anything when the time came, but she wanted to make John feel welcome. Travis held Davy to his shoulder and was pacing around the room, and she could tell he was feeling the same frazzled emotions.

The doorbell rang, and they both jumped.

"I'll get it," Daisy yelled from the dining room.

Lizzy moved to Trav's side, and they hugged with the baby nestled between them, his sweet face tilted up to look at them. That's how Daisy and John found them when they came into the kitchen.

John smiled at them. "Don't move. Stay just like that." He pulled out his phone and took their picture. "I couldn't resist, because—" He choked up and had to clear his throat.

Lizzy went to him, and even though initiating physical contact of this sort used to paralyze her, she hugged him.

He held onto her for a moment.

"I'll be upstairs," Daisy said and slipped quietly from the room.

Travis came over to them with the baby. "Would you like to hold him?"

"Yes." John took Davy into his arms. "Hey there, little man."

"Let's sit and talk," Lizzy said.

Both men did as she suggested, and as she brought over glasses of iced tea, Lizzy noticed that Trav and John could pass for brothers.

"Are you two engaged?"

Lizzy froze and held her breath.

Travis spread his fingers on the tabletop. "You saw the social media gossip about me, didn't you?"

"Yes, I did."

She shared a glance with Trav, having a quick and silent conversation. This was not a minor thing like the fake boyfriend incident or even what he'd told Crystal. They would be completely honest. It was the only way.

"We're not engaged, yet," Travis said and let his smile spread. "When I ask this beautiful woman a question that important, it's not going to be because of gossip on social media. It's going to be special and because we're both ready."

She reached for his hand and laced their fingers. "Sounds like a good plan to me."

"Lizzy, do you still want to adopt Davy?"

"Yes. Absolutely yes." Her nerves were practically sparking, and she squeezed Trav's hand so hard she was surprised she didn't crack a bone.

"Even if it's just you by yourself, you can give him a life I can't."

Lizzy sagged with relief against Travis. "Does that mean…?"

"I've spent a lot of time talking things over with my mom, and I'm giving up my parental rights so you can adopt Davy."

Lizzy jumped up from her chair, ran around the table and leaned over to hug him for a second time. "Thank you. Thank you so, so much. You won't regret this. I'll be a good mother to him. I promise."

To add to that point, she kissed the top of the baby's head, then feeling slightly embarrassed about her outpouring of affection, she blushed, but both men were grinning at her.

"Do you want to know why I took that picture when I came in?"

"Yes," they both said.

"I saw what looked like a happy family. I could see the love, and I'd like to have it as a reminder of the life my son will have."

Lizzy wiped her cheek, and only then did she realize, she was crying.

"I just have one request," John said. "I expect to be invited to the wedding someday."

Lizzy sat on the front porch swing with Davy on her lap and Travis by her side. The sun had slipped below the horizon and stars were coming out across the Texas sky.

"Tomorrow, will you take me over to see the Martin Ranch? I guess we'll have to stop calling it that."

"Yes, we will. I'd love to take you." He tightened his arm around her shoulders and kissed the side of her head.

"Since the brothers get the acreage with the ranch house, will you keep living with us?"

"Would you like for me to?"

She looked up at him, hoping he could see the truth of her feelings in her eyes. "Yes. I love living with you, but I'll understand if you want to live on your own land."

"At some point, I'd like to build a house on my new ranch, but until then, I'd like to stay here with you and this tiny dude." He put his big hand on the baby's tummy. Davy cooed and kicked his little feet. "I think he likes that idea, too," Trav said.

"Of course, he does."

"When we go over to see the ranch, want to help me pick out a good spot to build a house?"

Her heart picked up speed with what this could mean. "I would love to."

"Now that you're going to officially be his mom, what name are you going to put on his birth certificate or whatever paperwork it is when you adopt?"

Was he asking because he wanted to be part of the decision? That sounded good to her. "David for his first name, and I'm open to suggestions for his middle name." *And his last name,* she added silently in her mind.

"I do have a couple of ideas and maybe a name change."

"A change?"

He cleared his throat and seemed to tense before he stood, but then immediately dropped to one knee and pulled a ring from his front pocket.

She was filled with so much love she thought she might float away.

"My beautiful songbird, you are what I didn't know I was looking for, and I love you more than I knew was possible. Would you and Davy make me the happiest cowboy in the world and take my last name?"

"Yes," she said so fast he chuckled. "I would love to be your wife, and I'd love to be parents—together."

His smile was the one that transformed his face from

handsome to drop-dead gorgeous. "This belonged to my Great-grandmother Dorothy."

"It's gorgeous."

He slipped the diamond and sapphire ring onto her finger, took her hand and let Davy grasp a finger on his other. "I can't wait to share my life with both of you."

"Like a family."

He sat beside her on the swing and pulled her in as close as he could with an infant between them. "Yes, songbird, exactly like a family. I want to spend all my tomorrows with you."

"And all the days and nights and birthdays and holidays after that." She slid her hand around to the back of his neck.

"And all the dances in the rain," he said against her mouth.

"All of them."

"Promise you'll sing just for me when we are alone in our bedroom?"

"I promise. A special song, just for my cowboy."

Epilogue

"Elizabeth."

Lizzy froze, the voice out of place here in Channing, and she wasn't altogether sure how to feel about it. Slowly turning from the coffeepot, she faced him. "Dad. What are you doing here?"

"Hoping my daughter will let me walk her down the aisle tomorrow. You did send me an invitation."

"I didn't think you would come. You said you'd never come back to Texas." He wasn't wearing his usual business suit or khaki slacks. Instead he wore dark jeans and a navy blue polo. Since they were the same color as most of his suits, she supposed this was his version of ranch wear.

"I've heard people can change, and I'm trying to do just that. And along with being here for your wedding, I'd like to ask for your forgiveness."

Her jaw dropped in a very unladylike fashion. Change and forgiveness were words she couldn't recall ever hearing him say.

"I went about things the wrong way, and I'm sorry I..." He sighed and ran his fingers through his thick salt-and-pepper hair. "I'm not sure where to start."

She was tempted to say that was because the list was long, but he was making an effort and so would she. "Let's sit and I'll bring over some coffee." Lizzy motioned to the round table in the farmhouse kitchen where he'd grown up. The place he hadn't visited in sixteen years.

"Thank you, Elizabeth."

It took only a moment to pour his black coffee and add a bit of cream to hers. Once she was seated, neither of them seemed to know what to say, so she pulled out her new-found gumption and started the conversation.

"Are you sorry for interfering with my audition in Chicago?"

"Yes, I am." He ducked his head but then met her eyes. "I just wanted to have you in my life every day. But I went about things in the wrong way."

Wait. Every day?

"Why didn't you ever tell me this?"

"Damn good question. I'm sorry I was so selfish."

Her eyes widened, and her inner child was starting to perk up. "I suppose if you hadn't sabotaged my audition, then I wouldn't be getting married or be adopting the most precious baby ever."

"Well then, happy to help." He grinned.

"Did you just make a joke?" she said with a chuckle.

"Not a very good one. I would like to meet your baby and your fiancé, though."

"Davy is sleeping, but we can go look in on him in a minute. Travis went to pick up his mom, Beth, at the airport but should be back soon."

He momentarily closed his eyes. "Your mother would be very proud of the woman you've become."

The backs of her eyes pricked with tears. "Why don't you ever talk about her?"

"She was the love of my life and irreplaceable, so after…" His Adam's apple bobbed while he gathered himself. "I just didn't know how to do it without her."

She had no idea he felt this way. "Is that why you only dated and never married again?"

"That and the fact that several women ended up calling me a bastard or other choice names."

She pressed her lips together to keep from laughing. He never shared his thoughts and feelings in this way, and she didn't want to do anything to shut him down.

"I've also been told I have selective listening skills," he said.

"It's possible that's true on occasion."

"Someone recently told me that forgiveness isn't like having amnesia. It's more like giving someone a chance to fulfill a promise to be better. And I do want to be better, if you'll give me a chance."

"I like that way of thinking about it." She couldn't believe what she was about to say, but it felt right. "I'm happy to give you a chance."

"More than I deserve." His tone was low as if he was talking to himself.

"It's never too late to start over. Thank you for coming to walk me down the aisle."

"I'm very happy to do it," he said and then took a sip of coffee.

"We're back, princess," Travis said as he opened the kitchen door but then stopped short when he saw her father. "I didn't know we had company."

"This is my father, Joshua Dalton. And this is my very-soon-to-be husband, Travis Taylor."

Joshua stood and held out his hand, and the two men shook. "It's very nice to meet you, Travis."

"You, too."

The door opened again, and the twins came inside with a woman Lizzy had only seen in photos. Trav's mother, Beth, had flown in from whatever location she'd been living in this month. Her curly brown hair was thick and down to the middle of her back. She wore layers of long natural stone necklaces that looked lovely against her flowy white top. Her jeans and Birkenstock sandals were at that perfectly worn-in stage.

Now they both had their somewhat estranged parents here for their special day, and it was making her nervous. Maybe they should've eloped.

"Welcome," Lizzy said to Beth, and she was immediately pulled into a tight hug.

"I'm so happy to meet you, Lizzy." His mom held her by the shoulders. "You're even more beautiful in person."

"Thank you. I'm glad you could come." Honestly, she'd been worried having her here would upset Travis.

Beth wasn't at all what she'd expected. Not in her dress or her bubbly personality. Lizzy had been prepared to dislike the woman who'd hurt the man she loved, but as she'd just done with her father, she would listen and give her a chance before passing judgment. Along with love and celebration, this weekend would be about second chances and maybe at some point…forgiveness.

"Let's all move into the living room, and then I'll bring in refreshments," Sage said.

When Davy started crying, Lizzy and Travis went upstairs to change him before he met his grandparents for the first time. They were both worried about his mom's reaction to meeting a baby named for and so much like the one she'd lost over twenty years ago.

"Your mom isn't the way I pictured her." She picked up her sweet son and soothed his crying with cuddles and kisses.

"She's talking about moving back to Channing, but I'm not going to hold my breath waiting for that to happen. And that's another story for another day."

"Are you okay?" *Please don't let this interfere with our happy day!*

"Do you love me, Princess Songbird?"

"I do."

"Then I'm definitely okay." He wrapped her in a hug with their son between them.

When they rejoined the party, Travis was holding Davy. His mom pressed her fingers to her mouth but recovered quickly and held out her arms for the baby.

"Hello, darling," she said as tears began to roll freely down her high cheekbones. When she leaned down to kiss the top of his head, Davy touched her cheek gently as if sensing how fragile she was feeling. The whole room got teary-eyed.

Joshua handed Beth a handkerchief and held out a finger for Davy to grasp. "Hey there, big guy. I'm happy to meet you. I'm your grandfather."

A few minutes later, Joshua pulled his little sisters, Sage and Daisy, across to the dining room to talk. When they returned to the living room, Lizzy couldn't exactly say they were smiling but the tension seemed to be easing. It would take time for them to repair their relationship.

That evening they all gathered on the patio for a barbecue. Lizzy relaxed in one of the rocking chairs with a sleeping baby on her lap and Travis rocking beside her. *Happy* couldn't begin to describe how she felt as she watched everyone interacting.

Finn and Daisy laughed about something while they

manned the grill together. Sage had the other two Murphy brothers helping her move pots of flowers for tomorrow's sunset wedding ceremony.

But the most interesting ones of all were her father and Trav's mother standing at the opposite end of the patio. They held glasses of red wine and were smiling as they chatted. They were total opposites and Beth was not at all her father's type. When their parents laughed and Beth put a hand on Joshua's shoulder, Lizzy tapped Trav's arm and pointed. "What do you think about that?"

"Unexpected to say the least," he said.

"They appear to be hitting it off."

"This should be interesting."

The following evening, close friends and family were gathered in the backyard, seated and waiting for the ceremony to start. In only a few minutes Travis would be married, and he was so excited.

He was wearing black jeans, new boots and a crisp white button-up while standing in a sea of flowers and swags of sheer fabric—that were of course pink. Finn, Riley, Jake and Davy's biological father, John, were lined up beside him, and his best man was nestled in the crook of his arm.

Davy's tiny onesie was printed to look like a tuxedo and his booties were black cowboy boots.

"Are you ready for this?" Finn whispered.

"I'm ready." His nerves were jumping in a good way, and he couldn't wait to get his first look at Liz in her wedding dress.

Music began playing and first Sage and then Daisy walked down the aisle between rows of white chairs. The song changed, and his beautiful songbird came into view on her father's arm.

Her hair was loose and flowing around her bare shoulders in soft waves and she wore a small tiara—very fitting since he called her princess.

And her smile…

It took his breath away. Her white lacy dress was strapless and hugged her curves before flowing into a long full skirt that brushed the grass. When she got close, he saw her bare foot peek out as she walked.

His smile widened. He should've guessed that she wouldn't wear shoes to her own backyard wedding.

"Look, son. Here comes your mama. Can you believe she's ours? We're lucky guys."

The baby cooed and kicked his legs, which were now chubby and getting stronger every day.

As Liz neared, Davy reached for her, and she handed off her bouquet of pink roses so she could take her son into her arms. He immediately grabbed for her long hair and gummed her chin with so much excitement that everyone chuckled.

"I love you," Travis whispered to his soon-to-be wife.

"I'll love you forever, cowboy."

The ceremony was short, sweet and to the point. As Trav slid the ring on her finger, Davy started babbling, and he said something that sounded a whole lot like the word *mama*.

* * * * *

#3035 THE COWBOY'S ROAD TRIP
Men of the West • by Stella Bagwell

When introverted rancher Kipp Starr agrees to join Beatrice Hollister on a road trip, he doesn't plan on being snowbound and stranded with his sister's outgoing sister-in-law. Or falling in love with her.

#3036 THE PILOT'S SECRET
Cape Cardinale • by Allison Leigh

Former aviator Meyer Cartell just inherited a decrepit beach house—and his nearest neighbor is thorny nurse Sophie Lane. Everywhere he turns, the young—and impossibly attractive—Sophie is there...holding firm to her old grudge against him. Until his passionate kisses convince her otherwise.

#3037 FLIRTING WITH DISASTER
Hatchet Lake • by Elizabeth Hrib

When Sarah Schaffer packs up her life and her two-year-old son following the completion of her travel-nursing contract, she's not prepared for former army medic turned contractor Desmond Torres to catch her eye. Or for their partnership in rebuilding a storm-damaged town to heal her guarded heart.

#3038 TWENTY-EIGHT DATES
Seven Brides for Seven Brothers • by Michelle Lindo-Rice

Courtney Meadows needs a hero—and Officer Brigg Harrington is happy to oblige. He gives the very pregnant widow a safe haven during a hurricane. But between Brigg's protective demeanor and heated glances, Courtney's whirlwind emotions are her biggest challenge yet.

Get 3 FREE REWARDS!

We'll send you 2 FREE Books plus a FREE Mystery Gift.

FREE Value Over **$20**

Both the **Harlequin® Special Edition** and **Harlequin® Heartwarming™** series feature compelling novels filled with stories of love and strength where the bonds of friendship, family and community unite.

YES! Please send me 2 FREE novels from the Harlequin Special Edition or Harlequin Heartwarming series and my FREE GIFT (gift is worth about $10 retail). After receiving them, if I don't wish to receive any more books, I can return the shipping statement marked "cancel." If I don't cancel, I will receive 6 brand-new Harlequin Special Edition books every month and be billed just $5.49 each in the U.S. or $6.24 each in Canada, a savings of at least 12% off the cover price, or 4 brand-new Harlequin Heartwarming Larger-Print books every month and be billed just $6.24 each in the U.S. or $6.74 each in Canada, a savings of at least 19% off the cover price. It's quite a bargain! Shipping and handling is just 50¢ per book in the U.S. and $1.25 per book in Canada.* I understand that accepting the 2 free books and gift places me under no obligation to buy anything. I can always return a shipment and cancel at any time by calling the number below. The free books and gift are mine to keep no matter what I decide.

Choose one:
- ☐ **Harlequin Special Edition** (235/335 BPA GRMK)
- ☐ **Harlequin Heartwarming Larger-Print** (161/361 BPA GRMK)
- ☐ **Or Try Both!** (235/335 & 161/361 BPA GRPZ)

Name (please print)

Address   Apt. #

City   State/Province   Zip/Postal Code

Email: Please check this box ☐ if you would like to receive newsletters and promotional emails from Harlequin Enterprises ULC and its affiliates. You can unsubscribe anytime.

Mail to the Harlequin Reader Service:
IN U.S.A.: P.O. Box 1341, Buffalo, NY 14240-8531
IN CANADA: P.O. Box 603, Fort Erie, Ontario L2A 5X3

Want to try 2 free books from another series? Call 1-800-873-8635 or visit www.ReaderService.com.

*Terms and prices subject to change without notice. Prices do not include sales taxes, which will be charged (if applicable) based on your state or country of residence. Canadian residents will be charged applicable taxes. Offer not valid in Quebec. This offer is limited to one order per household. Books received may not be as shown. Not valid for current subscribers to the Harlequin Special Edition or Harlequin Heartwarming series. All orders subject to approval. Credit or debit balances in a customer's account(s) may be offset by any other outstanding balance owed by or to the customer. Please allow 4 to 6 weeks for delivery. Offer available while quantities last.

Your Privacy—Your information is being collected by Harlequin Enterprises ULC, operating as Harlequin Reader Service. For a complete summary of the information we collect, how we use this information and to whom it is disclosed, please visit our privacy notice located at corporate.harlequin.com/privacy-notice. From time to time we may also exchange your personal information with reputable third parties. If you wish to opt out of this sharing of your personal information, please visit readerservice.com/consumerschoice or call 1-800-873-8635. **Notice to California Residents**—Under California law, you have specific rights to control and access your data. For more information on these rights and how to exercise them, visit corporate.harlequin.com/california-privacy.

HSEHW23